ENTWINED DIMENSIONS

ARIEL GRACE

To Gretchen for showing me ways to reach beyond the known stars.

TABLE OF CONTENTS

Proverb

Fire forgets nothing; it transforms memory in form.
- Ignaran Proverb -

Prologue: Avaris

22 AFE *Linear Time (After the Fall of Ether)*
Planet: *Ignara* **Dimension:** *Pyron*
Galaxy: *Andromeda*

Lightning didn't typically behave like a fizzling bad first date, even here, but today wasn't a typical day. It sparked sideways, fizzled halfway down, then crawled into the cliff like it was embarrassed to be seen with me.

I tilted my head, smoke curling off my grin. "Bold move. Ghost me to my face."

The cliff didn't laugh; the lands rarely humoured me on purpose. Ember-veins under its obsidian skin pulsed off-beat; fast, slow, fast, fast, slow; clapping out the wrong rhythm and hoping no one would notice, cheeky gorge. In the air between the rhythm, an echo slipped through: *two-and-two, miscast.*

What in all of Ignara was that supposed to mean? The lands often pulsed and spoke with the beings here, as they did everywhere, I assumed. But they didn't usually use that ancient-sounding tongue. Still, you couldn't get much past me.

Below, the lava river turned in its sleep, offered a half-growl, and decided against it. Thunder arrived late, shuffling in like it had forgotten the address. That was when I saw it: a bubble hanging above the river, pulsing and gleaming where nothing should be. A blip; that was the nearest word to describe it. A bulge in the air, the skin of a drum pulled too tight over nothing. And around it, my home, my

2

sweet lands, they were freaking out from the disturbance. Heat snagged toward it. Light bent. Ash fell sideways to stare.

"Finally," I said, flexing my back a bit because I wasn't subtle, and I enjoyed an audience. Sparks slipped between my scales; little traitors skittering forward to race the fissures like they always did.

They didn't make it. They hit the blip and froze mid-leap, twitching like a constellation drawn by a tipsy Godhead. In their hiss, I caught a fracture of static, sharp and brittle as glass: *laws unbound*.

"Settle down," I coaxed my spark offspring to hurry up. "Don't just... hover."

They didn't listen. Sparks never did once they had left me. The ledge brightened under my claws where I gripped it; obsidian flashed orange in a quick, flattering mirror. I was every bit Pyron's favorite uproar; iridescent swirls of magnetic rainbow caught light ripples in my wings, feather-edges flickering to flame and back, and ember-veins traced across my chest and throat, flaring when I laughed. With smoke in my teeth and talons that ticked sparks out of stone without trying, it wasn't humility to say I looked good on a cliff. It was simply a service to accuracy.

"Alright then," I told the blip, wings fanning ash into confetti. "If you want attention, earn it."

I exhaled a clean ribbon of fire. It should have bitten the fissure and run through; spark, ignite, movement of form, singeing the rock into a new way. Instead, the flame broke into bright beads that rolled up the wrong face of the canyon like lightning lizards fleeing a party they had started. One bead bumped my jaw on the way past. Indignant.

"New choreography," I said, delighted, my attention piqued. "Risky."

Above me, the storm changed its mind out loud. A white fork dropped from the ashcloud, sharp as edgestone, then folded at the elbow and slithered sideways into the blip. Thunder tried to follow and got lost. The sound arrived out of order: a distant rumble first, then a small pop like a bubble wrapping quietly around itself, then nothing at all. The silence wore a grin it hadn't earned.

The canyon pretended it hadn't noticed, an obvious lie. Everything down to the cooled ore was watching. Another bolt fell and stopped, hung midair, and then turned into a dozen thin threads that braided themselves into a loop and fed back up into the cloud that had made them. Lightning was eating its own tail.

"That," I said, "was a terrible distraction." I prodded the lightning, and the blip oscillated, everything around it moving in strange, nonsensical responses I had never seen before. I angled myself directly in front of the blip, turning to face it with all of my might and flair. "Listen, whatever you are, I have plenty to enjoy around here without your interruption."

The blip trembled. Its surface wasn't smooth: it quivered with ripples that pushed light around like a lazy tide. For a blink, its skin thinned, and through it I saw a flash of something; an image of another world, then eyes and a face of some type. With a flash, the images left, soft and sharp all at once, and I was left pondering colours and shapes my eyes didn't usually get as morsels for free. Something like rain hovered in the back of my mouth, sweet and cold, gone before I could taste it properly. The hairline along my spine lifted, confused and amused.

"Tease," I said to whatever thought it could wave new worlds and colours at me without warning.

The bubble sealed. Sparks dropped out with little hissing apologies. The lava below tried to cough cool and failed; a belch of fire blurred up like an alibi. Heat licked my belly as I shimmied off the ledge, my wing skimming the surface of the river. The blip tugged at my edges as I passed, a current deciding whether to keep me. I put a talon up to it, grazing the surface. It wasn't air. It wasn't anything I had words for. It was the sensation of a beat that didn't exist, insisting I dance to it anyway. The membrane flexed and sent a tiny, eerie thunderclap up my bones. Lightning immediately tried again, furious at being interrupted by this otherworldly energy full of opinions.

"Okay," I laughed, wheeling up. "Now we're flirting." But the truth was, the blip was winning over the lightning in vying for my attention.

I circled back and then corkscrewed toward it, head on, ready to face whatever may come. Sparks peeled off my feathers and stuck, a rash of constellations nobody had asked for. The blip shuddered open wider than it had any right to, and the world leaned in without admitting it was doing so. Through the slit, I glimpsed movement. Not flame. Not stone. Lines stacked on lines, branching in a patient logic that felt like growing instead of burning. It wasn't my business. I grinned because that had never stopped me.

"Come on, then," I said to the slit, to the idea, to the strangeness, to the deliciousness of it. "Show me your best trick."

The slit closed like a mouth swallowing a secret. I landed back on the ledge, which looked offended that I had left. My talons bit and popped little orange stars from the glass. The cliff sulked, but I pretended not to notice.

"Alright," I said, and my voice came back a fraction after my mouth stopped moving. "Enough of this dance."

I sprinted to the ledge. The river keened an opinion and then apologised for having one. Lightning dropped like a dare. I jumped at the exact wrong time on purpose because wrong was the new right today, and timing was for those who needed it. My wing brushed the membrane again, and this time it gave. It didn't pop; it admitted me. The surface dimpled, remembered it was a door instead of a wall, and I shoved my muzzle through.

The smell hit me first; a cool, sweet edge that felt like a memory I had never had. The light was green again, but deeper, layered, confident. I heard leaves. I didn't know what a leaf was, but the word folded itself around the sound and sat there, pleased, like a spark that had found a new place to burn without burning. Something on the other side breathed. It wasn't a volcano, nothing like my world. The blip remembered I had invaded its space. It clamped shut on my muzzle with a soft slap that would have been insulting if it weren't so funny. I drew back with half a grin, dripping light that wasn't mine. It slid off me in threads and became nothing before it hit the ledge.

"Rude," I said, and my echo agreed ahead of me.

I stepped off the ledge again, the air blurring under my wings. A bolt dropped and split, and I was already through the gap it forgot to make. A bead of my own flame rolled along the big blip's skin, wrote my name in ash and flame: Avaris; then faded into the night. The blip wobbled in a new rhythm. For a moment, we all hung there: me, the river, the cliffs, the storm, the blip, and the idea of the colour green, pretending we hadn't just watched reality forget its lines.

I hovered, heat streaming off me in banners, sparks drizzling like streamers that had gotten lost on the way to a parade. My wings rustled. The ember-veins in my chest dimmed to a thoughtful glow.

"Alright," I said to the place where the seam had been, to the strange space of a floating world that tasted fresh, to the day that had bent. "You win the first round."

A small, treacherous joy answered me from inside my bones, where joy had no business being. Second round's mine. I climbed, coiled, and dove for the spot again, laughing as the storm remembered to be loud, as the river committed to a roar, as the cliff relearnt the beat it had once written for itself. The world tried to pull itself back into the shape it understood.

But the elders had been watching. They always knew when the rhythm of Ignara stumbled. I ventured toward their cavern to discuss the happenings of the day. Their voices met me in the carved dark inside the council cavern, steady as the veins that ran beneath all stone:

"A breach, a presence, a call. This blip is not a storm, not a fissure of rock or fire. It is a fold in the fabric of dimensions. Time-bending. Time and space, perhaps, miscast. What you touched is no mere anomaly; it is a wound where past and future spill together."

The cavern pulsed once with the ember-light of their truth. My wings rustled against my back. Time and her bestie, space, had found a new way to speak. And I was a novice at listening.

Part One

Tear

CHAPTER ONE

Daria: Dilemma

20 CE *Linear Time (Common Era, After the Fall of Ether)*
Planet: *Earth* **Dimension:** *Human*
Galaxy: *Milky Way*

I was born in the wrong dimension.

Parallel dimensions are zipping around us all the time, like rush-hour traffic on the Auckland motorway, just vibing at different frequencies. But because Humans are a bit slow, and their eyes are set to "potato quality," they can't see a thing. I was meant to pop out in the Fae dimension; way zippier, more sparkly, heaps of room for creative mischief. But at the last second, that cheeky sprite Nuvious pulled a fast one on me, swapped my time-space boarding pass, and bam — I opened my eyes in the Human timeline. Cheers, mate.

Sprites, as I recall, are absolute muppets; all tricks, no chill. To this day, I have no clue what Nuvious has against me. Maybe I stole his pixie dust in a past life. Ever since I was a wee thing, I've been haunted by flickers of Fae memories in daytime and nighttime dreams. I scribbled them down in cheap notebooks with my trusty fluffy pink pen (yeah, judge me). But I could never quite shake the feeling that I was tricked into this form. And I wanted to get back to the Fae dimension. I'm pretty sure it's possible to hop back and forth on the back of a hummingbird if one knows the way and is, well, small enough. It's not that the Fae themselves are small (though some are—

there are hundreds of species), I wanted to hitch a ride with a hummer. Those tiny, sugar-high speedsters are essentially living portals. They can flit between the Human and Fae dimensions like they're just nipping out for a coffee run. One second they're sippin' nectar, next, poof — gone. Off on a cosmic bender.

So here I am. Stuck. Big sigh.

And let me tell you, Human time-space is a proper drag. The majority of self-determined powerful are stuck on repeat: fear, greed, violence, rinse, repeat. Sure, most everyday folks are trying their best, but the system? Absolutely cooked. Meanwhile, other beings across the multiverse are out there thriving, living their best lives without trashing their planets. Trust me, I wouldn't have chosen this assignment if I'd had a say. I'd rather be gallivanting around as some glow-in-the-dark alien artist or a Fae forest DJ. But no, here I am, watching Humanity doom-scroll itself into oblivion. Meanwhile, races of far more civilised and advanced intelligence forms have been living peacefully and leveraging kindness throughout the multiverse for eternities. Human Earth time-space just can't seem to get the frequency right.

When I first began adjusting to my Human-dense existence, everything felt out of balance, and if I'm being honest, downright crazy. It is a magical place, too, don't get me wrong. There's plenty of magic here in the Human dimension, just not the kind of everything-interconnected kind I remember from the Fae dimension. As a kid and teen, I watched the systems on Human Earth crumble around me like a rusted machine sputtering its last breath. The schools weren't places for learning but breeding grounds for violence and indifference. Personalised care for youth was nonexistent; just a conveyor belt pushing out students without any regard for their individuality. The jobs were monotonous, stifling the natural creative impulse that I knew all Humans held within them. And don't get me started on healthcare. Broken, toxic, and designed more for profit than healing, it left people sicker than before. Most of the Humans I knew were addicted to something: alcohol, shopping, sex, drugs, or worse, just to numb themselves to the reality that previous generations had created.

You can see why I would have never willingly dropped into this drab looping disco party. I would much rather incarnate as a more advanced race to live out a life of meaning, freedom, and creative impulse. But I'm not giving up on Humans just yet. That's part of the reason I wanted to go to the Fae dimension; I knew they had some proper ways of living, and I figured I could bring it back to Humanity. As far as I've remembered, fairies are nothing like Tinkerbell from Disney movies. They are varied and vast in shape and form. But their dimension is less dense, and they have less form than what we experience as Humans. Think: living light-beams with a bit of form so they don't blow away.

In the Fae dimension, things moved with the rhythm of thought. The pace of manifestation was easy and flowed in harmony with the natural world. Their technology didn't oppose nature; it worked with it, informed by its intelligence. They are a civilization so advanced that waste doesn't exist in the way Humans know it. Everything was regenerative, every creation intentional.

It wasn't all perfect, though. The speed of life in the Fae dimension, as wonderful as it sounds, has its downsides. Relationships? Total bin fire. With things moving so quickly, commitment became almost impossible. Their kind didn't have time to bond as deeply as I see Humans do here. There's a particular sect of Fae that, like me, as far as I can remember, struggles with this. They're known as the Eura, and they are uniquely gifted and cursed. These poor sods have wings for ears, so they catch every single vibe in the room. Their ability to anticipate others' needs before they speak makes them excel in social situations. But it also overwhelms them, causing them to retreat into solitude. Eura rarely form lasting bonds because they feel too much, too often. As a Human, I exhibit Eura traits myself, which explains why I ghost people after a few mistaken sideways glances.

There are other types of Fae, too, though I've only been able to recall fragments from ancient mythology and deep meditation. The Learli are a race that glows with a more subtle ethereal light. Their bodies are semi-translucent, and their emotions radiate in colours visible to the naked eye. They are the keepers of knowledge and wisdom, often detached from the emotional pull of the present moment, choosing to live in contemplation of the stars, the future, and the vastness of the multiverse. Learli generally live in solitude, their brilliance isolating them from the rest of Fae society. Then, there are the Thelassi, sea-dwelling Fae who are fluid like the ocean itself. Their forms shift and change with the tides, and they can shape themselves into whatever they need to be. Their adaptability makes them hard to spot, as they are constantly moving. The Ekat, forest guardians with antlered crowns and bark-like skin, are deeply connected to the Earth, acting as protectors and mediators between the Fae and the natural world.

Unlike the others, the Ekat are slow to act, deliberate in their every movement; perhaps the only Fae who understand the value of patience. Their hearts beat with the pulse of ancient trees, and they are one of the few Fae capable of forming long-lasting relationships. There are too many types of Fae to list, but these were some of the ones I remembered in my memories.

Since I was a little bean, I've been trying to crack the code on how to shrink down enough to hitch a ride on a hummer. And I'm now a full-grown adult, so I'm told, at 29, and I still haven't figured it out. I'm a perfectly standard, run-of-the-mill female-bodied Human, with wavy brown hair, brown eyes, 5'5", and an 8-foot shoe size. I blend into all crowds, which comes in handy since I don't mind being invisible. I became a scientist, and that's what I do for my day job. But at night, I work on my plan to get to my real home. I've been working on a concoction just like out of Alice in Wonderland that would shrink me small enough to be able to hop on a hummingbird.

It's going pretty wonky if I'm being honest. I started with the potions, and they did teach me a thing or two. There was a time when I mixed in too much silicon with the conductor fluid and tested it on my hand, turning it into a flimsy, glue-like substance for a few minutes. Admittedly, my kea-like shrieks didn't help the situation much. Or, the time when I overdid the incinerator mixture and left it a little too long in the heat, and ended up with a dead leg for about two hours. I had mastered body transformation by the time I got through the last few years of experiments, but none of them shrunk me to a smaller size; they just warped my body into weird shapes. Thankfully, I could bounce back from all of the mess-ups, with a few tinctures and lots of Band-Aids.

After this much epic shrinking flop, I reckon it's time to give a new angle a crack. Now, my plans are moving more into quantum physics with a dash of fancy tech. I'm hoping to adjust my body's chemistry to be crystalline enough that I just hop in and out of the Fae timeline at will, and I can give up hitching a ride on a bird. The only quirk in my plan is that I need a helper. I hate having to rely on other people. There is only one person I would ever trust with such an important job. And I didn't want to bug her. But I picked up the phone anyway.

"Jeanie, can you, umm, can you keep this on the DL?" If there was one person I did trust, it was Jeanie, despite her ADHD.

"Of course, I can, my lips are a trap of glue, or a steel trap, or um, whatever they say," she sounded distracted.

"You ok?" I didn't want to tell her anything if I couldn't get her full attention.

"It's just that Darwin is kind of sick." Darwin was her pet frog. One of about 20 pets she kept illegally off-leash in her small apartment on 3rd Street. "I think he ate a bead from my latest project." Jeanie was a jewelry artist and made gorgeous retro-inspired handmade earrings, which had been flying off the proverbial online shelves lately, thanks to Etsy. We'd been best friends since college, and I adored everything about her power in an under-five-foot package. Her freckles and curls completed the adorable that had her popular with all the ladies, too. She came out in college. I was jelly of her on two counts. One, she had much simpler ways than my wild and weird parallel dimension dreams. Secondly, dating women felt way easier to figure out than my shambly love life.

"Listen, I need some help," I lowered my voice to a whisper for no reason at all because I was alone in my house.

"Oi, don't even start, Daria." Jeanie knew my so-called help requests were never straightforward. "I'm not getting roped into any of your nonsense again. Last time you had me helping, the neighbours nearly called the cops on me 'cause of that weird-as-purple fungus creeping down the hallway in my flat!"

"Don't be so dramatic, it was just a little overgrowth problem." I knew I needed to rein her in quickly, or I'd lose her to the frog and the bunny and the cats.

"Righto, so, here's the deal," I was choosing my words carefully, I didn't want to manipulate her into this. I wanted her to genuinely want to help me, and I knew she did; she's my BFF, after all, and she wanted the best for me.

"Please don't tell me I have to shoot you with a water gun full of an alien substance," she interrupted. Bugger, she does know me, doesn't she?

"I mean, it's not a water gun," I started to explain.

"Oi," she sighed. I could just picture her pushing up the glasses on her nose and squinting her eyes at me, "There's a gun involved?"

"I mean, it's not a gun it points a suspended light structure which allows the singularity of the dimensional field to open, the gravimetric signature of the quarks and glucons are detected, and then the filter targets the center of a particle to pull the matter and collapse it so I can then replace it with the crystalline frequencies to be able to hop into the Fae dimension."

"Still sounds like a bloody gun to me, a crystal fairy gun," Jeanie sighs more dramatically this time.

"I haven't named it yet since I don't know if it will work, but we can call it a Crystal Converter." That sounded way less dodgy than it actually was, perfect.

"Ok, when are we testing this thing?" she sounded distracted again, "I can't on Saturday, Bixby's got his jabs. No, Shar, don't do that, you can't eat that!" Bixby was her new cat. I had no idea which creature was the feral one she called Shar.

"Let's shoot for Sunday," that would give me a couple of days to figure out how to get this thing to turn on. No problem.

"OK, Shar is about to eat Sandy's meds, gotta go! See you then!"

"Bye!" I hung up the phone and had a moment of panic. Maybe I'm not ready. Maybe I'm jumping the gun again.

CHAPTER TWO

Daria: Tinker

Tinkering is a real thing we Humans, who should have been fairies, do. But not always in productive ways, I might add. Like today, I was avoiding the tinkering I needed to do with the Crystal Converter to adjust the mirror in the bathroom just so, to ensure my books were ordered by colour and first letter, and to count the grains of tiny rocks in the fish tank. Classic avoidance tactics for an only slightly OCD fairy Human.

I suppose I felt like this was my last chance. What would life be like if I could not go there, to the place where I knew was my true home? How would I learn to accept this terrible Earthperiment where most of the Humans were heart-crushingly disconnected and disenchanted with life?

I had tried everything one could imagine to enjoy being a Human. Meditation, present moment awareness, learning to be patient, building and losing many relationships that seemed to end in disaster despite all my best attempts at love and kindness. I'd tried to find solace in it being enough to have my "wings clipped." But it just always felt like my true home was elsewhere, and my heart longed to know whether it was a legit yearning or just a cheeky trick from my ego dangling a sparkly carrot. I was determined to find out. Today. No more mucking about.

Eventually, I made my way to the lab. Riley was always five steps ahead of me, anticipating my every move. She was already sitting patiently, panting, ready to nudge me in the right direction. I couldn't speak fluent dog to understand her tone when she lovingly growled at me, but I figured it meant to get moving. If it weren't for her furball fuzz, I am pretty sure she was made of pencils for bones, typical Pomeranian. Riley was my ride-or-die pup, and she was one of the few creatures on the Earth plane that got me, or at least I liked to think she did from the way her head tilted when I talked to her. Jeanie would be here soon, and off I'd go into the wild woods of a Fae forest or a hospital bed; it was a 50/50 coin toss.

I stared at the Crystal Converter, its sleek, reflective surface glimmering under the fluorescent lights. It looked almost normal, like a fancy salon hair dryer you'd find in Ponsonby, except it housed the most advanced laser tech available. I hadn't slept much since the idea took root, and now, it felt like my entire existence was bound up in this one device. I couldn't help but feel a pang of nostalgia for the simpler days when I dreamt of shrinking down, hopping on a hummingbird, and zipping into the Fae forests. But here I was, staring at a piece of tech that could either catapult me to my true home or disintegrate me on the spot.

Riley sniffed at the device, then looked up at me with those big eyes as if asking, "Are we really doing this?" I bent down and scratched behind her ears, more to soothe myself than her.

"I know, girl. I know." My voice was softer than usual, the weight of the decision pressing down on me. What if it didn't work? Or worse, what if it did? Would I lose Riley, Jeanie, and this strange, broken world that had somehow become my life?

But there was no going back. Not now. Not after years of experiments, failures, and fleeting moments of hope. I had to trust the part of me that remembered the Fae dimension, buried under layers of doubt and late-night ice cream binges. It was out there, just beyond the edge of this one, and I was determined to break through.

I pulled up the schematics one last time, my fingers trembling slightly as I scrolled through the blueprints on my tablet. Everything seemed in order. But there was still that voice that whispered, "What if you're wrong?" I shook my head, trying to dispel the fear. I couldn't afford to hesitate, not when I was this close. I had to trust that part of me that remembered and knew what to do, even if it was buried deep beneath layers of forgetting.

Jeanie's arrival was heralded by the chaotic jingle of her keychain and the clatter of her oversized bag against the doorframe. She stumbled in, juggling an overflowing mug of coffee, a pet carrier with Bixby inside, and what looked like a half-finished necklace dangling from her wrist.

"Don't ask," she said before I could even open my mouth. "Bixby wouldn't stop yowling, so I had to bring him. And yes, I needed the largest possible coffee; it's one of those mornings."

I just nodded, too wrapped up in my nerves to process the whirlwind that was Jeanie's life. Bixby's plaintive meow echoed through the room, but I was already turning back to the Crystal Converter, my mind racing. Jeanie took one look at the device, then at me, and her expression softened. "You ready for this, Daria?"

My head bobbed in affirmation, though I wasn't sure if I was trying to convince her or myself. "Yeah. I think so. I mean, it's now or never, right?"

She set her coffee down on the nearest surface and walked over to me, placing a hand on my shoulder. "Just... promise me you won't blow yourself up, okay? I'm not cleaning up that kind of mess."

I managed a weak smile. "No explosions. Hopefully."

We both stared at the Crystal Converter in silence for a moment. The air between us was thick with unspoken fears, but also an enlivening anticipation. The kind that had kept me going all these years, chasing after a dream that was categorically insane to everyone else.

Jeanie cleared her throat, breaking the tension. "So, what do I have to do?"

I took a deep breath and started explaining the process, trying to keep my voice steady. "It's pretty simple. I've set the parameters, so all you have to do is aim it at me and press the trigger. The light will do the rest."

She raised an eyebrow. "That's it? Just point and shoot?"

"Yeah," I grimaced, though my heart was pounding. "Just point and shoot."

Jeanie nodded, concern etched across her brow. "Okay, but if you start glowing or, I don't know, melting, I'm stopping this."

"Fair enough," I said, trying to sound more confident than I felt. "But I'll be fine. Trust me."

We both knew that "trust me" was a loaded phrase in our friendship, one that had been tested many times over the years. But this time, it felt different. This time, it wasn't just about some crazy experiment or half-baked idea. This was about everything; about finding my true home, about escaping the suffocating slowness of Human-Earth-ways, about finally, finally, being where I belonged.

Jeanie picked up the Crystal Converter, her fingers hovering over the trigger. "You sure about this, Daria?"

I swallowed hard, then nodded. "Yeah. I'm sure."

She hesitated for a split second longer, then aimed the device at me, her grip steady despite the tension that crackled between us. I closed my eyes, bracing myself for... I didn't even know what. The light? The shift? The end?

There was a soft click, followed by a whizzing noise that reverberated from the Converter with a growing urgency. The air around me seemed to shimmer, like the surface of a pond disturbed by a single drop of rain as a thunderstorm cleared. For a moment, everything was still. Then the objects around me began to warp, colours bleeding into each other, shapes distorting and stretching like taffy.

And then... nothing.

I opened my eyes to find myself still standing in my lab, the fluorescent lights flickering overhead, Jeanie's wide eyes staring back at me.

"It didn't work," I breathed, a mix of relief and crushing disappointment flooding through me.

Jeanie lowered the Crystal Converter, her expression a blend of confusion and concern. "What happened? Are you okay?"

"I... I don't know," I said, my voice trembling. "I felt something, but..."

I looked down at my hands, expecting to see some sign of change: glowing skin, shrinking limbs, anything. But there was nothing. I was still me, still trapped in this too-slow, too-solid Earth body.

"Maybe it's just a fluke," Jeanie suggested, though she didn't sound convinced. "We can try again, right?"

"Yeah," I said numbly, though the hope that had fueled me for so long was already starting to fade. "Yeah, we can try again."

But even as I said it, I couldn't shake the feeling that something had gone wrong. I had missed my chance, and now I was stuck here in this world that was never meant to be mine. Riley nudged my leg, her warm, furry body grounding me in the present. I reached down to pet her, grateful for the small comfort she offered.

Jeanie set the Crystal Converter down carefully as if it were a fragile thing that might break if handled too roughly. "Maybe we need to tweak the settings or something," she said, though her voice was distant as if she were speaking more to herself than to me.

"Yeah," I mumbled, fully knowing I didn't know if I had the

strength to try again. Not after coming so close, only to be pulled back into this reality.

The room felt too quiet, too still, as if the whole world was holding its breath, waiting to see what I would do next. But I didn't have any answers. All I had were the pieces of a dream that had shattered around me. Jeanie was still talking, something about recalibrating the device, about not giving up, but her words were a blur, lost in the fog of my thoughts. I wanted to believe her, to hold on to the hope that had kept me going all these years. But right now, all I felt was the weight of failure pressing down on me like a lead blanket.

"I need some air," I muttered, cutting Jeanie off mid-sentence. I didn't wait for her response, just turned and walked out of the lab, Riley trotting at my heels. The cool evening air hit me like a shock, clearing some of the haze in my mind. I took a deep breath, trying to steady myself, to push back the tears that were threatening to spill over. Riley pressed against my leg, her presence a small comfort amid my swirling emotions.

I wandered down the street, not paying attention to where I was going. The sky was a deep indigo, the first stars just beginning to peek through the twilight. The world around me felt too big, too vast, and I was a speck lost in an endless sea of time and space. Eventually, I found myself at the edge of the park, the grass cool and damp beneath my feet. I sank onto a bench, staring up at the sky, my mind racing with thoughts that refused to settle. What if this was it? What if I was meant to stay here, trapped in this suffocating world, forever cut off from the place where I truly belonged?

The thought was too painful to bear, so I pushed it aside, focusing instead on the stars, on the tiny points of light that seemed so far away, so unreachable. Maybe Jeanie was right. Maybe we needed to tweak the settings to try again. But deep down, a part of me knew that it wasn't that simple. The Fae dimension wasn't just a place I could reach with the right technology. Perhaps it was a state of being, a frequency that I couldn't seem to tune into, no matter how hard I tried.

I don't know how long I sat there, lost in my thoughts, before I heard a soft rustle beside me in a bush. I turned my head, expecting to see a bird or maybe a bat, but there was nothing there. Just the faint echo of a sound, like the memory of something long past. I shook my head, dismissing it as my imagination, and stood up, Riley following suit. The night was growing colder, and I could feel the chill seeping into my bones, a stark reminder that I was still very much a part of this

Human world, whether I wanted to be or not.

I started to head back, my steps heavy, when I felt it again: that strange, fleeting sensation, like a brush of air against my skin, or the whisper of wings just out of sight. I stopped, turning around, but again, there was nothing. Just the quiet of the night, the distant hum of the town, and the steady thrum of my heartbeat in my ears. Maybe it was nothing. Or maybe... maybe the Fae dimension was closer than I thought. Closer than I could ever have imagined.

The thought sent a shiver down my spine, but this time, it wasn't fear that gripped me. It was something else; something that felt a lot like hope. Maybe I hadn't failed after all. Maybe the Crystal Converter had done something, something I couldn't see or understand just yet. Maybe the Fae dimension wasn't a place I needed to find, but a part of myself that I needed to remember. And maybe, just maybe, I was already there, standing on the edge of two worlds.

"Nah," I shook it off and laughed at myself for going crazy, turning around to head back to the lab and apologise to Jeanie for running away. Just then, as I turned around to leave, I heard a voice that sounded strangely familiar, and eerily unique, rumbling with a thump and a bang from behind the blooming, fragrant lilac bush.

"Ouuuuch, where in the heck am I?"

CHAPTER THREE

Caelan: Maze

20 CE Linear Time (Common Era, After the Fall of Ether)
Planet: *Earth* **Dimension:** *Fae*
Galaxy: *Milky Way*

I hadn't had as much as a drop of elderwine since the wedding, and I still felt like I'd been whacked over the head with a taleni branch. I couldn't think straight, and my ears rang — never a good thing for a fairy with a heightened sense of hearing. The dull hum of Faierodon's bustling energy raced through me, making it harder to focus. And the maze... what in all the realms was I still doing in this maze?

But it's not a surprise that I participated in the festivities a little too much, given that I was supposed to be the groom only weeks ago. Beyond the shock and heartbreak that came with your fiancé breaking it off with you for a musician from the West Villas, it didn't help that he also used to be my best friend. But, hey, what's new with Eura, am I right? We tend to flit about from relationship to relationship, or so I'm told. My heart never really got on board with "the way it is." I fluttered unsteadily, narrowly avoiding a wall of glimmering thistles. "You think you can help out here, Spitz?"

Sure, Spitz was a glowbug no larger than a dewdrop, but he sure had the wit of a sprite at times. Zipping into view, he carefully perched on my shoulder with a huff. "Help? You're the one who decided to face-plant into that elderwine barrel last night. I'm just here to make sure you don't get stuck in a hedge."

I groaned. "Remind me again why I agreed to come?"

"Watching Remidia fall epically on top of her sister in the conrea dance is heaps of fun, but, admittedly, it was not worth the side effect."

I shook my head, trying to make sense of the maze and failing miserably. Faierodon was typically an orderly realm, but everything about this wedding had been designed to confuse, disorient, and, quite frankly, dazzle. I'd been noticing that more and more lately — this constant dizzying light show of extravagant events and excess that didn't use to be the norm. Anyone who tried to see something more meaningful beneath the surface would get distracted immediately by the glimmering show. The iridescent towers of the city spiraled in the distance, an architectural marvel of crystal and energy beams. Floating platforms whisked away guests, flickering with bioluminescent lights. Hovering gardens, spires made of pure crystal, and invisible passageways... it was breathtaking — and chaotic. But it always felt so dizzying to me, and I felt so alone as an Eura who was supposed to enjoy this stuff. Our kind had always prided ourselves on our tech and how it was in harmony with natural law, but it seemed like something had shifted in the last several gaelons as I was growing up. I couldn't help feeling like there had to be a way to enjoy the natural world more than this, to slow down like the Ekat in the wooden glens. Sure, we had built our world into the fibers of nature with our tech, but it was still moving so quickly. Ever since I was small, I remembered feeling a longing to slow down, to pause, to be able to use my senses at full capacity and enjoy things longer.

But that was not the way of the Eura. We were proudly the three F's: feely, flighty, and flashy. We had become show-offs, and the rest of the Fae avoided us most of the time because of our self-absorbed ways, though they benefited greatly from our innovation. I never felt like I fit in, so I had spent much of my youth studying other civilizations, trying to find the source of my discomfort.

As I was pondering my studies momentarily, Spitz buzzed in front of my face. "You're doing it again."

"Doing what?"

"Zoning out. Thinking about Humans again."

I shot him a look. "I am not." Nonetheless, my hand went to my pocket just to check that the Eurometer was still there, just in case. I kept it on me at all times. Among its many functions in interdimensional species communication, it helped Eura convert the speeds of other species speaking to a pace that could be interpreted by the Eura eardrum. It had a range from the slowest of creatures, such as the Lakdeo that live in the slowest known dimension, so slow that our entire concept of the multiverse's timeline happens while this dimension is in its earliest evolutionary moment of creation. Humans' Earth speed is slow, but it's in its quickening phase of evolution. The device was there, right where I always kept it. I flipped it on just in case; its nearly indistinguishable hum started to rumble in my pocket.

"You are. You've got that dreamy glaze in your eyes." He zipped ahead, lighting the way, gently teasing. "I don't get why you're so obsessed. Humans are just a myth."

"And yet, we exist to them as myths," I muttered, cautiously hopping on the strange floating blobs leading us forward on this glowing trail. "I mean, if they didn't exist, why do we have documentation of them in our Field Anthologies? Why do we have them on the time-space Eurometer? They must be in one of the dimensions."

Spitz hovered before me, spinning in a lazy circle. "So what if they exist? The Field talks of races and dimensions in every time-space. Why do you care about the Human one so much? They are supposed to be rather slow and dull anyway, aren't they? You're wasting your energy, Caelan. Focus on something more important, like surviving this maze or, ooh, I don't know, moving on from your heartbreak."

"I'm moving on," I lied, fluttering lower to avoid a particularly prickly branch of enchanted nettles. "I don't know, I guess I feel pulled to them."

"It's a distraction," Spitz argued, zigzagging back and forth. "And you need fewer distractions right now. Remember what happened last time you got obsessed with a Human myth?"

I rolled my eyes. "It wasn't that bad."

"You ended up stuck in a mirror for three days, Caelan! You keep getting yourself into trouble that I had to get you out of, I might add. Quit trying to figure out why we banned them from our logs."

"Okay, maybe it was a little bit of drama," I muttered. "But this is different."

"Oh sure, different," Spitz teased, lighting up a pathway that twisted sharply to the left. "At least this time, you're making it more interesting by getting lost in an actual maze, not just the Human maze of dead ends."

We turned the corner, and I had to admit the maze wasn't nearly as fun as I'd thought it would be last night when I'd accepted the dare. Faierodon's labyrinth was famous for its enchanted traps, shifting walls, and mischievous Fae illusions. Under normal circumstances, it might've been a thrilling challenge, but today, it felt like another headache that matched the one pounding through the mush between my ears. Spitz's glow dimmed as we reached a narrow clearing lined with glowing flowers that sang faint melodies. He perched on a nearby petal and glanced at me. "Look, I get it. You're distracted because you're heartbroken, and your mind's wandering to old fantasies. But maybe it's time to let the Human thing go."

I opened my mouth to argue when a strange sensation prickled at the edge of my senses. I froze, wings fluttering silently, and strained to listen. There it was, a faint voice, far off and distant like a whisper carried on a gust of wind. It wasn't any Fae language I knew. It was... something else. My heart pounded as I strained to catch the words. It was the faintest sound, a seemingly feminine-sounding voice, but not any creature from the Fae.

"...I need... some air..."

I blinked, trying to focus. I understood it. I looked down at the Eurometer; it was blinking on the Human setting.

Spitz's glow brightened as he noticed my reaction. "Caelan? What is it?"

"I... I heard something."

Spitz buzzed closer, interest flickering in his tiny voice. "What kind of something?"

I looked around wildly, trying to pinpoint the sound. "It was a voice. I think... it was coming from somewhere not in our world. It sounded like a female, perhaps. The Eurometer is glowing on the Human setting."

Spitz scoffed. "Here we go again. Caelan, you've really got to—"

"I'm serious!" I interrupted, my pulse quickening. Having always-on-alert winged ears was both an asset and a curse. "It sounded... it sounded a little like the noises I heard that were Human in the forbidden library. They have old audio clips. And this voice just now — it felt like, almost like... she was trying to reach me. Or calling for help? I don't know, I'm probably hallucinating." I shook my head and paused, bending down to catch some air.

Spitz blinked twice, his wings shimmering with disbelief. "You're sure?"

"I don't know," I admitted, my mind racing. "But it felt real. And I know what you're going to say, but this time—"

"No, no, I'm with you, mate," Spitz said, surprising me. "If you think you heard something, maybe we should investigate. I mean, what's the worst that could happen?"

"Besides getting trapped in another maze dimension?" I muttered.

The voice came again, fainter this time, as if drifting away. It sounded like muffled crying. Spitz's wings buzzed, uncomfortable. "Okay, that was definitely something." My heart leapt at the confirmation. I wasn't imagining it. Somewhere, somehow, a Human was reaching out.

I glanced at Spitz, who had shed his usual sarcasm for a rare moment of seriousness. "We need to follow that voice." Spitz hesitated but nodded. "Alright, but if we end up stuck in some interdimensional limbo, I'm not begging the elders to save you this time." There he was, back to his usual self.

We darted down the glowing path, the maze seeming to twist and shift with us. Each turn felt more urgent as the voice grew fainter, slipping through the cracks in reality. I couldn't explain why, but deep down, I knew this was the moment I had been waiting for; proof that Humans existed, that the myths weren't just stories. It was like my obsession had finally opened the door to something real. I shook my head again, trying to make it work properly.

But the maze wasn't giving up easily. Just as we rounded another bend, the walls shifted with a loud groan, sealing off the path ahead. I ignored the strange sound, staring at the smooth stone wall that had appeared out of nowhere. The voice was gone now, but its echo lingered in my mind. She had sounded lost... and scared. What if this Human were stuck somewhere between dimensions? I wanted to figure out how to help.

"We have to find her," I said, my voice resolute.

"Right," Spitz sighed. "Because chasing down mysterious voices in enchanted mazes always ends well for us."

Spitz's fear couldn't quell the excitement bubbling up inside me. Maybe this was it. Could this be the adventure I had always dreamt of? Finding proof that Humans were more than just legends, that they were out there, waiting to be discovered? The question now was... where? And how could we break through the maze's endless tricks and traps to reach this voice? Or was this just an illusion of the maze? Was I making it all up?

Suddenly, a wasp of glowing green and blinding pink lights blocked our path. I'd recognise this creature anywhere; it was a Learli. They usually don't leave their homes in Gredarr, so what could have drawn one here? I hadn't seen one before outside of picture books at school as a wee Fae. They were never among us common Fae, and it didn't bode well to see one now. Was that the voice I heard?

"I must intervene," the Learli whispered, radiating and extending a large, white glowing spiral grid, blocking our path. I took a step back, distracted. This was not the voice that I had heard in the distance at all.

"How did you get in here?" I asked with a gentle firmness to hide my insecurity. "Are you an illusion? I'm beginning to think that elderwine was laced with something."

"Kindly refrain from proceeding, Eura boy," the Learli continued. "I fail to understand why you would drink the elderwine anyway, given you don't need a physical substance to survive."

It's a common misconception among the Fae that the Eura don't partake in physical sustenance because we are translucent and can mostly live off the biofumes of the city's naturally produced energies. In reality, we chose a long time ago to continue to partake in the physical sensate experiences that races like the Ekat and Thelassi still enjoy because, frankly, we got bored otherwise.

"Do you have a point, lady?" Spitz intervened.

"I must implore you not to proceed forward. There has been a dimension tear detected here just now; we must be extremely cautious," the Learli pressed. "To my recollection, it has never occurred before, and I was sent immediately to mitigate."

"A dimension, what?" I was feeling a bit dizzy now.

"Tear," the Learli repeated, sounding exceedingly bored. "You don't have to understand it, just please do not proceed."

"But I heard a voice. She sounded like she was in distress." I was not giving up so easily. I felt a sure pull that I needed to find this creature. Was she on the other side of the tear? Was that why I heard her? I pressed my hand against the stone wall, the cold surface humming beneath my fingertips. "There's got to be a way through," I murmured, glancing at Spitz, who was flickering uncertainly beside me.

"And what, you think you're just going to wish your way through?" he snorted, wings buzzing irritably.

Before I could fire back, the wall beneath my hand trembled. A shiver of energy passed through the air, and I instinctively took a step back. The stones rippled like water disturbed by a single drop, and then they... vanished. One moment, there was a solid barrier, and the next, it was as if the maze had simply given up its game.

"Okay, that was weird," Spitz muttered, hovering closer. "Even by Fae standards." I leaned forward to look and lost my footing.

"Stop! Don't do it!" the Learli sounded alarmed as Spitz and I were instantaneously whisked into another place.

Beyond the wall, an eerie glow pulsed in the distance, drawing me forward. My wings fluttered with excitement and apprehension as I stepped through the space where the wall had been, the air thick with the scent of damp earth and moss. Spitz zipped ahead, his tiny glow flickering nervously. "This is not normal. Are you sure about this, Cae?"

I nodded, my heart pounding in my chest. "There's something here, I can feel it."

The ground beneath me shifted, and suddenly, the world seemed to tilt on its axis. I stumbled, losing my balance as the ground dropped out from under me. My wings beat frantically, trying to catch me, but it was no use. The air felt thick and unfamiliar as I gasped for breath.

With a jarring thud, I landed on solid ground, groaning as pain shot through my leg. "Ouch, where in the heck am I?"

CHAPTER FOUR

Caelan: the Tear

The words echoed strangely in the air, and when I opened my eyes, the vibrant, glowing maze of Faierodon was gone. In its place, solid, dense-looking trees loomed overhead, their leaves rustling in a soft breeze that felt entirely foreign. The sky above was a dull grey, unlike the ever-shifting hues of the Fae sky. I blinked, trying to adjust to the strange stillness, the unfamiliar gravity weighing down my wings. I sat up, rubbing my sore leg, which felt heavier than normal. Suddenly, a soft gasp caught my attention. I turned quickly, only to freeze at the sight of a girl—a Human girl—standing just a few feet away.

Her reaction was immediate. Her eyes widened to the size of full moons as she took an instinctive step backward. She wasn't just staring at me; she was *staring* at me. And why wouldn't she? I wasn't exactly subtle. My whole body was illuminated, radiating a faint blue glow that shimmered across my skin like ripples of light in a pond. I could see the reflection of my iridescence in her eyes, making her look even more stunned than I felt.

Her lips parted slightly, her breath catching as she struggled to process what she was seeing. Until this moment, I'd never thought about how strange I must look to a Human—a being made of pure light, hovering, multiple pairs of wings fluttering softly as blue tendrils of shimmering energy cascaded around me, catching the dim light filtering through the trees. Though looking down at myself, it appeared that my body was adapting a bit to this dimension, more solid, more physical.

"You…" she breathed, barely audible. "What are you?" Her voice trembled, not from fear but from disbelief, as though she couldn't wrap her head around the fact that I was standing there, glowing like some ethereal apparition.

"I'm Caelan," I said softly, trying not to startle her more than I already had. My wings fluttered behind me, the soft, rhythmic glow dimming a bit as I tried to make myself seem less... well, otherworldly. "And I don't think I'm supposed to be here."

Her hand went to her mouth as if she were trying to hold in a gasp, and her eyes flickered over my form, taking in the shimmering hues that danced across my skin. I watched as her gaze moved from my wings to the faint glow that emanated from every inch of me, her expression wavering between disbelief and wonder.

Her voice, when it came, was soft, almost a whisper. "Umm, I'm Daria. Are you... Are you some kind of angel?"

I blinked, caught off guard by the question. "I am unfamiliar with the term," I said gently. "I'm referred to as a fairy—I believe Humans call us that. I'm an Eura, to be specific. I come from a realm called Faierodon, and, well, I accidentally ended up... here."

Her hand fell slowly from her mouth, and she took a tentative step forward, her eyes never leaving mine. "You're glowing," she said, almost to herself, as if she still couldn't quite believe it.

I couldn't help the small smile that tugged at my lips. "It appears that I've morphed form a bit to fit into your realm," I explained, glancing down at my body. For some reason, I was nearly her size.

She blinked, and a faint blush crept up her cheeks as if she suddenly realised how intensely she'd been staring. She shifted her weight awkwardly, tucking a loose strand of chestnut-coloured hair behind her ear. "I... I've never seen anything like you before. Well, except in my memories," she admitted, her voice softer now, less startled, more curious.

Spitz finally buzzed into view, his tiny glow flickering with annoyance. "I should hope not; I think we broke dimensions to get here. We are in big trouble, Cae."

The girl blinked again, her gaze shifting to Spitz, who was hovering in front of her face. "And what's that?" she asked, her voice a mixture of fascination and disbelief.

Spitz huffed, crossing his tiny arms. "I'm not a *that*—I'm Spitz, a very underappreciated glowbug who seems to have gotten dragged into yet another one of Caelan's Human-hunting adventures."

Daria let out a breathy laugh, the tension in her body easing slightly as she processed the bizarre situation she'd found herself in. "Well, this is definitely… something." She looked back at me, her gaze softer now, the awe still lingering but mixed with something else—concern, maybe? "Listen, I think I may have had a part in this dimension issue," she offered, her voice steadying as she took another small step toward me. "I feel like I'm responsible for this. I want to help you figure it out."

I met her gaze, and for the first time since I'd had my heart blown up into seven million star particles by Remidia, I felt like I wasn't entirely lost. There was something in the way she looked at me—like she wasn't afraid to understand what she didn't know—that made me feel at ease and strangely connected to her in ways I was not willing to think about at this moment.

"Responsible, how exactly?" I asked, an eyebrow lifting in wonder.

"Well, I may have, um, run an experiment that maybe, possibly, could have created this dimension problem you're referring to and landed you here." She looked a puzzled mix of pride and concern, her eyes glimmering with the reality of talking with us here in the twilight of a park somewhere in her world.

"What kind of experiment?" Spitz demanded, sounding a bit impatient.

"It's a long story, but basically, I've always felt like I wasn't supposed to have been born as a Human, and I knew there was a way to get to your dimension." She looked down sheepishly at her shoes, trying not to show the embarrassment on her face in admitting her truth. "So, I've been tirelessly working to find a way to get to your world, to your dimension. And, from the looks of it, I somehow succeeded. But not exactly the way I had hoped." She stumbled over her words.

"I mean, no offense, I'm happy to meet you." She glanced up again, and my heart did a little flip as her eyes pierced into mine. "It's just that I wanted to go to your world, not the other way around. Also, I'm surprized you're so large. I thought you'd be small, like in our myths."

"It's the strangest thing," I began to explain what had happened. "I heard you. I could hear you speaking before we even realised what was happening. I don't know about the size, but we shouldn't be able to hear each other. Our dimension is much faster paced, but this device I have, it's called a Eurometer. I turned it on for some reason right before this all started. It must be adjusting my entire time-space experience to be able to adapt to this dimension and interact with its creatures, even for Spitz."

The moment felt surreal; I couldn't believe I was really here.

"I'm sorry," she interrupted. "I didn't mean to have you sent here." I felt her trepidation, and my concern for her well-being was increasing, uncomfortably disproportionate to how little I knew her.

"No, don't worry at all. I am quite keen to be here. I've always been rather obsessed, as Spitz would say, with trying to find out if Humans were real. This feels like a dream come true." I saw her shoulders relax a little as I spoke.

But now I had to tell her the hard part. "The thing is, Daria, before we were whisked here, a Fae from an ancient and wise race from our dimension was warning us that we tore time-space. She was telling us not to proceed, and then, wham—we were here anyway."

"Exactly!" Spitz burst out. "We're probably mucking up the whole of existence just 'cause you two wanted to prove the other one's real. Well, sweet as, mission accomplished. So... how do we get home then?"

"Do you feel that?" Daria looked uneasy, her face pointed upward. "What's happening in the sky?"

The air around us started to feel heavy, weighing us down as if the very fabric of reality was warping. I clenched my fists, my heart pounding in my chest. The excitement of meeting this dazzling creature was quickly overshadowed by a growing sense of unease. Just then, out of nowhere, from the shadows of the trees, a figure emerged.

"I can assist you with returning."

It was a woman's voice. Her figure became more visible as she approached. Dressed in midnight blue, her hair slicked back, she looked like someone who would definitely have a *don't mess with me* tattoo on her forehead if you lifted her bangs. She had some weird label, "IGSTA", on her shirt. "Returning to your home can be arranged, but I'll need you to sign off on some forms."

"Uh, where did you come from?" Daria looked startled and uncomfortable.

The woman looked up, annoyed, from behind her notepad and dark-coloured sunglasses. "Just your run-of-the-mill Intergalactic Space-Time Agency clean-up crew."

"Are we in trouble?" Spitz was zooming frantically in circles at this point.

"Standard protocol must be observed with an incident like this," the time-space agent explained. "I'm going to see if we can create a repair, or how bad the damage is. Hang tight."

Spitz buzzed frantically, darting back and forth. "I told you this was a bad idea! Now we've got some interdimensional bureaucrat ready to zap us into oblivion!"

My mind raced. I had no idea how to fix a tear in dimensions. I wasn't even clear what Daria had done to cause it. But I knew one thing for certain: we couldn't stay here. This woman from the Agency was giving my senses all sorts of absolutely-do-not-trust activations.

"We need to get out of here," I said, grabbing Daria's hand. "Now."

Daria's eyes widened with fear, but she nodded, her grip tightening on mine. "But where do we go?"

Before I could answer, the ground beneath us began to tremble violently. The trees around us twisted and warped, branches reaching out like gnarled hands. The sky above darkened in swirling, ominous clouds of disapproval. The agent stepped closer, her voice monotone. "You cannot run from this. The tear you've created will cause far larger problems unless we find a way to close it." The agent stepped forward and tried to give me a pen. "Sign here, and we'll get it cleared up in no time."

I had no idea how to fix what we'd done, but I knew one thing: something about this was not right. With a burst of energy, my wings flared to life, and I hoisted Daria onto my back before taking off from the ground. "Hold on!" I tried to soothe her as we darted into the sky, narrowly avoiding the grasping branches of the twisted trees below.

Spitz buzzed alongside us. I could feel how irritated he was with me. "Do you even know where we're going?! Why are we running again?"

"No idea!" I shouted back. "But anywhere's better than here!"

As we flew higher, the air around us started to shimmer and warp, like the fabric of reality was unraveling. The IGSTA agent below watched us, annoyed.

"You cannot escape what you've set in motion," she called after us, her voice echoing in the darkening sky. "The tear will follow you. We will follow you!"

My heart was racing the diantyo tango as we flew farther away, the agent's ominous words echoing in my mind. I didn't know how, but I had to find a way to fix this, to close the tear before it destroyed everything. But as we soared through the sky, I couldn't shake the feeling that this was only the beginning.

What if we couldn't repair what this innocent desire to discover another dimension had set in motion?

CHAPTER FIVE

Daria: Flies

"Where are you taking me?" I sputtered loudly at Caelan.

I was trying, truly, not to lose my cool while being hurled into the sky by a winged creature for the first time in my Human life. My cheeks stung from the ice-slick wind that had whipped up. The ground fell away beneath us, revealing a vast stretch of ocean curling beyond the horizon and mirrored by fiery storm clouds I didn't know how to avoid but hoped Cae could figure it out up here. I wasn't panicking, at least not about the strange agent who might be chasing us (hopefully they couldn't fly like an Eura). What had me awe-struck was the sheer fact that I had done this. My experiment worked. Possibly in a catastrophic, tear-in-the-multiverse sort of way… but still. It worked.

"I think we lost her," Spitz announced, zipping along beside us and squinting down through the cloud line.

I mean, I did trust this Fae. The second we locked eyes, I knew he was Eura—the way you recognise someone you've never met but have always known. I had been confused by his morphed form from my memory of what they would look like. But I hadn't accounted for how my heart would respond to this particular Eura. It pulsed with some memory I couldn't place. I wasn't scared of being carried away by this interdimensional winged stranger. I was trying to figure out where in the multiverse we could land that was even remotely safe.

And now we were soaring, escaping… something. Or someone. Not to mention, a very moody weather system that was not messing around. I glanced down; the northern tip of New Zealand rolled out beneath us in all its wild, quiet beauty. Kaitaia. Still small, still sweet.

Still somehow untouched. Its orchards and grazing hills shimmered below the roiling sky. But the air felt off, like the world's edges were bending, overlaying with something that shouldn't be there. My stomach flipped. I'd torn time-space. And I had no idea what happened next.

"You still haven't answered me!" I shouted over the wind.

Caelan leaned in close to speak, his voice calm and low. "It's your dimension, aye? I knew we had to get away from that lady. The lands are similar to ours, but everything else is different. Got any ideas?"

I peeked back at him. His wings weren't flapping; they were pulsing, like waves of light keeping us aloft in rhythm with some invisible current. For a moment, I forgot the chaos. We were flying, just the two of us, suspended in this momentarily quiet air-dance.

"Not exactly," I admitted. "But Jeanie will help us. Head that way." I pointed toward the town. As if summoned, my phone buzzed. Still airborne, I flipped it open to Jeanie's voice crackling with anxiety.

"Daria, where the hell are you?!"

"Jeanie, I need your help," I blurted. "The Crystal Converter worked, just… not the way we planned. Can you meet us at your house? We're almost there."

"We?" she repeated, voice pitching up.

"No time to explain! See you soon."

We landed gently on her apartment steps, tucked into the most populated part of sleepy little Kaitaia. But it didn't feel like the same town anymore. The sky above was rippling, trying to hold its form as something foreign pressed in. I had this feeling, quiet and insistent, that something else had followed us through the tear. I didn't say anything.

Jeanie answered the door faster than I thought possible, ushering us in with a look that could melt steel. Inside, her flat was a jungle of chaos. Filbert the ferret was scaling the curtains. Ollie the parrot was squawking something about a "door to the stars." And my favorite of her pets, Darwin? Nowhere in sight.

"Jeanie, where's the frog?"

She gave me a look. "Daria. Really? Now?"

Fair.

Then she spotted Caelan and did a double-take. "Okay, hold on. Who the hell is this? Is he an alien? Are we under attack? Because the sky looks like it's having a full-on meltdown."

"This is Caelan," I said quickly. "He's from the Fae dimension. We were chased here by someone from this… intergalactic cleanup crew called IGSTA. Long story."

Jeanie didn't blink. Just nodded. This is why I love her. She rolls with it.

"We need to see Eleana. Now."

"Eleana?" I asked.

"She's the Oracle. Runs the local pet shop. Come on."

"Keen as," Spitz buzzed, nodding his head vigorously in anticipation.

If Jeanie said we needed to see the Oracle, we needed to see the Oracle. We cloaked Caelan in a hoodie, which honestly just made him look like a seven-foot luminescent Smurf trying to blend in at a midnight rave. But whatever. It was still dark out.

The shop smelt like herbs, catnip, and mystery. Eleana was waiting for us, sharp-eyed and utterly calm, her frazzled hair pulled back in a light, waspy bun.

"The Human dimension's Field Anthologies," she said before we spoke. "You need to find it. It holds the Golden Prophecy. It's veiled. Hidden. But it's in Motueka, South Island. And you'll need more than magic to retrieve it."

"Motueka?" I blinked. "Crikey, that's not too far."

I'd lived in Aotearoa most of my life. Mum and Dad moved us here from Canada when I was a wee kid. But mostly, I stuck to the North Island. I always loved the South Island, though—those cruisy, rolling hills and slower pace. The quiet.

Eleana's gaze softened, though her voice stayed firm. "The IGSTA doesn't want that prophecy to come to pass. They'll stop at nothing. And they believe you're the one the prophecy names."

My stomach lurched. "What even is the prophecy?"

"It foretells the merging of dimensions. A time when all beings; Fae, Human, what we call 'aliens,' even the Lakdeo, would unite. But the IGSTA? They fear the chaos that could bring. They believe in separation."

Caelan spoke up. "An agent found us recently, she tried to make us sign something. It felt… wrong."

"Of course she did," Eleana said. "That signature would have erased the timeline you're meant to fulfill. And now that the tear is open, you'll need to be careful. Others will come through. Creatures. And Humans… they may wander in where they don't belong."

I swallowed. "And what happens if they do?"

Eleana only tilted her head. "That, you'll have to discover yourselves."

She turned to deal with a rogue cat knocking over dog-biscuit displays. Jeanie and I exchanged a look. Darwin. Could he have…?

"One more thing," Eleana said, almost casually. "You'll probably run into the Crow Network. If you do, make sure they know you support neutralizing false light. That's what they're working toward."

Whatever did that mean?

"Brilliant," I muttered. "More cryptic riddles."

"Take this." She handed me a rolled parchment. "A spell to unveil the Golden Prophecy." I tucked it away.

Caelan asked, "And how will we get there?"

Eleana sighed, already done with us. "I'll put the map into your minds. Telepathically. Obviously."

I turned to Jeanie. Her eyes were watery. "Be careful out there," she said. "I'll hold down the fort. And… I'll look after Riley."

I wrapped her in a hug. "Thank you. We'll be back. Promise."

Outside, the storm raged, winds spiraling with the pull of something ancient and vast. The next part of our journey was calling, a bit violently, from the looks of the sky. We were going to find the prophecy.

"You ready?" Caelan's arm stretched out, waiting for me to take that leap into the night sky again.

If this were under different circumstances, I might've found it… romantic. Flying through the sky, held by someone so unexpectedly dashing. Who even says *dashing* these days? But there it was. My heart always had a soft spot for old-school gestures. Heat rose to my cheeks before I could stop it. I nodded, gripping his arm tighter as we lifted off. Below us, the world looked so calm, but I could feel it—the pulse of everything shifting, the tear growing. It wasn't just my world anymore. It was both worlds colliding and twisting in ways I couldn't even begin to imagine. The wind roared past us, cold and wild, buzzing with urgency. We had to find the Field Anthologies, and fast. As we neared the ferry docks at the southern tip of Wellington, the city lights behind us flickered like distant stars. Finally, the wind eased a bit, as if even it was taking a breather. Below, the water shimmered in the night, and I felt my adrenaline ebb, leaving behind a shivery kind of calm.

"Flying over water at night? Nah, not a great idea," Cae said, shaking his head. "Especially with the tear playing up. The sea here…

it can call in all sorts of strange stuff, eh. We're better off keeping to land-based areas."

We decided to take the ferry in the morning so we could plan our next steps. We landed softly by the docks, in a quiet spot where the stars felt close enough to pluck from the sky. As we walked, I could feel his watchful presence beside me, steady and warm.

"Strange like meeting you?" I teased, giving him a gentle nudge.

He flashed a grin, his eyes catching the starlight. "Oi! You reckon I'm strange? That's rich, coming from the girl who cracked open dimensions just to skip the 9-to-5."

I laughed, rolling my eyes. "I didn't mean to rip open dimensions, okay? The plan was just to get me to your world, not start an intergalactic crisis."

"Yeah, yeah," he said, giving me a knowing look. His wings fluttered softly behind him. "I'll say this, though: your world's bloody fascinating. I'd love to see it properly. And you... the Human who managed to yarn with me across dimensions, break the time-space barrier, and still reckon she wants to be a fairy. You're a bit more choice than I expected."

A warmth sparked in my chest, catching me off guard. I glanced at him, a shy smile sneaking in. "I can't tell if that's a compliment or a cheeky dig, but I'll take it. You're not so bad yourself. Even if I'm still a bit jealous of those wings."

He tilted his head slightly, ear-wings twitching; I realised I'd been watching them far too closely. He noticed, too, and smirked, leaning a little closer. "You like them? The wings, I mean."

I flushed, caught out. "I—yeah. They're... beautiful. And practical. You make it look easy. But I still don't get how you're Human-sized. Can we circle back to that?"

"In my dimension, form is fluid," he explained. "But I had the Eurometer on when all this kicked off." He pulled out a small gem-like device, softly glowing. "I thought it just sorted time perception, but it looks like it shaped me to fit your world, too. Mean as."

"That's incredible. Do all your lot carry one of these flashy gadgets?"

He laughed softly, eyes going distant for a moment. "Nah, that would be chaos. I've got mine 'cause of my family—big science lineage. My dad passed it down before moving on to the other realms."

"Oh... I'm sorry," I said, eyes fixed on the gentle light.

"Sorry? What for?" he asked, looking genuinely puzzled.

"Don't you miss him?"

"Miss him?" He paused, then shook his head. "Nah. He's more present now than he was before. Can ask for a chat anytime. When he was here, he was always flat-out busy."

"That's... comforting," I whispered, a swirl of feelings tumbling inside me.

Caelan studied me, his voice softening. "It's not just the flying, you know. We Eura feel the energy of the land, the vibe everywhere. Here, it's slower... peaceful. Feels like a proper breather from home. I can even sense your energy signature, if you'd like. But only if you're keen."

The way he asked, so gentle, so careful, felt more intimate than any touch. I took a shaky breath. "My energy signature?"

He nodded. "Yeah. It has a shape, a colour, and a feeling. But I only tune in with permission. Gotta respect that."

I met his gaze, heart hammering. "Okay. You have my permission. What do I feel like to you?"

His fingers brushed my arm, featherlight. Blue light shimmered under my skin, glowing softly before fading. My breath hitched.

"There's a sway in you," he whispered. "Like someone caught between tides. You're steady underneath all that movement, just waiting to anchor somewhere. You're ready to come home to yourself."

My eyes welled up. "That's... exactly how I feel," I admitted, voice barely above a whisper.

He nodded, gaze deep and kind. "Whether we like it or not, we're in this together now. The tear, the prophecy—all of it. But don't worry," he added with a soft grin. "I don't mind the company. As long as you can keep up."

There was a quiet pull in the air between us, almost lyrical, like a melody waiting to be remembered through a forgotten pocket of time. Then, of course, Spitz had to break the moment. "Ahem, excuse me?" He zipped up, unimpressed. "While you two were busy sharing starry-eyed stares, I sorted us a place to crash for the night. Over there."

Caelan's gaze lingered on me for a heartbeat longer before he let out a low laugh. "Cheers, mate. Right then... let's just try not to draw too much attention tonight, eh?"

As if on cue, the night split open behind us... screams, splintering wood, and a low roar echoing out into the dark.

CHAPTER SIX

Caelan: Protects

I should've sensed the disturbance sooner. But truth be told, I'd let my guard down. I was too focused on Daria; this radiant, bewildering Human woman standing before me. And for once, I hadn't been using my Eura senses to scan the horizon for trouble. I felt the ground shiver before I heard the low rumble echo across the darkening shoreline. I turned sharply, adjusting my hearing to a higher range, my wings bracing for what lay ahead.

"Hang on," I called to Daria, motioning for her to stay behind me as I sharpened my focus.

Through the haze, I could see a massive silhouette lumbering toward us. My stomach dropped. It couldn't be… could it? This moss-covered, broad-shouldered giant, half stone, half living, moving with slow but unstoppable force. It could only be a Rekel. A Rekel, *here*?

I'd heard stories about them since I was just a youngling back home, usually as cautionary tales to keep us out of Simsora, the land of roaming giants. I had never expected to see one, much less encounter one on the Human Earth plane. I swallowed hard. As far as I could sense, no Humans or animals had been hurt yet, but it was only a matter of time. Trees lay splintered in its path, rooftops crumpled like discarded leaves.

"Do you have creatures like this here?" I asked Daria, my voice low, hoping she wouldn't catch the rising tension vibrating through my wings.

She was frozen, eyes wide, her breath coming in short, sharp bursts. "Not since the dinosaurs," she whispered.

My heart sank. "It's got to be a Rekel," I muttered, mind racing back through old memory scrolls, trying to recall how we were taught to deal with them, or rather, avoid them at all costs. The Rekels had driven entire Fae populations out of Simsora ages ago, thousands of gaelons before the Fall of Ether (BFE). They were unpredictable, impossible to reason with, and unstoppable once they were awake. Not like the Yeti, those adorable, sweet creatures that protect the Ekat in the forests. The Yeti seemed to be nearly as big as the Rekels, but 180 degrees opposite in character.

"We're gonna have to figure out a way to send this big fella back!" Spitz buzzed, nearly shrieking, his tiny glow darting around in frantic loops. "If we could come here, and it could come here, surely we can send it back too!"

"I'm sure there's a logical explanation," I said, trying to stay grounded, though my thoughts were moving a million directions at once. "It seemed like the weather calmed as we moved away from the tear. Maybe it followed us through… maybe it's lost."

"And why would it be following us specifically?" Daria's voice cracked, but her eyes stayed locked on mine. Brave, even in fear.

Before we could even finish the thought, a thick, milky mist began to curl along the edges of the bay. It rose so quickly it felt alive, coiling around the Rekel's massive form, winding up its mossy shoulders and swirling around its heavy head. I felt the energy shift immediately; the air turned dense, humming with an old magic. The Rekel slowed, its massive shoulders slumping as if all at once overwhelmed by sleep. It groaned, the sound echoing over the water like a mountain sighing, before collapsing into a sitting position. Branches cracked under its weight, and a crumbling barn gave way, its last beams snapping like dry twigs.

"Snrrgg…" The giant let out a slow, thunderous snore, sending a wave of displaced air toward us.

Daria clutched my arm, half hiding behind me, eyes wide.

"You have more allies than you know," a deep voice called from behind us.

I whirled, wings fanning out instinctively, shielding Daria. "Who's there? Show yourself!" I demanded, trying to keep my voice steady, even as adrenaline zinged through every nerve.

Out of the fog stepped an Eura, bulkier and older-looking than most. His beard was long and twisted with tiny crystalline beads that shimmered faintly in the misty moonlight.

"The name's Faelearo, but most folks call me Ro," he said with a half-smile, raising one palm in a gesture of peace.

"I'm Caelan, or Cae," I managed, pulling my wings in slightly but keeping my guard up. "How did you get here, Ro? You don't look like anyone I know from home."

Ro chuckled, deep and slow, a sound like pebbles tumbling down a riverbed. "Ah, mate, I'm not too sure myself. One minute I was tending to the seasonal fluxes in Faierodon, next thing—poof—I'm here on your beach with this sleepy big boy."

Daria, now breathing harder but trying to stay composed, stepped forward.

"Don't worry, lass," Ro said gently, his eyes softened. "I'm a friend, not a foe."

"Did you do that to the Rekel? The mist?" I asked, suspicion still lacing my words.

"Aye," Ro nodded. "Back home, I'm a Sophos. We manage elemental flows and nature's shifts. Thought this fella needed a nap more than a scrap."

Daria tilted her head, confused. "What's a Sophos?"

"In our world," I explained quickly, "they're a bit like your wizards or elemental sages. They work directly with the energy currents of nature."

"Spot on," Ro said, giving me a respectful nod. "That Rekel shouldn't cause a fuss for a while now... though how long that spell lasts is anyone's guess."

Daria crossed her arms, still eyeing him warily. "How come you're Human-sized too? Do you have a Eurometer?"

Ro looked offended, puffing out his crystalline beard. "Eurometer? Nah, don't need such clunky old kit," he sniffed. "And who might you be?"

"I'm Daria," she said, her voice a little small, "just a regular Human, I guess."

"Lovely to meet you, Daria," Ro said warmly, bowing slightly. "I've been time skipping and dimension hopping a while now, though I've never meant to land here. Maybe the multiverse thought I might lend a hand."

I squinted at him, my senses prickling. "Skipping dimensions isn't exactly common practice," I pushed. "I've never heard of our kind managing that."

"Well," Daria piped up, her voice almost sheepish, "I always thought hummingbirds could do it…"

Ro looked down, a shadow passing briefly over his features. "There's more to it, sure. But that's a yarn for another day," he said, shifting his weight. "For now, I'm on your side, if you'll have me."

I glanced at Daria. She gave me a small, steady nod, her unspoken code for we'll trust him for now.

"Alright," I said. "We're staying at that inn over there tonight. Tomorrow, we head to Motueka."

Ro looked out at the still-sleeping Rekel. "I'll see what I can do about getting him home."

"Cheers, that would be appreciated," I said cautiously. "We'll meet at the ferry first light."

Ro nodded once, then stepped backward into the mist until he vanished completely.

It was impossible to sleep after that. Not that I slept much anyway; being half-adapted to Human life was the only reason I even tried. But sleep played hard to get. My mind spun with visions of other Fae creatures slipping through the cracks of reality like mischievous possums in a compost bin, each one primed to cause fresh chaos in this already fragile world. And through it all, my urge to protect Daria kept pulsing louder.

I tried not to hover. Humans had odd boundaries, I'd read about them in the books I wasn't technically supposed to read. I didn't want to offend her by getting too close. Across the room, Daria murmured in her sleep, her hair tangled around her face like she'd wrestled a cyclone.

"Snrr-ruhmm," she mumbled, flinging a pillow to the floor. "Yes… it's a beautiful sunrise…"

I stifled a laugh. Could this creature get any more endearing? Eventually, the first golden rays of sunrise slipped through the thin curtains, seeming to promise a quieter start to the day than I expected.

"Think she's awake?" Spitz buzzed above her head, eyes wide with curiosity.

"Shh! Don't startle her!"

Before I could formulate some gentle, Fae-appropriate wake-up strategy, she sat bolt upright, hair everywhere, looking bright-eyed, like she hadn't just shared a room with an elemental creature and his quirky sidekick.

"We'd better get moving!" she chirped, a morning person if I'd ever seen one.

"What about Ro?" I asked, still wary.

She glanced at me, gave a little smirk. "We've got a saying here: 'innocent until proven dodgy,'" she added a little wink that made my stomach do a weird fluttery backflip.

"Before we see him, we should sort out our plan," I said, trying to sound practical.

"The map in our heads gives us the general area, but no exact spot," she mused, brow furrowed. "I thought it'd be hidden in an old library or something."

"Could be a hidden door or a puzzle," I offered, already imagining levers and cryptic riddles.

Her eyes lit up. "A puzzle! Yes, like a game. Maybe if we treat it like that, it'll make more sense once we get there."

"Exactly," I said, relieved by her spark returning. "We should head out early, get to the dock before Ro. Keep an eye out."

She looked me up and down, then burst out laughing. "You're not exactly blending in with that hoodie, love. Let me fix it." She rummaged in her bag and pulled out a small pot of makeup.

"I don't know what that is, but alright," I said, staying very still as she dabbed at my face like I was a reluctant canvas.

When she was done, she stepped back, squinting. "You look... seasick. But it's better than glowing like a disco jellyfish." I caught sight of myself and cracked up.

"Better than nothing, eh?"

"We don't have time for a fashion show!" Spitz chimed in. "Let's crack on!"

The morning felt suspiciously calm as we walked. Birds chirped like they were getting paid for it, and a soft breeze carried the smell of salt and early blooms.

"For a second, I thought maybe I dreamt the whole thing," Daria said, her tone teasing. "But then I look at you, and, well... here we are."

"Yeah, it's oddly peaceful," I agreed, scanning the landscape for the next uninvited creature.

"It's not calm. Don't let it fool you," a voice crooned above us.

We both jerked our heads up. A sleek black crow sat on a low branch, head cocked like it had gossip to spill.

"What were you referring to?" I asked cautiously.

"Name's Quinley. I'm with the Crow Network," he said, giving a dramatic fluff of his wings. "We're guardians, neutralisers of the

Megalight."

"Megalight?" Daria echoed, eyes wide like she'd heard a brand name for a shady supplement.

"It's a deceptive energy; a false light," Quinley explained. "Looks pretty on the outside, but it's all manipulation and control underneath. Real slippery bugger."

Daria's face lit up. "An Oracle told us about you! I'm so glad to meet you."

"We perch on the power lines, balance the flows," Quinley said proudly. "We're not the only birds in the biz, but we're the classic model. Stewards of truth, feathered edition."

I nodded. "We've got similar networks back home. Ours are more tech-tree-based. Less beak."

"How do you stop it? This Megalight?" I asked.

"We're still working on that," Quinley admitted. "It's kind of a group sport. Think of our network like a magical firewall. It disrupts the energy's feeding habits."

"Feeding habits?" I winced.

"Everything in the multiverse is energy," Quinley explained. "Some beings forgot how to fuel themselves generatively of their own creative force. So now they freeload, grab what they can, where they can. Works for light and dark. Humans feed on plants and animals. Feeding isn't the issue; it's that it has gotten out of hand and greedy, at a galactic level. That's the Megalight at work. The creatures of Earth are susceptible because they haven't learnt how to rebalance it, though the Fae dimension is a lot closer—where you come from." Quinley gestured at me. "Most have just forgotten how to be in harmony with their natural impulses in an ecosystem that thrives as a whole."

"Dare I ask what these false energies feed on at the multiverse level?" Daria said, one eyebrow raised.

"Don't panic," Quinley replied, smoothing his feathers. "Ironically, it feeds off attention and has a heyday with fear. Activates its feeding time through unaware creature's genetic vulnerabilities. It gets in through the DNA and messes with motives. Never consent based. Real passive-aggressive, that."

"It feeds off fear and messes with our genes..." Daria murmured, her curiosity spiking.

"Right. It nudges behaviour, manipulates, and slowly convinces beings to hand over their will. Like the multiverse's worst pyramid scheme," Quinley said. "Then they forget who they are, their soul's signature, their Lightbody."

"Are you saying it eats souls?" Daria asked.

"Not quite. It drains their life force and identity. Nibbles away at the core."

"Can they get it back?" I asked.

"Yes. They've got to renounce any sneaky alliance and start acting in alignment with the truth. Kindness is the best compass, always has been."

"Thanks, Quinley," Daria said, looking a bit like she'd been handed an intergalactic syllabus. "That's... a lot."

"One last thing," Quinley added, "there's no evil overlord behind this. No boss to take out and fix it all. So be mindful of who you trust. Lots of neutralisers out there. You're never really alone."

"Thanks, Quinley," Daria said, softer now.

"We've got your back," he replied, with a wee feathery pat on the back.

"Cheers, mate!" Spitz piped up. "But if we don't leg it now, we're missing that ferry!"

"Thank you, Quinley!" we called as we dashed off.

At the dock, Ro was already there, lounging like he owned the tide. He was leaning against a post with a spread of pastries and steaming mugs arranged on a wee folding table.

"Morning, team!" he called, raising a flaky croissant. "Hope you're keen on brekkie. You'll need it for what's coming next."

CHAPTER SEVEN

Daria: In the Dark

Boarding the ferry felt a bit like entering another dimension in itself, but this time, one filled with awkward glances and barely contained curiosity from strangers. People shuffled past, their eyes darting to Caelan, then quickly away, like they'd seen a ghost they didn't want to acknowledge. The makeup was only halfway doing its job; he looked like some poor lad on the brink of hurling overboard after a dodgy fish and chips. But still, he had this undeniable... magnetism. Even as he tried to blend in, there was an otherworldly shimmer about him. I couldn't stop glancing at him.

It wasn't just the way he looked, though, let's be real, even under a badly smudged foundation, he was distractingly handsome. It was the way he carried himself, that protective, unwavering gaze that felt like a silent promise. A promise that maybe he'd still show up, even if I chucked myself headfirst into another bonkers science mishap with wires crossed and common sense left at the door. And that scared me. It made me feel downright uncomfortable. I wasn't used to having someone care for me that much, particularly someone I'd just met. I needed to keep my wits about me, to stay on guard, even with him. I trusted him so far, but I had been hurt in the past.

I sighed, staring at the churning waves below as we boarded. My mind was a tidal wave of its own. Distortions in DNA. Energy feeding on genetic vulnerabilities. Multiverse overlaps. And what had Ro meant about time skipping? That sounded strange indeed. The idea that my life wasn't just about dimensions on Earth but about a whole multiverse—it felt like someone had dropped an ocean into my teacup brain.

I leaned against the railing for a second, trying to breathe it out. My mind spun back to that film *Everything Everywhere All At Once*, where the daughter starts losing her sense of self under the weight of infinite knowing. The thought made my hands tremble. Was I becoming like her, losing my center, my sanity, beneath the flood of cosmic information? I pressed my palms together, feeling them clammy, and tried to ground myself. Meanwhile, Ro was all chipper and chirpy, bustling around with a ridiculous breakfast platter like a jolly uncle at a kids' soccer game.

"It's just an hour or so across, I reckon," Ro was saying to Caelan while handing him a bright red strawberry like it was a miracle invention. "And what brings you down that way?"

We'd found a relatively quiet corner of the boat. The sea breeze smelt crisp, salty, almost cleansing, brushing away some of yesterday's chaos.

"Thanks for the breakfast," Caelan said cautiously, eyeing the fruit like it might sprout wings and fly away. He took it politely but didn't answer Ro's question. I could tell he was still suspicious. So was I. But I couldn't quite place why. After all, Ro had helped us with the Rekel. He seemed a good sort.

A couple of crows hovered nearby riding the gusts beside the boat, the Crow Network, watching. Ro tried to keep up the cheerful small talk, fumbling with a strawberry and sniffing it suspiciously. "So this is a 'strawberry,' is it? Remarkable." He held it up to the light like he'd just discovered a new star.

I giggled despite myself, feeling a flicker of joy in the weirdness of it all.

"How do you drink this vile liquid?" Caelan was scowling at the coffee cup in his hand, his nose wrinkled adorably. "It tastes as if soil had an existential crisis and decided to become a beverage," he declared.

I nearly spat out my coffee laughing. "Humans love it because it helps them stay awake. They sort of... grow to like the taste," I explained between giggles.

"It's probably like dagel," Spitz buzzed, looking smug at making the comparison.

"Dagel?" I asked, curious.

"Ah, yeah," Caelan replied, squinting at his cup. "A strong root drink in Faierodon. Tastes like sadness and tree bark, but very energizing."

"Indeed," Ro nodded sagely. "Exactly like that! So, remind me, what brings you down south?" His persistence was starting to itch at me.

Caelan shot him a cool look but kept quiet. I felt a strange tension creep into my chest, like a string pulled too tight. At that moment, I noticed the crows beginning to form a pattern, circling tighter, moving in sync like a living net. My pulse picked up. Ro seemed to notice, too. Then came a weird fizzing sound, like soda pop being poured too quickly, followed by the smell of burning metal. Ro clutched a small bag at his waist.

"What the—?" he stammered. A loud pop exploded from the bag, blue sparks shooting up like tiny fireworks.

Suddenly, everything tilted. Stars burst around the edges of my vision. The air felt like it folded in on itself.

And then... nothing. Darkness.

My awareness floated somewhere heavy, viscous. It felt like being stuck in syrup, like I was too slow to swim out. A voice slipped around my ears, low and slippery, like a snake wrapping around my thoughts. I tried to turn away, but it kept following me, weaving closer, coaxing. I swiped at my ears, desperate to block it out. To my shock, I felt them —long, delicate wings instead of Human ears. Eura ears.

What on Earth?

The voice didn't sound kind. It wasn't guiding me. It was using me, trying to burrow its way into my mind and take up residence. But why? I wanted to scream, to claw it out, but no sound came. Then another voice managed to get through, warm, soft, familiar—slipped through the blackness.

"Daria... Daria, can you hear me?"

Caelan.

My eyes fluttered open like slow blinds in a dusty room. Light stabbed at my retinas, but his face came into focus, his hands on my shoulders, steadying me.

"What happened?" I croaked. My voice felt like it belonged to someone else.

"You fainted," Caelan said, his eyes full of worry. "I think you were psychically attacked. Are you alright?"

He helped me sit back in my seat, moving with a gentleness that almost undid me.

"I think so," I said shakily. My mind felt like a room someone had broken into and rifled through, leaving everything in chaos. "How long was I out?"

"Just a few moments," he said, glancing around sharply. "But Ro vanished as it happened. His aura, it changed. He wasn't who he said he was."

My stomach clenched. Ro had felt off from the start, but I'd wanted so badly to believe he was helping. Just then, a familiar black shape swooped down, perching neatly on the railing.

"You sure do get yourself into a pickle fast," the crow remarked, preening its wing.

"Quinley?" I asked, relief flooding me.

"At your service," Quinley bowed slightly. "We detected an Aura Scrambler. Thought you could use a hand."

"Ro?" Caelan spat the name like a curse.

"Yep," Quinley confirmed. "He was using the Scrambler, makes an aura look harmless, even friendly. Clever trick. But the crows saw through it."

"What was happening to me?" I asked, hugging my arms around my chest, still shivering inside.

"He was trying to manipulate you," Quinley said softly. "Pull you into a mental dimension, warp your perception, possibly even plant commands."

I shuddered. "I... I heard whispers. I couldn't understand them, but they felt... wrong. Like they wanted to hollow me out."

"You resisted," Caelan said, pride glowing in his voice. "You knew not to let it in. That's powerful."

I met his eyes, feeling something warm unfurling in my chest.

Quinley bobbed his head. "Tuning out false voices is key to resisting the Megalight. You passed an important test."

"Megalight," I echoed. The word felt like a weight. "I thought that was just an abstract idea. But it's real. And invasive."

"It feeds on doubt, too, not just fear," Quinley said, his feathers fluffing. "You've got to stay vigilant. Once you sense that heaviness, that unkind pull, you'll know. That's when you hold your center."

I nodded, even as the ship rocked gently beneath us. A thought flickered in my mind: how much easier it was to trust external voices than to trust my own. But maybe that was the point. Maybe all this was a brutal invitation to come home to my inner knowing.

Quinley flicked his head. "Stay sharp. You'll need that discernment soon enough." With that, he launched into the sky, merging with a flock of crows that danced like black ribbons above the waves. Caelan sat next to me, his presence grounding.

"You alright, love?" he asked softly, brushing a stray hair from my face and tucking it behind my ear.

My heart stuttered. "Yes. Thanks to you. And Quinley."

I watched his hand hover by my cheek for a heartbeat longer before he pulled back.

"I don't understand," I said, my voice barely above a whisper. "Why did Ro target me? Why now?"

"Your aura," Caelan explained, shifting closer. "It's bright, and shifting. You're on the brink of something. That makes you vulnerable... and powerful. He wanted to sway you before you learnt to use it fully."

"Aura," I repeated, tracing the word with my tongue. "How is that different from my energy signature?"

Caelan's eyes lit up, his wings twitching slightly beneath his cloak. "Your energy signature is like your soul's personal fingerprint, the unique melody only you carry. Your aura is the light you broadcast in each moment, constantly changing. Your emotions, your thoughts, what you eat; they all tint it. Eura can see and feel these shifts."

I took that in, feeling simultaneously exposed and seen in a way I'd never known.

"What does mine look like to you now?" I asked, curiosity tinged with anxiety.

He studied me, his eyes softening. "Warm reds and purples around your core; that's your passion and curiosity. But around your arms and shoulders... there's something else. Blues and silvers, shimmering patterns I've only seen in other Eura. It doesn't make sense."

I sucked in a breath. "I... I always felt like I didn't belong here. Maybe it's more than a feeling."

Caelan's gaze softened even more, as though he could see the raw pieces inside me, scattered but yearning to come together.

"I think you carry Eura patterning in your field," he said finally. "How? I don't know. But it's part of why you can perceive us, maybe why you could reach me through the dimensions."

A warmth spread through my chest. For a moment, it was as if the waves around us quieted, the ferry gliding through a soft hush.

"Attention, everyone," the captain's voice crackled overhead, breaking the spell. "We'll be arriving at the port in ten minutes. Please prepare to disembark."

Caelan's eyes didn't leave mine. "You're more than you know,

Daria. And you're not alone in this."

I swallowed, feeling tears sting the edges of my eyes. I looked away, embarrassed, but he reached forward, catching my chin with a gentle touch.

"Heya," he murmured, voice low and laced with warmth. "You don't have to tuck that part of you away. Vulnerability's not a weakness; it's brave as hell."

I let out a soft, wobbly laugh. "Says the interdimensional Fae with sparkles in his hair, looking like a seasick supermodel."

He laughed then, a sound like wind chimes in a summer breeze. "I'll take that as a compliment."

The deck crew started to appear, readying the ropes and preparing the ramp. Passengers gathered their bags, the normalcy of it all feeling surreal after what had just happened inside my mind.

Caelan stood, offering me a hand. "Ready?"

I took it without hesitation.

"Ready."

We moved toward the exit ramp together, my hand secure in his. A subtle buzz of energy thrummed between our palms, like a shared secret. As the boat docked and the scent of earth and damp moss drifted up from the South Island, I felt the world tilt in a new direction inside me. There was no going back now. My life wasn't small, or ordinary, or perhaps even only Earthbound anymore. It was as vast as the multiverse, as unpredictable as a hummingbird's flight.

And for the first time, even amidst fear and confusion, I felt the tiniest spark of something else, it felt a lot like belonging. We were a quirky crew, but somehow we had found each other.

CHAPTER EIGHT

Caelan: New Friend

The moment our feet touched the shore of the South Island, the soft, damp air enveloped us, and I could feel the calm of this land resonating through my limbs. It wasn't just slower; it felt older, wiser. Like every stone and leaf carried secrets too heavy for words. Beside me, Daria's amber eyes flickered with that quiet curiosity I had come to adore. She kept stealing glances at me, and each time, I felt a warmth spark somewhere deep in my chest. I was about to ask her more questions about being Human when a sharp, sudden crack rang out.

"What on Earth is that?" she gasped, turning toward the sound. "Do you think this is from the tear, too?"

We both spun to see an ancient kauri tree split straight down the middle near the shoreline. It looked as if lightning had cleaved it in two, but there were no clouds, no sign of a storm. Just a perfect, violent rupture. I took a breath, trying to center myself despite the waves of grief echoing from the tree.

"Let's go check it out," I said, already stepping toward the wounded giant. The closer we got, the harder it became to move. My chest felt tight, as if I had plunged underwater, the weight of unseen currents pressing in from all sides. I knelt and pressed my fingers to the bark. It wasn't just wood under my hands; it was a living symphony. I felt echoes of storms, whispers of moonlight, the slow stretch of seasons, and the bright laughter of young leaves. The kauri's aura shimmered in shades of deep emerald and bright turquoise, unraveling in chords like the final notes of a song. Daria dropped beside me, her knees hitting the damp ground. Tears gathered in her eyes faster than she could blink them away.

"I didn't mean to do that, I swear it," a voice crackled out, rasping and scratchy from behind a pile of branches.

I turned sharply. From the rubble shuffled a small creature with oversized eyes, a wild white tail, and tufts of fur that stuck out every which way. He was covered in tiny metallic gadgets clinking with every step. A sprite. Of course. Mischief incarnate.

"How did you get here?" I demanded, keeping my voice level, though every sense was on high alert.

"Oh, I was just minding my business with the Ekats, at the Sadekial festival, and then, wham! I'm here!" he chirped, bouncing on his feet as if none of this was serious.

Sadekial was the festival where the Ekats gave thanks to the Earth and gave offerings to the soil and winds.

"That doesn't explain the tree," I pressed. "Listen. I'm Caelan. And you?" I also noticed a device on this sprite with the initials AMD engraved on it; I didn't recognise it from anything I had seen. He seemed to be pushing it away into a pouch.

He hesitated, shifting from foot to foot. "Nu. Call me Nu."

Beside me, Daria inhaled sharply, as though struck in the chest.

"Nu... Wait. Are you... Nuvious?" she demanded, her voice trembling.

His eyes darted toward her, and in a flash, his hand shot to a small pouch at his side. Before I could stop him, POOF! A thick cloud of shimmering dust burst out, clouding our sight. When it cleared, he was gone.

Daria fell forward, bracing herself with both hands on the bark. Tears streamed down her cheeks, mixing with flecks of moss and wood dust.

"Nuvious..." she whispered. "He's the sprite who switched my timecard at birth. I remembered it in my dream logs as a child. Why would he be here now? Why destroy this tree? And how did he disappear just like Ro did?!"

I stared at her, my mind a swarm of questions as well. Why would a sprite from my world meddle with a Human birth? And how did Ro and Nu move so easily between dimensions?

"It must be the prophecy," I muttered, feeling a shiver ripple through me. "That device he hid, it said AMD on it. I don't recognise it. It looked nothing like anything from my dimension."

"And this disappearing act," she added, her voice distant, "how is that possible?" Her gaze dropped to the fallen tree. Her hand trembled as she reached out to stroke the broken trunk.

"This poor kauri… It's hundreds of years old," she sobbed. "I'm devastated."

I could feel the kauri's sorrow vibrating under my palm, a heavy, thrumming grief that pulled at my own heart.

"Do you hear it?" I asked her quietly.

"I… I think I do," she whispered back.

I placed one hand on the trunk and the other gently on her back. I closed my eyes and let the old words flow from me, ancient syllables rising from deep in my bones:

"Ka oric und a hlet, an tuodal, Ent tualte humah…"

The Eurometer shimmered faintly at my side, translating for her:

"Eventually the river returns to the sea,
but here in eternity, there's just you and me."

"That's… beautiful," she breathed, wiping tears from her cheeks. "What does it mean?"

"It's a release," I explained, my voice low. "A way to honor a life that has given itself completely. We witness, we remember, we hold space for its passage, back into the sea."

She bowed her head. "I doubt I'll be remembered," she mumbled. "I have connections… but I still feel so small. Like, none of this will matter in the end, with so many stars and worlds out there."

I turned to her, my chest tight. "*I'll* remember you," I said, almost in a whisper. "I know that might not be exactly what you mean, but to me… that's everything."

Her eyes lifted to mine, wide and soft. A moment passed between us that felt impossibly delicate, like a thin strand of silk holding back an ocean.

Finally, she nodded, a fragile smile breaking through. "Thank you," she whispered. "I… I needed that."

We stood there in silence, the sea breeze carrying the scent of salt and the grief of a forest that lost its heartbeat, until she finally took a shaky breath and straightened.

"Well… we should go before someone sees us here," she said, her voice steadier now.

"Yes," I agreed, rising with her. "We still have the prophecy to find."

Spitz zipped into view, buzzing around our heads. "So… walking again? Fantastic. Can't wait. Truly."

Daria gave him a watery laugh. "Yes, we walk," she confirmed, wiping her face with her sleeve. "Before dusk. There's a path there, see?" She pointed toward a winding forest trail that disappeared between the trees.

We stepped into the forest, the canopy closing around us like a protective cloak. The air shifted, cooler and rich with the scent of wet leaves and pine. Sunlight broke through in playful shards, dancing on the soft ground. I reached out and touched the bark as we walked, feeling the vibration of life beneath my fingers. Here, the world was alive in a way that felt almost familiar, a gentle echo of my realm, though slower, denser.

Beside me, Daria's steps softened, her body relaxing into the rhythm of the forest. Every so often, she would pause to listen to a birdcall or watch a leaf drift lazily to the ground. I could see her aura settling, the sharp reds of grief fading to soft violets and gentle gold.

After a few miles, we found a clearing where thin ribbons of light spilt down in rainbow silk threads. Daria dropped her pack and turned in a slow circle, her eyes wide with wonder.

"This is… It's magic," she whispered. "I didn't think we had that in my dimension, the Human one."

I smiled. "I think you're starting to tune in," I said.

She glanced at me, her face open and earnest. "Cae… earlier, you mentioned my aura. You said it looked like an Eura's. What did you mean?"

I paused, choosing my words carefully. "It's… unusual," I admitted. "Your aura isn't fully Human. There's a pattern, an undercurrent, that resembles Eura energy. I don't know how it's possible, but it's there."

Her brows drew together, her fingers fidgeting at her sides. "Do you think… could it be connected to Nuvious? What he did to me at birth?"

"It's possible," I said slowly. "Sprites are tricksters, but Nuvious interfering with your timecard… that's a deep manipulation. It could have altered your energetic blueprint."

She swallowed hard, looking down at her hands. "I always felt like I didn't belong. Like my body was too heavy, my senses too dulled, like I was meant to be something else. Maybe… maybe I wasn't just imagining it."

I stepped closer, my instinct to comfort her almost overwhelming. "I don't think you were imagining it at all," I said softly. "I think you've always been more than you knew."

She looked up at me then, her eyes soft with wonder. For a moment, everything else fell away: the prophecy, the tear, the uncertainty. Just her, and me, and the quiet balm of the forest. I lifted my hand, hesitated, then brushed my fingers lightly along her cheek. She closed her eyes, leaning into my touch, and a shiver of blue sparks danced briefly beneath her skin. When she opened her eyes again, they shimmered with a quiet, fierce light.

"I'm scared," she whispered.

"I know," I replied. "So am I."

We stood like that, suspended in the clearing's hush, until Spitz cleared his throat loudly behind us.

"Ahem. Hate to interrupt yet again," he said, "but we should keep moving if we want to avoid more visitors."

Daria pulled back, her cheeks flushed. She gave me a shy, crooked smile that made my heart stutter.

"You're right," she said. "Let's keep going."

We picked up our packs and moved deeper into the forest. As we walked, I couldn't help but marvel at how this Human, this almost-Eura soul, could hold so much strength and softness at once.

Around us, the forest began to shift. The path narrowed, the trees grew denser, their trunks twisting in strange, intricate patterns. Vines hung like curtains, and small white mushrooms glowed faintly at the base of old roots. The air grew damper, heavy with the scent of dew and soil. Daria's steps slowed, her eyes darting from shadow to shadow.

"Do you feel that?" she asked suddenly.

I nodded. "Something's watching us," I said.

Spitz zipped ahead, his glow dimming slightly. "It's too quiet. I don't like this."

I motioned for Daria to stay close. The tension in the air coiled tight, like a held breath. Somewhere ahead, a branch snapped sharply. We froze.

A large shape loomed ahead in the dappled shade. I tensed, shifting slightly to stand in front of Daria, my wings pulsing softly under my hoodie. Out of the hush stepped a towering figure, covered in long, reddish-brown hair, gentle eyes shining like polished amber stones, and broad shoulders that radiated warmth with not a hint of menace.

Daria's eyes widened so much I thought they might pop from her skull.

"Is that... Bigfoot?" she whispered, incredulously.

The figure let out a soft, rolling sound, something between a purr and a gentle thunderclap, and held up a massive hand in greeting. I could feel their vibration immediately, calm, protective, ancient beyond measure.

"Ah, they don't like being called that," I corrected quickly, turning to her. "I read about them back home! They prefer 'Yeti,' or other terms that are too sacred to mention out loud. Their feet are perfectly sized to them, eh."

The Yeti's wide mouth stretched into what could only be called a kind smile. The being stepped forward, each movement impossibly fluid for its size.

"You know of us?" the Yeti asked, its voice a gentle rumble that vibrated straight through my limbs.

I nodded, bowing slightly in respect. "I've only heard stories among my people. You're protectors of the great trees, the star frequencies. You work with the redwoods and pines in the Northern Americas, right? And in the Arctic poles as well."

The Yeti nodded, looking pleased. "We do. But we help the Ekats as well in your realm. We help the trees retune the messages to and from the stars. The soul recycling program has been distorted for a very long time here; we help filter and re-amplify clear frequencies, protect the signals that reach the Earth and her creatures. We hope to free more souls this way."

Daria was staring, mouth slightly agape. "Wait... you're telling me... You... talk to the stars?"

The Yeti chuckled softly, a warm sound that made the whole clearing seem to brighten. "Yes. We work with the star codes, the high trees. We are fortifiers and magnifiers. We coat the redwoods with energetic fortifications that are flexible, living membranes, not rigid, but strong. We help them endure the attacks on the natural life force from the Humans, from the Megalight."

Daria stepped forward tentatively, eyes shining like a child's. "I... I don't even have words," she said, breathless.

The Yeti lowered to a squat to be more at eye level with her. "Words are not always needed," it said, touching a giant hand to the earth. "Feel."

A vibration pulsed out gently from where its fingers touched the ground. Daria swayed slightly, her eyes closing as if she were listening to a distant, beautiful song.

"They're speaking to her energy signature," I whispered to Spitz, who was hovering cautiously above us.

Daria opened her eyes, tears slipping down her cheeks. "I felt… the forest… the stars… everything…" She pressed her hand to her chest. "I felt a profound sweetness like I belonged, like I've always belonged here."

The Yeti tilted its head kindly. "You do. You've always been part of this web, even if your Human mind didn't remember."

I stepped forward then. "Why are you here, in this form, in this moment?" I asked, my voice respectful.

The Yeti stood, towering again but never threatening. "We roam where we are called," it said. "Our Trobins - what we call our family group - travel lightly, harmonizing where distortions appear. We sensed the dimensional tear and came to aid the forest, to comfort the trees. This kauri…" It glanced back down the path. "It cried out. We heard it. We came."

Daria sniffled, wiping her nose with her sleeve, her aura a shimmering blend of tender pinks and soft golds now.

"Are you alone?" she asked softly.

The Yeti shook its head slowly. "No. My Trobin is nearby. We never stay in groups larger than ten. We prefer the open sky, the night grasses, the moon's kiss. We do not need to consume creatures. We thrive mostly on the moon's clear light and the sun's gentle rays, sometimes on berries and tender foliage."

I felt my heart bloom open even further at this. These beings, these kind, star-attuned protectors, were the living embodiment of the balance we had lost.

"I am so honored to meet you," I said, bowing my head again.

"And grateful for your help," Daria added, her voice trembling.

The Yeti inclined its head to her. "You carry seeds of many worlds within you," it said softly, addressing Daria directly. "Your path is tangled with the old trees and the bright stars. Be patient with yourself."

Daria let out a shaky laugh, tears still slipping down her face unexpectedly. "I… I'll try," she whispered.

The Yeti stepped closer to her, reaching a gentle hand toward her shoulder. She hesitated, then nodded, and the Yeti placed its large palm lightly over her heart. A gentle pulse of light shivered out from its hand, wrapping her in a kind of shimmering glow for a brief moment before fading.

Daria gasped softly. "What… what was that?"

"A small blessing," the Yeti explained. "A fortification for your journey ahead. It will help you discern what is true and what is false when the path becomes muddled."

She nodded again, pressing her hand to her chest as if to keep the glow there.

"I wish we could stay and learn more," I said honestly, feeling the moment slip away like morning mist.

"You have your quest," the Yeti replied gently. "The Field Anthologies await. But we will remain near. If you listen closely to the wind in the pines or the hush of the moss at night, you may hear us."

Daria beamed through her tears. "Thank you," she whispered, her voice small but full of awe.

With one last warm, rumbling chuckle, the Yeti stepped backward into the deeper shadows. The form seemed to ripple and blur, until only the swaying of leaves hinted at where it had stood. For a long moment, we stood in silence. The forest felt different now, more alive, more aware, as though it was holding us in a gentle embrace.

Finally, Daria turned to me, her face flushed, eyes sparkling with a mixture of wonder and relief.

"That… was the most incredible encounter of my entire life," she said, her voice trembling but strong.

I reached for her hand, my own heart echoing with a quiet, steady joy. "I've never met anyone with that calming of an aura," I admitted.

We stood there a little longer, hands intertwined, letting the feeling wash over us, soaking it into our core. Then, slowly, we turned back to the trail ahead, stepping forward together into the emerald hush, the prophecy still waiting somewhere ahead, the forest alive with whispered blessings all around us. Though danger still loomed, for that moment, we were simply two beings walking among giants, carried forward by the kindness of stars and trees, and the quiet strength of a Yeti's gentle heart.

CHAPTER NINE

Daria: Weavers

"Are you familiar with the Field Anthologies of your world?" Caelan asked as we ducked under a curved branch, stepping softly over a surprise patch of wildflowers that looked like they'd shown up just to welcome us. I was careful to avoid getting too covered in dirt, squishy mud, and leftover puddles from yesterday's rain.

"Hang on," I said, pausing mid-step. I turned my face upward and let the hush of the forest settle over me like a soft wool blanket. For once, I didn't want to rush. I wanted to savour this, breathe in the mossy smell of the earth, dazzle at the sharp emerald green of the ferns, soak in the heady fragrance from the faint salt breeze rolling inland. It wasn't just peaceful, it felt alive in a way I hadn't expected. I gestured for Cae to sit with me on a fallen log. My heart was thumping, not in fear, but in deep recognition.

"Is everything alright?" he asked, his soft, careful voice wrapping around me like a cloak.

"Yes," I breathed. "It's this place... it feels like... home. Not the home I've been chasing all my life, where you're from, but one that was here all along and I just didn't know how to experience it. It's disorienting, in a good way. Like I've been running for so long and didn't realise I could just stop and delve into my body and truly feel how wonderful it can be to be alive as a Human."

Cae nodded, his silvery wings shifting gently behind him. "I feel it too. Back in Faierodon, we have beauty, breathtaking, yes, but it's always pulsing forward, fast and bright and restless. Here, the land breathes with a slow heartbeat. It wants you to linger, to listen. Even the trees hum with richer, lingering stories if you're patient enough to hear."

A hush settled between us that felt less like silence and more like communion. I reached out and rested my hand on top of his, and he didn't flinch or flutter away. In that moment, it wasn't about romance, or missions, or tears in dimensions; it was just two beings who understood each other beyond words.

I felt a warmth rise in my body, and then I saw them: blue sparkles dancing just below my skin, tracing delicate lines along my arm and hands. They didn't fade this time. They shimmered softly, like moonlight on wet sand, content to stay.

I didn't need to figure it out right then. For once, I wasn't scrambling to define it or box it up. Whether I was turning into an Eura fully or remaining Human, or living in both, it didn't matter. I let the sparkles be part of me, part of the forest, part of everything. After what felt like both a single breath and a thousand lifetimes, I felt ready to stand.

Cae looked at me with wonder. "Your sparkles," he murmured. "They're staying."

I gave him a small smile. "I think so."

He returned the smile, his whole face lighting up in that gentle, slightly mischievous way of his. "Are you ready to keep going?"

"Yes," I replied. "And to answer your question about the Anthologies, I've heard whispers of them in old stories and history books. Nothing concrete. Just fragments."

Cae tilted his head, considering. "Where I'm from, we have our own Field Anthologies; great libraries that document the universal laws of all dimensions. I think your world's Anthologies might be similar. I keep seeing a library, but it feels... hidden."

An image rose in my mind: an underground chamber, quiet and alive with the hush of ancient words.

"I think it's underground," I said softly. "Somewhere close."

Spitz zipped around anxiously, his glow flickering. "We should make camp. It's nearly dark."

"Yes," I replied, winking at Spitz playfully, "we wouldn't want to stumble into a Yeti's nest without permission, eh?"

I gestured to a small side trail. "Let's check this path."

We followed the sound of water, a sweet gurgling that felt like a forest lullaby. Soon, we found a stream winding around mossy rocks, leading us to a gentle waterfall. The rocks were slick and charcoal-coloured, the whole place smelt fresh, like ferns after rain. I edged carefully along the covered stones behind the waterfall, feeling the spray on my face. My hand brushed against something cold: a golden metal ring embedded in the rock wall, like it had been there for decades. Curiosity pulsed through me. I reached out to gently touch it. Suddenly, the world around us began to shift and warp. The ground turned to liquid beneath our feet.

"Hang on, Daria!" Cae grabbed my hand.

We were caught in a cyclone of light and sound, spinning and tumbling downwards, underground. My stomach flipped like I was on the worst roller coaster at Rainbow's End. When it stopped, I was on my feet again, sort of. The space we landed in glistened with silken fabric in purples, teals, and blues. A walkway of pure light glowed beneath us. My body felt light and floaty. I looked down and nearly gasped, I was translucent, shimmering. I looked like... like Cae. He was there too, smaller, his edges fuzzy, his form shifting with the colours of the space.

"Where are we?" I asked, my voice echoing like it was coming from a canyon.

Spitz buzzed past. "Oh, you know, just another Tuesday. Portal? Tear? Maze? Who can keep up anymore!"

"This looks like somewhere in Faierodon," Cae said, turning slowly. "But I've never been here."

Before I could ask more, a voice rose from the shimmering veils.

"You activated the Overlay between the Dimensions with that ring, because we called you here," it sang, airy and echoing.

We turned, and there she stood. A figure approached, shaped like a Human woman but clearly so much more. Her hair danced like river stones at dusk, short and smoky grey, glasses perched on her nose like a librarian. Her gown looked like night skies woven with starlight, twinkling endlessly in folds that seemed to spill into forever. She moved like mist across a moonlit lake, and behind her, two more beings followed. There were two other women with her, each as mysterious and inviting. The second had wild, flowing brown hair that tumbled around her like a waterfall in a Nor'Wester. Her gown flickered with dawn colours: corals, greens, golds, alive as a Tui's morning call. She seemed constantly on the verge of giggling, eyes bright with mischief and warmth. The third had crimped grey hair in a sharp bob that would make any Ponsonby hair stylist jealous. Her gown shimmered in deep purples and silvers, like the last streaks of twilight on a frosty Otago evening. Her expression was no-nonsense, but her eyes sparkled with kindness and curiosity in equal measure.

"We are the Weavers," the bob-haired one announced, her voice layering over itself like waves on a stony beach.

The wild-haired one gave a cheeky grin. "Some call us Fates, but that's just one of our many nicknames. We've got more than a possum has hiding spots."

I stared, dumbfounded. They had all sorts of strings and yarns rolled up in baskets, connecting to their elaborate, glowing gowns as if they were weaving something, but I couldn't see anything concrete come from their chaotic and colourful efforts. "You lot look like a cosmic knitting circle," I blurted.

The brown-haired Weaver burst into laughter, doubling over and wiping starry tears from her eyes. "Finally! Someone who sees it! Cosmic knitting circle. I'm keeping that one."

The first Weaver stepped forward again, her gown shifting with tiny galaxies spinning beneath its surface. "I'll get right to it. You are a dyphoros, Daria," she said, her voice gentle and powerful at once.

My knees nearly gave way, though I had no idea what it was; it sounded like a mouthful. "What's that?"

The bob-haired Weaver leaned in, her eyes glinting a dewy mist. "A dyphoros is a being who begins a particular journey in form, living two full lives at once, across two dimensions, holding both worlds within but not in union, initially. Not just dreaming, not metaphor. You are both, simultaneously. It's why you have been experiencing this dual tug of war within you, Daria."

I felt my breath catch, it was like they unlocked something deep within me. Tears welled up, but they felt more like a blessing than a burden. Images slammed into my mind, years of experiences I had been blocking, flashing one after another, and then fading into one recent memory. I was laughing under the stars as a being named *Daer* in Faeirodon, I was an Eura. I had an entire other family there, friends, rich and beautiful memories of a life as a fairy.

"Think of it sort of like a dolphin's mind; one side can sleep while the other is alert and working." The Weaver, wearing glasses, put a hand on my shoulder to steady me as I was starting to feel dizzy, even in this lighter form. "You are this way, except that you get to choose whether you are experiencing both lives at the same time, muting one in your consciousness for a moment while the other is active, or dropping in and out of both like visiting a close friend and catching up on the story. You will keep living in both dimensions at the same time, whether you realise it or not, and have been your entire life. Unless of course, you choose to merge."

Cae watched me soak in what was being said in silent awe, his face resonating gentle hues of care.

"That's a lot to take in," I finally spoke, "but I feel it all now, it's starting to come alive inside me."

Suddenly, my life clicked into place. Was it possible that Nuvious's timecard switch was supposed to have happened? Was all of this just as it was supposed to be?

"If you are the Fates, do you know everything that's going to happen already?" I asked, confused.

"We are not omniscient, darling," the bob-cut Weaver jumped in. "Our job is to orchestrate extremely interwoven stories, but we can't possibly derive all the exact outcomes."

"So we don't have everything pre-ordained about our lives, then?" I asked.

"Of course not, there are simply keystone moments and important opportunities for your growth as a soul."

The wild-haired Weaver hopped forward, eyes sparkling. "You're not chained to fate. You're a dancer on a wobbling boardwalk. You can leap, pause, even slip and laugh your guts out before climbing back up."

"So... fate isn't fixed?" Cae asked, his voice almost reverent.

"Nothing is fully fixed," the first Weaver said. "We set the equations; your free will sets the variables."

"Thank you," I whispered. "I don't know what to do with this yet, but thank you."

The Weavers exchanged glances; the brown-haired one giggling, the bob-haired one tsking, the first simply watching me with a soft, endless patience.

"You're as strong as that kauri that you blessed as it gave its last breath," the laughing Weaver said, stepping forward and gently squeezing my hand. "Strong enough to hold all the stars and the sea in your chest."

Their laughter, warmth, and wisdom hummed around us as they slowly stepped back, dissolving into the starlit folds of the air like mist at sunrise. Cae reached for me, his hand trembling as it touched my cheek. "You are incredible," he breathed softly, tucking back a curl from my glowing hair.

I leaned into him, my forehead resting on his. "I don't know what all this means, but we'll figure it out," I whispered. "One heartbeat at a time."

And for the first time, I felt fully at home; not in one world or the other, but in the space between, held together by love and the glistening threads of something far bigger than fate.

CHAPTER TEN

Daer's Dilemma

20 CE *Linear Time (Common Era, After the Fall of Ether)*
Planet: *Earth* **Dimension:** *Fae*
Galaxy: *Milky Way*

I was born in the wrong dimension.

I always knew I didn't quite fit the mold, even by Faierodon standards. And let me tell you, this place is no stranger to out of box ways. Our cities breathe with bioluminescent rivers, trees hum secret songs at midnight, the bees have informed our hegaxon building structures, and entire villages shift shape with the moon cycle. But even among the Ekats or Thelassi, I always felt like I was peeking over a fence into another life, another rhythm. I was born with the pull of another heartbeat. A warmth that didn't belong to the winged, fast-paced Fae dimension. I'd dream of heavy rain on concrete, of crowded bus stops and burnt coffee. Things I'd only ever heard of in the Field Anthologies about Humans, but never actually seen. I was tortured by constant nostalgia for the life I knew I was supposed to live in the Human world that had no place among the starlit meadows and shimmering sky gardens of the Eura.

Parallel dimensions swirl around each other; not far, just hidden, like a door you almost remembered how to open, but then forgot you were looking. Eura like me move too fast, too lightly, to catch Human eyes. We flicker on the edge of perception, a shimmer in a puddle or a sparkle just out of reach. Humans? Their eyes are set to dense mode, their senses dulled by centuries of distraction. They wouldn't see us even if we tap-danced across their breakfast table. Oh, and don't get me started on their beliefs about fairies. They think we exist if *they* believe or babies fart? Where do they get this stuff?

I was meant to enter the Human timeline, to guide them away from self-destruction, to gently nudge them back toward the Earth's pulse and their heart's truths. But at the last moment, that dodgy sprite Nuvious slipped in, snatched my time card, and swapped it with a sly maneuver. And just like that, I blinked awake in Faierodon instead.

Nuvious. His name sounds like a daft whisper through a keyhole, doesn't it? Sprites like him thrive on trickery. They're the sort to lead you in circles on a misty trail. But what grudge does he hold against me? I still don't know. Maybe I outshone him in a starlight weaving contest, maybe I laughed at the wrong joke, or maybe he felt like causing chaos that day.

From my earliest moments, I felt the pull of another life. Visions of rain-slicked footpaths, the gentle buzz of city lights, and the smell of toast and jam in the morning. The warmth of old jumpers, the taste of salty chips on a beachside bench. These flickers filled me with an ache that tugged at my chest like a half-forgotten song. I wrote them all down in journals; each vision a thread, each memory a shimmering bead.

We Eura are sensitive, almost unbearably so. Our winged ears hear the murmur of moss, the sigh of starlight, the tremble of hidden emotions in a friend's smile. We sense everything before it's spoken; a gift, and sometimes a curse. We drift apart easily, retreating into our glowing caves to process the endless waves of feeling. Yet through it all, that other rhythm called to me. The Human rhythm.

What's more, I was miserable in my life here as an Eura and mostly invisible. Here's how it usually goes. I say hi. They say nothing. Then they vanish. That's it. That's the pattern. Back when I was younger, I thought it was bad luck. Maybe I was standing in the wrong crystal corridor, or maybe my hair had gone all static again. But after the hundredth time of someone bolting like I'd just announced the apocalypse, I had to admit: it's me. It's not my looks. Plenty in Faierodon shimmer brighter. It's not my form either; some days I'm more ripple than most, and no one seems to mind. It's my voice. Something about the way it lands, the way it cuts through all the polite illusions people like to wrap themselves in. Even a simple "hello" snaps them out of their comfort zone, and then I'm left talking to the echo.

I've tried being gentle. Tried shortening my sentences to a single word. Even tried not speaking at all, which is great for keeping friends. But sooner or later, the moment I open my mouth, it's like pulling a lever: poof. Gone. The elders call it the Origin Chord, something about Ether and the Fall. They act like I'm supposed to be proud of this trick. Destiny, prophecy, blah blah. Honestly? It feels less like destiny and more like a curse designed by a bored prankster.

So I drift through Faierodon like a shadow in a hall of mirrors. The markets glow, the spires sing, whole plazas blaze with light, and I walk through all of it like I've got a permanent "do not disturb" sign stuck to my forehead. The worst part isn't the ghosting itself. It's the silence afterward, when you're left wondering if you were ever really seen at all. Born of Faierodon's light, sure. But cursed to be invisible the second I open my mouth. Some beings get adoration. I get the world's fastest disappearing act.

Then, one dusky evening, as I sat tracing the constellations in my journal, Nuvious burst in. Covered in bark, twinkling sap, his hair wild and sticking out like a startled hedgehog.

"Listen, Daer, it's not what it looks like," he sputtered, eyes wide and darting.

I put my pen down, slow and careful, my glow steady but cool. "What are you talking about?"

He flinched, brushing sticky leaves off his tunic. "I didn't want it to get this far. I mean… I did, but I didn't think it would last. The swap. The veil."

"The veil? The swap?" I echoed, my voice low.

Nuvious shifted his weight, wings flicking. "The IGSTA, Intergalactic Space-Time Agency, they ordered the swap and the veiling. They were afraid. Afraid you'd merge."

I felt the forest pause. Even the soft glow of the starroot tea leaves on my table seemed to lean in.

"Merging," I whispered. "You mean… my memories?"

He nodded, his eyes shimmering with regret. "You are a dyphoros, Daer. A being who can fully inhabit two dimensions at once. Your other self exists inside of you, right now. Her name is Daria. You were meant to bridge the worlds, but they feared the collapse of the separation. So they had me do it, they had me switch you both to separate you from, well, yourself."

I closed my eyes. In the dark, Daria was there. Her grin crooked and wild, her eyes bright with impossible questions. I felt her frustrations, her heartbreaks, her deep, relentless love.

When I opened my eyes again, they were brimming with electric tears. "You veiled me from myself."

Nuvious crumpled. "I thought it would keep you safe. Keep us all safe. But now… the Weavers have begun unraveling it. You're seeing her now, aren't you?"

I nodded, the glow of my skin intensifying as memories tumbled together; her late-night tinkering, my moonlit dances. Her science journals, my forest songs.

"It's begun," I said, my voice echoing like two songs layered over each other.

I breathed a sigh of something similar to anticipation mixed with relief, and the halls of my home answered back. Each wall sang my name in a different octave. Faierodon does not forget. It is memory spun into living legend. Yet today the notes warp. A thread out of tune. Slower, duller, as if some other world is trying to press its rhythm into mine. That's when I feel her, like a twin heartbeat, half a measure behind. She fumbles, she laughs, she runs. Human time, heavy and cooked. My time, sharp and cutting. And between us, the tear.

I thought I was whole, just lonely. But the Field whispers otherwise: dyphoros. Split, not by mistake, by design. I am Daer, and I am not alone in myself. The Field knows far more than whatever prophecy Daria is chasing.

Nuvious sank onto a plush, floral cushion, his small hands trembling. "I'm sorry, Daer. I truly am."

A long hush stretched between us. The vine walls of my home pulsed gently, breathing with me. Finally, I stood, feeling the merging pull at every cell. My wings flickered, then softened, blending into the new weight of my form. I wanted this, I wanted to become all of me.

I looked down at him. "I don't know if forgiveness is the word. But I understand. You were afraid."

He nodded weakly. "What now?"

I tilted my head, listening to the new heartbeat echoing inside me. "Now, I become whole. We do. Together. It's time."

He looked up, tears clinging to his lashes like morning dew. "And the IGSTA?"

A wry smile touched my lips. "Let them tremble. They can't stop what's true."

I reached for him, my fingers shimmering, the bridge between dimensions alive in my touch. "No more meddling. If you come with me, you come honestly."

His face brightened, the mischief softened by relief. "I promise."

With one final glance around my sanctuary, the mossy walls, the gentle glow of a thousand lifetimes, I closed my eyes and opened to the merge. Daria's presence surged within me, warm and bright. Her humor, her defiance, her hunger to learn. My softness, my connection to starlight and laughter, my patient watchfulness. We flowed together like two rivers finally meeting after lifetimes apart. The ache of separation unwound, replaced by an electric wholeness. The world folded around me in waves of colour and warmth, each tone a note in a new symphony. My being rearranged, my cells shimmered, my heartbeats aligned.

And then I was kneeling on a different mossy forest floor. My hands glowed faint blue and white, with the soft luminescence of moonbeam caught in rippling tides. My body felt denser but equally enlivened with starlight. I heard a voice, so familiar, so grounding.

"Daria!"

I turned, slowly and deliberately, in my new merged form. There he was: Cae. His eyes were wide, brimming with an emotion I couldn't name.

"Goodonya," I confirmed, my voice layered like two waves crashing together.

He knelt, his hands hovering, trembling. "You're... you're different," he stammered. "But you're you."

I laughed a bright, sparkling laugh that spilt from my chest. Tears streaked down my face, each one catching the light in iridescent hues of sparkle like tiny falling stars.

"It's me," I breathed. "All of me. Daer and Daria... together. Daer is an Eura from Faierodon, as I'd always felt."

He exhaled shakily, brushing a glowing strand of hair from my cheek. "You blacked out again. For a moment, I thought I'd lost you," he admitted, his voice catching.

I pressed my forehead to his, feeling the heat, the anchoring solidity of him in his Human-adapted form. "No. You never did. I just had to find all of me first."

He held me tight, his heartbeat thundering against mine, the forest pressing close, listening. In Faierodon, we don't hold each other like this. We share light, scents, quiet pulses. But this, this raw, Human closeness felt like finding warmth after a thousand winters. I felt

Daria's snark rise, her cheeky grin pressing against my mind. I felt Daer's endless patience, her knowing smile. Inside me, their essences braided into one: the sharp wit of Human joy and the ancient glow of Fae magic.

When I finally pulled back, he searched my face. "So… what now?"

I looked at my hands, turning them over slowly, the dancing glow settling into something both wild and steady. "I think… I can move between them now. The ways of being. The softness, the sharpness. The science, the starlight."

Cae's face split into a grin, tears glittering at the corners of his eyes. "Only you would merge two entire lives and then say it like you've just decided between flat white or long black," he teased.

I laughed; a sound so full, so whole, it felt like the multiverse laughing through me. "Only me," I giggled, "Look at you and your knowledge of Human coffee orders at Starbucks."

He pressed a kiss to my forehead. "Welcome home… both of you."

I tilted my head back, letting the gentle drizzle of a soft rain that had begun to caress my skin, as the forest's ancient melody vibrated through my entire being. For the first time in all my lifetimes, I felt fully alive, fully here.

I looked at Cae again. His eyes held mine, steady as the earth.

"So," he said with a crooked grin, "Daria? Daer? Or… D squared?"

I snorted, shaking my head. "Let's just go with D."

"Alright then, D," he said, his hand warm on my back.

Rising to my feet, I felt the radiance dim to a gentle luminescence, my toes gripping the velvet moss beneath me. It felt really good to be able to sense with the Eura ways I had always known and embody them into the Human pace, together. For once, I wasn't torn between worlds.

"This is going to take a bit of getting used to," Spitz buzzed. "What now?"

"We've got to find the Golden Prophecy, finally," Cae said what we were all thinking. Then, as if in deep contemplation, he turned to me, "I can't believe there was a version of you living in my hometown all along, and we never met!"

"I'm glad we have now." I responded, blushing a bit, "I was a bit distracted during the merge. What happened to the Weavers?" I looked around, hoping to find a clue.

"They were telling us to find the prophecy here after your merge was complete," Cae recounted. "They said that you needed to go to the

Fae dimension to be able to merge, and the tear made it possible to be in both forms simultaneously until the merge. If you hadn't gone there, you'd never have been able to unite. The IGSTA has wiped out most of the dyphoros in the multiverse, and they are keen on blocking you from activating the prophecy."

"I still don't understand. Why is the prophecy scaring them?" I asked.

"Because a morphing genetic union of inter-dimensional beings has never occurred to their recollection, he began. "Sure, galactic same-dimension species have mated and created variant species, but never from completely different dimensions. Even the rare dyphoros they know of tend to be same dimensional. So, this union of your selves signifies the first step in the potential for a unification of both the Human and the Fae dimensions. Of various dimensions uniting across time and space."

"And that is bad because?" I pried.

"If dimensional beings were to merge, each species would have to adjust time-space paces to come to a middle ground," he continued, "inter-dimensional rules would have to shift in the fabric of each dimension's universal laws. The Field of each dimension tends to prevent this, but they are mysteriously updating with the tear, and the IGSTA is scared. There would be more access to nuanced ways of being and doing not available before. The IGSTA is afraid of the level of chaos they feel it will create."

"But what about the prophecy?" I pressed, "Why do we need to physically retrieve it if they already know what it has predicted?"

"I guess we have to find out," Cae's lip curled up, and he gave me a teasing look. "It seems important. It's just a piece of the puzzle, I assume."

I smirked. It was amazing to be able to find humour and comfort with Cae amidst all this uncertainty and information that was beyond mind-bending. It was completely changing not only my lived experience and sense of identity at lightning speed, but also the fabric of existence. You know, nbd.

"Cae, I have to tell you something. I saw Nu in the other dimension, and well, I am both creatures, as you can see. Anyway, Nu was part of the IGSTA; he had an AMD device. It stands for an anti-matter device. It's what allows the IGSTA to dimension hop."

"Well, that explains a lot," Cae nodded, contemplating the news.

"Now that I'm merged," I began, "it's clearer than ever, Cae. The

Fae dimension is intricately connected, I just know it has a big role to play to help the Human one before it collapses and both dimensions are destroyed," I pondered, almost to myself.

"That kind of talk could get you locked up," a deep voice drawled from behind us.

CHAPTER ELEVEN

Caelan: Prophecy

I felt the shift in the air before I heard the voice. That prickly, cold shiver that slides down your back when you know someone's watching. And sure enough, there he was: Ro, strutting out of the shadows like he owned the place.

"Oh, for goodness' sake," I muttered under my breath. "Ro, mate, ever think about taking up rugby instead of being a professional nuisance? I hear the Humans love it."

Ro tilted his head, all casual, like we'd bumped into each other grabbing pies at the local dairy, not that he knew what any of that was. "Figured I'd find you here," he sneered, gesturing toward D. "She's all kinds of a problem, you know."

I snorted. "A problem? She's the heart holding this whole mess together."

I shifted slightly, putting my body between them. Not that D needed protection, she could probably outwit a whole squadron of stray agents before lunchtime, but still. My instincts kicked in. Was he IGSTA, too?

"You still playing mystery man, or are you gonna tell us what this is really about?" I asked.

Ro sighed, as though we were keeping him from his afternoon nap. "I'm just here to help. I said it before, I could be an asset. But you two keep making things difficult."

D raised an eyebrow, "Are you with the IGSTA or not? Stop mucking about. Who runs it? What do you want?"

Ro winced, looking up at the treetops as if waiting for a bird to drop on his head. "Doesn't matter who runs it," he said finally, almost whispering. "Point is, you're both about to paint a target on your backs the size of the Sky Tower if you keep this merging business up."

I felt my shoulders tense. "Right then. Because someone's watching?"

Ro nodded, as if we were finally catching up. "You're a beacon now. They'll come for you. Not just the IGSTA."

"And you expect us to trust you?" I snapped.

Ro looked almost hurt. "I get it. But I'm telling you, you keep pushing, she'll end up locked away, lost to both worlds. Remember the Rekel? That was Grison. He is about as close as you get to someone in charge here in our dimensions on Earth from the agency. And I think I pissed him off by helping you. So, you might not trust me, but I was trying to help. Until you made it impossible by merging."

D stood a bit taller, eyes glinting gold. "What's done is done."

Ro threw his hands up, his face twisted like he'd bitten into a rotten feijoa. "Disgusting. Inter-dimensional merging shouldn't exist. You've broken nature."

I took a step forward. "Your meddling's grown mold. Why don't you head back to Faierodon and find a mushroom council to charm or a wind to quarrel with? But stay out of our path."

He scowled, glanced up at the sky, then at us. "Don't say I didn't warn you." And, poof. Gone again.

I turned to D, who looked like she was holding the weight of two worlds in her chest.

"Choice," I said, shaking out the tension from my arms. "Let's keep going. I feel like we're close."

The path wound through ferns and towering mossy trunks, the forest whirring around us like a soft lullaby. The dusk wrapped us in its indigo shawl, with only the soft shimmers of our skin lighting the path. Spitz zipped ahead, glowing like a living lantern, mumbling to himself about "dodgy agents" and "useless inter-dimensional politics."

A few minutes later, D tapped my arm and pointed. "Oi, look, that wee mailbox thing with the porch light on."

I couldn't help but grin at the sight. Nestled under a giant silver fern stood what could only be described as a wee cottage, no bigger than my hiking boot. Its roof, decorated with acorn caps arranged in neat little rows, curved gently over walls that seemed to be made of polished bark. A soft golden glow spilt from the windows, warm as a campfire on a cold night.

"Let's have a nosey," I whispered, crouching down. Peeking in, I saw two creatures sitting inside, legs dangling over a tiny table, drinking from acorn caps.

D leaned over my shoulder, eyes wide. "Oh my stahs. Are those gnomes?"

Before we could ponder more, the door swung open with a creak, and out stepped the tiniest creature I've ever seen, well, besides Spitz. He was wearing a hat shaped like a mushroom cap, spotted with blue and lavender. His cloak was woven from spider silk and tiny petals; his boots looked like they'd been carved from acorn shells. His round nose glowed slightly at the tip, and his cheeks were rosy as if he'd just finished a cheeky brandy.

"Evening!" he chirped in a surprisingly deep, velvety voice. "Name's Suzako. Who might you folk be?"

D straightened up, looking enchanted. "Hi, Suzako! I'm D, and this is Caelan and Spitz." She gestured at us. "I thought your kind were not from this dimension. How did you arrive here?"

"Things have been shifting, right fast," Suzako explained, "We have been here all along, but not visible to your kind," he gestured at her. "Well, not to the Human part."

Spitz buzzed down and landed on Suzako's tiny porch, inspecting him like a grumpy customs officer.

"We're looking for the Field Anthologies," I said, squatting down so we were eye to eye. "Might you know of the keeper?"

Suzako twirled his mushroom hat with pride. "Aye! That'd be me. Keeper of stories, songs, histories, recipes; you name it. Always happy to share with those who respect the old ways."

I let out a breath, feeling my chest loosen. The veil that was hiding Suzako and the Anthologies must have lifted! "Brilliant. We're after something called the Golden Prophecy. Ever heard of it?"

His face fell faster than a jandal off a dock. He shuffled backward, hands trembling. "Oh, no, no, no. Not here, not here," he stammered, nearly tripping over his tiny boots. Before I could say another word, he bolted inside, slammed the door, and yanked shut a dried flower petal curtain.

"Wait!" D called gently, tapping lightly on the window.

We crouched in silence, listening to cicadas buzzing a mesmerizing tune and the distant murmur of a waterfall. My knees started to ache, but I held still, not wanting to scare him more. I was recalibrating how to coax Suzako out when a nose poked through the curtains. His voice was trembling. "I can't trust you. Some nasty folk came before and hurt my friend Mae. Left her bed-bound for weeks."

My heart squeezed. "I'm so sorry, Suzako. Who were they?"

He hesitated, looking around like he expected shadows to pounce. "Not Human. Not Fae. Sharp eyes, cruel words. They broke things… broke her spirit."

D leaned closer, her voice soft and melodic. "We aren't here to harm. We just want to understand. We don't even fully know why this prophecy involves us. Please, help us."

Suzako sniffled, ducked inside again. Silence. He reappeared a few moments later and looked directly at D, his eyes seeming to bore into her soul. "You have it already, just unveil it, unlock it." And with that, he ran back into the hut.

"What does he mean?" She looked confused, and yet her eyes looked different, like a fleck of something had appeared inside them. I gazed closer, a golden flicker washed across a maple syrup pupil, like amber sparks lit aflame.

"D… your eyes…" I stammered, holding up my lantern to see better.

She tried to focus, but her gaze seemed to be dancing between worlds. "I feel… so much. Like I'm seeing everything at once. Oh boy, it's just like the film, I'll go insane and my head might pop off." Her joke landed a bit flat.

My hands trembled as I touched her arm. "Is it the prophecy? Inside you somehow?"

She shuddered, closing her eyes tightly. "There's a scroll… words I can't read… and me."

I held her tighter. "Breathe. You're safe. Just feel it."

Her breath came in shaky waves. Then, like a dam breaking, golden light burst from her chest, spilling out into the night in radiant ribbons. It wasn't harsh; it was soft, warm, gentle, like dawn breaking through thick mist.

D's voice cracked. "I see myself… Daer… Daria… all the fragments. All the futures, pasts, pieces."

I clung to her hand as the ground started to hum beneath us, the forest quivering, holding its breath. She reached out into the sparkles, and I instinctively grabbed her other hand, steadying us both as the world tipped sideways.

"This is it!" she gasped, her hair glowing like a halo, her whole form shimmering in and out of focus.

I had just enough time to mutter, "Ah, here we go again," before we were both swallowed by the golden wave, the air around us shimmering and pulsing like a living song.
*****

I knew exactly where we landed, though stars help me, I had no clue why.

Ryheadyl.

I recognised it the instant I felt the thick, warm hum of the forest floor vibrating beneath my boots. The towering trees, with their wild violet leaves like giant feathered cloaks, were unmistakable. Up above, the bark spikes, sharp as a Dalesta's back, jutted toward the sky in a protective crown. Those were there to keep the Tesree away; big, winged nightmares that thought everything smaller than them was a snack on legs.

The Ekats had made this forest their sanctuary ages ago, and they'd done it without cages or weapons, just quiet negotiations with the trees. The Ekats didn't force or conquer; they asked, listened, and adjusted. The forest adapted because it loved them, a kind of relationship I'd rarely heard of in the Human dimension. They didn't bolt tech onto roots or slap solar panels on tree bark; they just were together.

I'd visited Ryheadyl once as a boy, and even back then, I'd felt a weird pang of envy. The Ekats lived with such gentle simplicity, a deep ease with themselves. Now, standing here again, it felt like stepping back into a dream that smelt of care and damp, earthly joys. But why now? Why here?

Before I could say anything, a voice floated from the trees, sweet as honey but with an edge that made my shoulders tense.

"It's truly a mystery," it mused.

"Who's there?" I called out, sliding in front of D instinctively. Even sweet forest folk could get weird when startled.

Out stepped a small creature, almost blending right into the tree trunks. Its skin looked like layers of soft, rippling bark, its green hair braided into loops that bounced with every step. Huge amber eyes peered at us, bright and curious, shimmering like sap catching morning light. Behind it, more Ekats trickled out, their movements fluid and graceful, almost like they were made of water and leaves at the same time. One had tiny mushrooms growing on its shoulders like ornaments; another had small vines coiled around its wrists like living jewelry. A ripple of excitement ran through the Ekats. They began circling us, clapping their small, bark-textured hands, humming softly. One started a dance, its feet skimming the moss so lightly that it looked like it was floating.

"It's her! The prophecy is real!" one shouted in a squeaky, flute-like voice.

"They know?" D gasped, her golden-amber eyes wide, her Fae form shimmering. Recognition sparked, and she bent down suddenly, arms outstretched.

"Mills!" she exclaimed, her voice breaking with emotion. "Oh my stars, Millie! It's been so long!"

The Ekat she embraced, Millie, apparently, let out a little squeak, her round eyes filling with tears. She launched into D's arms, wrapping her thin, viney fingers around D's shoulders and nuzzling her cheek like a long-lost sibling.

"Daer it's you! You remember when you were just a few galeons, and your mum brought you to us for summers? We thought you'd forgotten us forever!"

D held Millie so tenderly, her forehead pressed against the little Ekats. There was something so impossibly soft about it, a tender recognition that defied time. I felt a lump crawl up my throat.

D looked back at me, eyes shining with lovely childhood memories. "This is Millie; my childhood bestie here in Faierodon."

I blinked, brain whirring like a broken drone. "I'm still adjusting to you being in both lives, I must admit. My head's doing cartwheels."

She giggled, that snort-laugh she does when she's truly unguarded. "Was I worth the mess?" she teased, her eyes dancing.

I felt my whole body go warm and heavy at once. "You're worth every portal, every mind-bending puzzle, every terrifying creature," I said, barely above a whisper.

Millie beamed at us both. "We have it here!" she squeaked, tugging at D's hand. "We never believed it would be you. The Weaveborn; the dyphoros! We grew up on those stories! Before the Gerasa's Dyphoros Eradication wiped them nearly out... we thought it was all gone forever."

D's eyes lit up, tears brimming at the edges. "I remember everything now, Millie. You're right, the dyphoros was common once. And I know the spell. I know how to open it."

Millie's tiny shoulders shuddered with excitement. "I was hoping you'd say that!" She scurried behind a giant root and emerged holding a long, moss-wrapped box. "We've been keeping it safe... but it wouldn't open. We tried every song, every moon chant. Nothing."

D took a trembling breath. "It's me. It always had to be me. The merge… the prophecy… I think it created the final key inside me."

"Give it a go!" I urged, my voice cracking. My heart pounded so loudly I swear the Ekats could hear it echoing through the leaves. D closed her eyes, her shimmering hands cradling the box as though it were a baby bird. The forest fell silent, even the usual gentle creaks and hums of Ryheadyl pausing as if the entire place was holding its breath.

"Nora seviet, alofesne respinel. Nora seviet, alofesne respinel. Awaken to the Truth of One."

She whispered it like a prayer, soft and lilting. The words barely made it past her lips, but they curled through the air like morning mist. The mossy box began to twitch. Then it shivered, bouncing gently as if laughing at a secret joke. A soft crack echoed, and then, pop! The lid shot open, releasing a sparkling explosion of glitter so dense I couldn't see my fingers in front of my face.

I started coughing, sputtering, trying to wave away the sparkling confetti. "Oh, for the love of, can someone turn off the glitter tap?!"

As the shimmering cloud began to clear, a scroll slowly unrolled itself mid-air, spinning like it was dancing to its silent music. It hovered between us, turning until the delicate letters shimmered into view. Together, D and I stepped closer. The Ekats gathered around, tiny hands clasped over their mouths, eyes huge and shining.

And then the words began to glow, weaving themselves into our hearts:

In times unseen, the threads of all shall weave as one,
mingling the laws beyond the stars in union.
Harmony of two hearts in two dimensions, an infinity bond warps time,
and once more, peace will guide the galaxies.

A hush. I could hear the blood rush in my ears. Each word of the prophecy echoed inside me, a vibration that started in my chest and rippled outward until even my fingertips tingled with its truth. D's fingers laced into mine, strong and trembling at once. I turned to her, my mouth dry, my heart threatening to break my ribs. I couldn't pretend to understand what it meant. It seemed coded with meaning more than what D was experiencing, more than what any of us could know now.

"You okay?" I asked, voice rough.

Her golden eyes searched mine, glowing as bright as a thousand dawns. "I am," she whispered. "For the first time… really, truly… I am."

I pulled her into my arms, feeling her warmth, the gentle tremble of her breath. Around us, the Ekats began to sing, soft and melodic, a song older than stars.

Millie tiptoed forward, pressing a tiny hand to D's leg. "Welcome home, Daer. Welcome home, Daria. Welcome home… D."

I felt her smile against my chest, her whole body melting into me like water returning to its river. Now I felt what it meant to be embraced and emboldened, held in the balm of the Golden Prophecy.

CHAPTER TWELVE

D: Infinity Bond

"An infinity bond," I echoed softly, almost to myself. The words shimmered off the scroll like a heartbeat. I traced them with my eyes again and again. "What could that mean?"

I glanced up at Cae, cheeks going warm and only slightly wishing I could have an off button for my senses giving me away. He looked back at me with a paradoxical, gentle intensity that almost knocked the wind out of me. For once, my usual snark piped down, and I just let myself feel that sweet, magnetic pull between us. A quiet knowing that crackled like a soft fire.

"Ooo, pick me, pick me!" an eager voice squeaked next to Millie, jolting me right out of my emotional puddle. An Ekat's wee hand shot up so quickly that it nearly toppled a mushroom lamp. The move was so genuinely enthusiastic it made me giggle, and a quiet tension began to release from my limbs, a relief after all the chaos we'd been through.

"Of course," I encouraged him, my voice wobbling between laughter and curiosity.

Millie stepped forward, her braids bouncing like viney tree sprigs as she walked. "This is Jis," she announced proudly, patting his head like a prized squash. "He's our Weaveborn lore master. Been reading up since he was just a sprout!"

Jis puffed up, eyes glimmering like emerald pāua shells. "Yes, yes! Thank you, Millie. The infinity bond is from the Golden Age records, recovered in early times After the Fall of Ether (AFE), according to the Galactic record. It doesn't mean romance like those sappy Human anthologies!" He paused, suddenly bashful, peeking up at me from behind his scroll.

"Oi, you do realise part of me is Human, right?" I teased, raising an eyebrow, a smirk curling at the edge of my mouth.

Jis nearly dropped his little scroll bundle. "Oh, branches! My apologies, Weaveborn, didn't mean a lick of offense!" He shuffled his tiny feet, looking like he might disappear into the moss.

I snorted and waved him on. "All good, carry on. I'm all ears."

He took a deep, shaky breath and found his rhythm again. "The infinity bond isn't about fleeting feelings. It's a mathematical, energetic imprint. Like a cosmic thread weaving two beings together across all time and dimensions, unbreakable. It opens new access points between realms, places we couldn't even imagine before. There are layers: first, your integrated self as dyphoros, then your family, then your community." He paused for a beat, as if he wanted to be sure I was following.

Then he looked right at Cae and me. "Your bond, you and this fine chap here," he gestured at Cae with his vine-wrapped hand, "isn't just personal. It's the ignition of love as an eternal force across the multiverse. A spark to guide every dimension. The dyphoros sets the spark, but the flame? That ignites infinite variation."

"The bond of eternal love made accessible..." Cae whispered, rolling the words around his tongue like a good drop of elderwine. His eyes danced in wonder, twin moons reflecting across rippling water.

"That's beautiful," I murmured, softly, pondering. "Why would the IGSTA and all those other creatures want to stop something like that? It makes no sense!"

"They misunderstand," Millie cut in, her bark-textured hands wringing anxiously. "They think merging and diversity mean chaos and disorder, when actually, it just means more love, more expansion. More possibilities."

"Also, some races," Jis chimed in, "such as Humans or the Lagas, as examples, are often afraid of expansion, of what they do not understand. Some of their kind, at least, prefer conformity and old ways to change and expansion."

I paused. Their words settled into me with the quiet certainty of the evening tide pulling at you while standing in the sand, not demanding but persistent. A gentle force that doesn't shout but won't be denied either.

Spitz hovered over the scroll, his wings creating a soft thrum in the air. "So what happens next?" he asked, glancing nervously toward the treeline. "Kinda weird we haven't been ambushed by now, isn't it?"

"Oi, don't jinx it," I muttered, my eyes scanning the treeline just as a voice sliced through the air, sending my senses into alert.

"I wouldn't speak too soon," came Ro's smooth-as-kerosene tone. In a flash, IGSTA agents slipped from the trees, dark shapes moving with an eerie, clinical precision. I felt my spine stiffen, every nerve awake. Cae instinctively stepped in front of me in his typical protective stance.

"It's too late," I said, squaring up despite the tremor in my knees. "The prophecy's opened. You can't unbloom a flower once it's opened."

A hulking agent lumbered forward, its skin a violet lime that might glow in the dark, a voice rumbling like an earthquake underfoot. "That doesn't mean we can't take you in for questioning."

Before the creature could get any closer, the scroll zipped shut with a sharp snap and dove into its mossy box, sealing itself with a satisfying click. The Ekats snapped into formation around us, bark skins shifting and flexing like living armor.

"We won't let you take them!" Jis shouted, his voice shaking but fierce as a young kōtare defending its nest.

"Oh, but you will," Ro purred, stepping forward, that smarmy calm twisting my stomach. "They'll come willingly. Trust me."

"Why's that?" Cae demanded, his voice cutting through the chaos with ease.

Before Ro could open his smug mouth, a shriek split the canopy. The forest erupted as massive black and green birds swooped in, wings slicing the air with terrifying grace.

"Oh no, the Tesree!" Millie gasped, her eyes wide as saucers. "Daer or, D, your part's done. We'll handle this!"

She shoved an AMD into my hand so fast I nearly dropped it.

"Go!" she urged.

I didn't hesitate. I grabbed Cae's hand, felt Spitz latch onto his shoulder, and slammed the button. The world twisted and folded in on itself, a sensation like being squeezed through a fern frond, and then, we were spat out into the Human dimension forest, my lungs gasping for air.

"Don't tell me you actually found it," came a small, grouchy voice.

I turned, squinting through the dark. "Suzako," I breathed, a weird mix of relief and dread washing over me. "How wonderful you're safe."

Suzako stepped out of his mossy hut, hat cocked sideways, face pinched with worry. "Wonderful schmunderful," he scoffed, throwing up a stubby hand. "My family's been threatened. Whole village nearly flattened!"

"By who?" I asked, my voice snagging on my tongue.

"A green giant," he whispered, eyes darting around. "Taller than the canopy. Could come back any tick."

Cae's brow furrowed, softening his whole face into something tender. "Grison. Is there anything we can do?"

Suzako sighed, his shoulders drooping like wet moss. "We'll burrow underground. Maybe one day it'll be safe topside again."

Cae reached into his pack and handed him a tiny glowing gem, blue as a midnight pool. "Take this. If you're in strife, we'll come."

Suzako's eyes glistened like dew on new leaves. "Thank you." He slipped inside, closing his tiny door behind him with a soft click.

I let out a shaky laugh, leaning into Cae's chest. His warmth grounded me like a root system in a storm. "That was a close shave," I mumbled. "Hope Millie and the rest are alright."

"They're scrappy," Cae said, though I heard the fret hidden under his calm. "But the IGSTA… they won't give up easily."

Spitz flopped onto my head like a deflated balloon. "I need a lie-down. And maybe a lamington the size of my whole body. Cae told me about them in this Human realm, it's the only reason I wanted to come in the first place."

I snorted, feeling the queasy tension ease just a smidge.

"I know a spot," I said. "Jeanie's South Bay cottage, she won't mind."

I fumbled for my phone, fingers trembling.

Jeanie, we found the prophecy. Too many yarns to spin. Staying at your South Bay place tonight. Code?

Three dots appeared.

3530#. Be safe. Spill it all later!

Relief whooshed through me, a place to hide, even if just for a moment. I didn't need Cae to lift off anymore. I could fly on my own now, fully. We soared into the night sky, trees shrinking beneath us. The Human dimension felt thick but oddly welcoming now that I was integrated from the merge, each gust like a cold sea plunge that jolted me alive. At the cottage, willow branches swayed in the moonlight as if they knew us, old friends waving us in. I threw open the windows, letting the salty tang of the ocean push the mustiness out. Once the fire crackled to life, I slumped down, muscles and mind uncoiling. I stared into the flames, watching sparks dance like tiny prophecies, each one a possibility.

Cae sat next to me, his fingers tracing the glowing line on my arm. "So… what now?" he asked, voice low, curious.

I watched the embers pulse and fade. "We don't hang about. The IGSTA's coming. We stay ahead, keep moving."

Cae's eyes flickered with a strange mix: excitement and apprehension braided together. "And the prophecy… do you think they'll try to destroy it? Or twist it for their gain?"

I sighed, my fingers drumming a restless beat on my knee. "Who knows? I don't think they can now that we enlivened it. But I know one thing: the next move is ours. We move before they can."

A gust rattled the window, bringing the scent of wet pines and earth. It felt like the forest was leaning closer, listening in.

Spitz let out a theatrical click from the mantle. "You two had better sort your business quick. I'm too pretty for an alien holding cell."

I smirked, standing up, stretching my new flexbody that still felt like a suit two sizes too big and somehow perfectly mine at once. The old felt like a too-heavy rain jacket I'd finally donated. Only forward now.

I turned toward the door, feeling the spark coil and snap inside me. "Let's show them what this bond really unlocked. Make them question every move they make."

Cae stood too, grin crooked, eyes alive with fierce warmth. "Now that's the D I know."

I paused, my thoughts swirling like wind-blown dandelion seed. Blending my two lives felt like a storm rolling in and a sunrise cresting the horizon at the same time; a wild dance and a quiet peace stitched together.

"An infinity bond warps time," I murmured again, trying the words on my tongue.

Cae closed his eyes, tilting his head like he was tasting them too. "Yeah… reckon I still don't fully get it."

I shook my head. "Not just dimension jumping. More like weaving timelines… bending time, feeling it differently."

Cae tapped his chin. "Maybe it means time's no longer a straight path. You can mend it, twist it… even heal old wounds."

I laughed softly, leaning into him, feeling his warmth run into me like a creek in spring. "Finally explains why I've always felt so bloody impatient here."

Cae chuckled, shaking his head. "Like trying to sprint through a swamp wearing gumboots."

"Exactly!" I giggled, my chest lighting up with a warmth I hadn't felt in ages.

Cae fell silent for a moment, then looked at me with a soft wonder. "Humans… they get all these chances to grow. Even when they muck it up, they get to try again. Maybe that's the real magic here."

I nodded, pressing my forehead to his, letting the moment stretch and glow, even if it was fleeting. It was long enough to log it in my archives of joyful moments, and that was beautiful. He was right, the Human realm's slow pace… it gave space to mess up and start again. Maybe that was its true gift.

CHAPTER THIRTEEN

Caelan: Caught

"You're glowing," I admired, watching her in deep contemplation. Suddenly, out of nowhere, a lightning bolt of pain shot straight through my forehead. It was so sharp and sudden that I had to lie down on the couch.

"Are you okay, Cae?" D leaned over me, his brow furrowed in the cutest way. Her hand brushed my forehead so lightly I barely felt it. "Sorry, that's a Human thing, checking for fever or heat."

I chuckled weakly. "That's sweet of you," I managed, trying to grin through the pain. Even in moments like this, she knew how to disarm me. Leave it to D to make a blinding headache feel like a shared moment rather than an infliction.

"What happened?" she asked, her voice like a gentle wave on a still lake.

"I'm not exactly sure," I said, trying to focus on the images that had flashed behind my eyes. Shapes, lights, maybe even memories, but so jumbled I couldn't untangle them. "I'm fine... don't fuss."

"Okay," she whispered, leaning down closer. Then she brushed her lips against my cheek. Barely a whisper of a kiss, so subtle I might have thought I imagined it if not for the warm spark that lit up my chest like a soft sunrise over the ocean, pink and teals melding into pure beauty.

It was the kind of touch that said more than any fancy poetry or grand declarations. It wasn't a wild lightning-strike sort of passion; no, that stuff just fried you alive. Kind of like this headache. I knew that kind well enough, and it always led to heartbreak. With D, this was different. It was quiet, almost shy, but it roared louder in my heart than any thunderclap. There was no hunting, no proving, no fixing. Just two beings feeling each other in their fullness. I realised in that moment that real love might not be about fireworks at all. It might be about ease. About sitting next to someone and feeling your breath finally settle.

When I recovered, we sat by the fire, yarned about life, about our families, about what we hoped for. We laughed a lot, full-belly, silly, nose-snorting laughs that felt healing in a way no potion or tech could ever manage. She shared stories about her past Human relationships, and each one twisted my stomach tighter. The ways she'd been treated... I couldn't wrap my head around it. I'd seen a lot of rubbish in my day, but the way some Human men could turn love into ownership, cruelty, violence... it made my senses stand on end.

In Faierodon, there was no "controlling" love or gender bias. It wouldn't have even been on the menu or registered as love. You didn't "possess" someone. You just stood with them, side by side, like two tōtara trees in a storm; supporting each other, not leaning too hard, just... being. I wanted to tell her that. I wanted to tell her that she deserved all the softness she had given out, that she shouldn't have to shrink herself to fit someone else's small world. But instead, I just listened. Sometimes that's what love looks like: shutting up and listening.

Then, out of nowhere, she blurted out, "Maybe a time warp is when dimensions blur, so time does too. Maybe time itself doesn't know how to catch up to the changes."

I laughed. "Sounds like something my uncle would say after a few too many pints. But aye, maybe you're right."

She cracked up, tossing her head back, and for a moment, I saw that wild, electric energy ripple around her. A shimmer that only I got to see in this moment. My mind wandered back to her stories of old relationships. In Faierodon, we didn't even really have "gender roles" like Humans. You just were who you were. You showed up with your gifts, your energy, and everyone accepted it; no questions, no policing. The idea of needing to dominate or "prove your masculinity" would have been laughed right out of the forest. There were genders for variety and procreation, but there were no rules to follow, because that would have wasted creative resources.

Of course, not all Fae were perfect; Ro had proven that plenty well. But at least in our world, when someone meant harm, their aura would show it plain as day. It was honest, even if it was dark or false light, I suppose. I pondered what had happened to Ro that he had strayed so far from his natural ways of the culture to join the IGSTA separation mission.

I realised I'd drifted over to the window while I'd been lost in these thoughts. D had dozed off nearby; Humans, even hybrid ones, needed their sleep. Frost edged the glass like delicate lace, and outside, I saw a crow perched on the lamppost, mist swirling around its wings. I felt a rush of comfort knowing the Network was still watching.

Then, a shadow flickered. A massive shape, shifting and reforming, until, in a blink, it vanished. My wings twitched, my senses snapped to high alert. The ground rumbled, the walls trembled, and suddenly D was at my side, eyes wide, trying to stay upright.

Thud. Thud. Thump.

"It's a Rekel," I hissed, my body tensing. I could feel his energetic signature. "Grison."

A deep voice boomed outside. "You should submit. I don't want to tear this lovely cottage to shreds."

"Where will you take us?" I yelled back, trying to sound braver than I felt. We were trapped. We could keep finding ways to hop dimensions, but the race would be endless, and they had agents in both places. We had no safe home base, not really. When was this time warp going to help us bend our reality in a better outcome than being endlessly chased? D and I exchanged knowing glances, alert.

"To Simsora headquarters," Grison answered. "We won't harm you, but you've broken more intergalactic laws than I can count. We need to analyze the girl."

"Analyze what?!" D snapped. "I don't want you poking me with your weird tech!"

"Come willingly. It will make things easier," Grison rumbled.

D turned to me, her eyes clear, fierce, golden even in the low firelight. "They're just going to keep hunting us. Maybe we can work with them instead of running. The tear, the prophecy... It's all in motion. They can't rewind it now."

I swallowed hard. "Are you sure?"

She squeezed my hand. "I think so. We'll go, but on our terms."

I turned back to the window. "Alright! We'll come. Just stop wrecking the cottage, for goodness' sake!" Grison had already pulled off an entire section of the roof over the kitchen.

We stepped outside, the cold hitting us like a salty Wellington southerly. Grison's massive form loomed, and in a blink, he grabbed us and threw us over his shoulders like we were sacks of sweet bao. The world blurred as we zipped through spacetime once more, everything warping and folding. My head spun, but I clung to D's hand as tightly as I could, Spitz holding onto my shoulder.

*****

Grison had been lugging us like wayward bundles of luminescent kelp over his shoulders. With a sudden thud, we were promptly plopped onto the fragrant grounds of Simsora. It felt like my entire Lightbody had been squeezed through a star gate backward; my senses flared and fizzed as I tried to steady myself, sparks zipping through my wings. My senses snapped back online, ready for whatever was coming.

"Pixie's gambit," Spitz chirped, wings flaring with false triumph. But even he knew; this wasn't the clever turn we'd counted on moments before. The trick had trickled too soon.

Ro stood at the gates of the Hidden Boulder Estates, fidgeting like restless thistlekin weed in the breeze. We landed in a bed of bright floral blooms; fragrant, with a heady mix of rain-slicked crystal pollen and old starroot. Almost enough to distract me from my post-portal daze.

Oddly enough, I felt a pang of sadness being back in this form. I was missing that dense, grounded Human form. I'd barely had time in it, but there was something solid and sure about that weight. Now, back in my Fae form, I felt too light, like I could drift away, a mist on the morning breeze.

Ro stood waiting for us, grinning like a Fae engineer who'd finally taught starlight to behave. "Welcome," he drawled.

I didn't know what waited inside, or what game Ro and the IGSTA were playing. But as I stood, bracing myself, I felt the heat of D's hand in mine, the wild tangle of prophecy and possibility moving through my being. Whatever came next, I wouldn't let it stop us.

"It's about time," Ro snapped, waving us forward. The entrance spiraled above us, glass and shimmering crystal etchings that climbed higher than any canopy I'd flown through in Faierodon.

Walking inside was like drifting into a star cavern lit with aurora threads. Every surface shimmered, reflective lights danced like spirit-fish weaving between worlds. Hallways twisted and arched in impossible angles, floating stairs carried creatures of all shapes and densities. Why had we feared this place? The resonance was sweet, almost lullaby-like. I shot a glance at D. She looked as mesmerised as a glow-lantern insect.

"You see, it's not so bad here," Ro smirked, his teeth catching the light like cracked moon shards.

And I almost believed him. The caution and tension I carried felt like it melted into the walls, leaving me weightless, agreeable, and open.

"Wait up!" Spitz zipped after us, wings buzzing so fast he blurred in and out of view.

We followed winding corridors until we reached a lounge space. I helped myself to a small chalice of deep violet nectar wine; heady and smooth, like liquid twilight. I nearly lost myself in the intricate fractal etchings on the cup, each line glinting with stardust patterns. D seemed equally adrift, her movements slow and serene, like she was floating through a dream sequence in happily ever after fairytales.

A faint itch pulsed at the edge of my mind. Something was off, but it felt like trying to catch mist in your hands.

"Why are you two acting so docile?" Spitz hissed, darting close, his small eyes shifting between us.

"We're fine," I mumbled, flicking him away with a careless motion. I didn't want to lose this sweet humming feeling. Ro and a few agents drifted over, swirling luminous tea in shimmering cups. Grison loomed behind, silent and dense as a shadow at the edge of a moonwell.

"Thank you for receiving us so well," D started, her voice gentle, if not a bit dazed. "But we still don't fully grasp why we're here."

"It's simple," Ro replied, words sliding like silk-lichen off wet stones. "We have a device to activate, and you two are the ideal catalysts."

"Catalysts for what?" I managed, curiosity poking through my haze. "What does that mean?"

"Better to show you," Ro motioned, "once we finish these brews, we'll move to the Revetron."

"The Revetron?" I echoed, half-aware.

"It's a machine from these parts, deep in the ocean's waters," Ro explained, strolling with the ease of a ripple through starlight. "The Thelassi designed it to rewind dimensional time-space, not jumping to other timelines, but returning the entire weave to its origin point. It was hidden in the Calistrea Abyss, protected by mindseals and distortion currents. Only the highest keepers even knew it existed."

"That's wild," D whispered, eyes wide, her aura flickering golden hues.

"Yes," Ro continued, "but we retrieved it. We believed it should not stay bound to Fae alone; the entire multiverse needs protection. Now is the moment to prevent total collapse."

"Collapse?" Spitz interjected, voice sharp.

"The tear you all triggered has destabilised the balance," Ro explained, his tone too smooth. "The Revetron will fix it, send everything back, before it unravels."

"Wait," D's voice trembled slightly, "You mean... undo everything?"

"It's of no consequence," Grison purred softly, soothing her, "You will still be honored in your Fae form and Human form, we won't stop that. All is well."

"Guys, wait," Spitz was getting annoyed, but didn't know what to do. His voice hummed into the background, a nuisance in this wondrous place.

"This way, I'll show you." Ro gestured, standing up and pointing towards the large archway.

We finished our tea and began to meander down the lavish hallways as Ro guided us toward the Revetron as promised. The ornamental hallways boasted every kind of beauty found in the Fae dimensions. Gallant crystaline gems, jewels, artwork, and statues of every variety. Everything was pristine, glowing, iridescent beauty and ornate glory. Eventually, we made our way to a room with lots of protection warnings and locks. We watched Ro enter his biometric and passwords as the doorway swung open.

We stopped in front of the device, the Revetron. It wasn't as monstrous as I had expected. Instead, it shone softly, decorated with delicate engravings, like a shell woven from cosmic dew. Small crystalline dials and knobs hummed with quiet energy.

"That's it?" I asked, blinking.

"That's it," Ro confirmed, pride gleaming. "Place your signatures and essence prints. We'll begin."

"Yes," D breathed, stepping forward dreamily.

We hovered, our joined hands reaching for the glowing surface. But just as we were about to touch it, an alarm shrieked, like a thousand shimmering crystals shattering at once. I clutched my ears, stars exploding behind my eyelids.

"What's happening?!" D cried.

A surge blasted through me, a stinging, electric slap of my senses — a wake-up. My wings twitched, my mind clawing back clarity. What in the cosmic whirlpool were we about to do? Undo everything we had become?

"This way!" Spitz shouted, wings slashing through the chaos. Mist sprayed across the room, tech agents scrambled like scattered mooncrabs. Ro? Nowhere to be seen. Typical. We bolted down the endless spirals of light, feet barely finding purchase. We ducked into a narrow supply chamber, packed with glistening cloths and scent-globes.

"You nearly let them erase it all!" Spitz yelled, his voice sharp enough to cut mana threads.

"What in all the worlds got into us?" D asked, eyes wide, skin pale as ghost bee pollen.

"The flowers," Spitz snapped. "Sense-stunning agents, you were charmed into obedience."

"And you?" I asked, shaking.

"Not sure. Might be because I'm bug-born," he muttered, rubbing his antenna. "Lucky for all of us."

"What did you do?!" I pressed, my hands shaking.

"I cracked the water conduits, flooded the inner chambers, tripped alarms. Classic distraction," Spitz shrugged nonchalantly.

"Thank you," D whispered, pulling him into a hug. Spitz squirmed, his wings twitching furiously, awkwardly patting her arm.

"That's enough snuggling!" Spitz snapped. "We don't have time to sit around like dew blossoms."

"We need an exit," D urged, voice steadying now.

"That was too close," I sighed. I took a breath, my head clearing cobwebs of dusty lies. "I reckon… I might just have an idea."

CHAPTER FOURTEEN

D: Escape

Cae's idea was nuts, a real bonkers kind of brilliant. But what choice did we have? We were stuck in a shimmering honey trap of lies, nearly tricked into reversing all of time and space in not just one dimension but who knew how many. Cae's delicate touch was suddenly softly above my hairline as he plucked out a small white petal that had been entangled from landing in the enchanted flower beds. His fingers brushed my curls so lightly that it made my whole scalp tingle.

"This little potion-maker might just get us out of here," he said, holding the petal like it was pure magic, eyes glinting with mischief. "If we convince it to guide us back to its source, maybe it'll show us the safest route out without getting tangled in this labyrinth of corridors and enchanted treachery."

"It could actually work," Spitz buzzed, his wings clicking anxiously. "But you do realise we could still get spotted, or worse."

Cae tapped his chin. "Aye, true. Hmm... what if we..."

"What are you thinking?" I prodded, my voice hushed but eager.

"If we dim our sense reflectors in Fae form, we'll be seen as sort of... shadows. Not invisible, just... not important enough to be noticed," he said, raising an eyebrow, as though daring me to find a flaw.

"Brilliant!" I shifted immediately, my skin softened into a bluish translucent glow, dimming until it looked almost like moonlight slipping through mist. Cae's hue deepened, his energy signatures muffled down to a low thrum. Spitz pressed himself against my back, his tiny body trembling from the effort of staying quiet.

Cae held the petal gently in his palm, whispering a few words in the old tongue. I felt the pulse of magic ripple through us like a subtle electric wave. Within seconds, we were weaving through the crystalline halls, following the petal's slow bobbing like a ghost lantern in the night.

I could hardly believe how close we had come to catastrophe. We nearly reversed timelines just because we were enchanted by some fancy flowers and posh wine. My heart pounded as we tiptoed past guards, each one towering and bristling with strange appendages and shiny weapons. At one point, Spitz almost sent a tall vase full of holygro flowers clattering to the floor. He jerked back just in time, his wings beating so hard I thought he'd faint. My hand shot out to steady him, our eyes locking for a split second; terror, relief, and a silent agreement to keep moving.

Near the grand entrance, I felt a wash of something that felt like the smell of fresh rain, a mix of relief and raw adrenaline. We were so close. My body ached for the open sky. I craved the wildness of flight and the soft, familiar pull of the forest at Jeanie's cabin. And then…

A hulking bear-like guard stomped forward, his fur an electric rainbow current, and slammed a paw out in front of Spitz.

"Oi, you there!" he rumbled, voice echoing like thunder rolling through the hills. "What's your jurisdiction, bug?"

Spitz stammered, his tiny glow flickering in panic. "Ah! I'm with the Enchantment Oversight Committee, sir. Just, uh, checking the integrity of the, er, floral enchantments."

The bear squinted, nostrils flaring. I could almost hear the gears grinding in his head.

"Right… right then…" He blinked a few times, clearly not wanting to look daft. "On your way, then. Be quick about it!"

Spitz nearly fainted from relief, wobbling forward with the tiniest of bows. I kept my arms wrapped tight around myself, even though I knew the guard couldn't see me, as if I might evaporate if I let go. We spilt out into the early morning air. The sky was smeared in shades of lavender and periwinkle, still waking up, still soft enough to feel like a safe cocoon.

"How do we avoid getting buzzed by those blasted flower fumes again?" I asked, glancing nervously at the beds lining the path.

"We could… fly," Spitz suggested flatly, rolling his eyes as though we were the slowest learners in the galaxy.

"Obviously," I muttered, feeling my cheeks warm even in my shimmered form. "Just making sure we were all on the same page."

Cae snorted beside me, his shoulders shaking. "Aye, love, we'll fly. Let's get out of this mess before our luck runs out."

The moment we left the ground, the rush of air against my skin felt like drinking the purest water after days in the desert. I let my wings expand fully, each shimmering feather catching the first pink kisses of dawn. For a few blissful seconds, there was no prophecy, no agency, no looming doom; just us and the wind.

But the multiverse had a way of interrupting. A sudden crack of light shot across our path, and a doorway materialised mid-air. It looked so mundane; a simple Human door, white, with a golden knob. It was so perfectly ordinary and out of place.

We all skidded to a halt, hovering awkwardly like newborn geese learning to fly.

"What do you make of it?" Cae asked, eyes narrowed.

"It's definitely for us," I said, my hand hovering near the knob. "It feels… good? Not slimy like the last trap."

Spitz covered his face with both wings. "Oh no, not again! I'm not opening any sky doors today, thank you very much."

"Loosen up, Spitzy," I teased, winking. "It'll be fine. I can feel it."

With a slow, deep breath, I turned the knob and peered inside. Immediately, I felt the warm pull of a room built entirely from pale rose quartz crystal, shimmering softly like the inside of a seashell. In the center stood a table, around which the Weavers sat, their long gowns flowing in patterns mapping constellations across their laps.

"It's been a minute," the bobbed-haired Weaver grinned, her eyes crinkling. "We're impressed, truly. Come in and rest, darling ones."

I stepped inside, my feet tapping lightly against the smooth crystal floor. Cae followed, his eyes wide and curious.

"Can we finally know your names?" I asked, hoping this time they'd share.

The long-haired Weaver laughed, her voice like a hundred tiny bells. "Names are funny things. You don't really need them, love."

"But I want to honor you," I insisted, feeling my heart thud with sincerity.

"Questions are good; answers are generally trouble," giggled the third Weaver, flicking her wrist as though brushing away a cobweb.

"Just know that we are Weaveborn, just like you, D," the bobbed-haired Weaver leaned forward, pulling out a strand of my hair that shone halfway between silk and stardew. "It means that we also were once dyphoros, before the Fall of Ether. Now we are infinite. Do you see this?" she asked, holding it between delicate fingers.

I nodded, though I didn't really understand.

"This is what the time part is from the prophecy," she continued, weaving it between her fingers like a cat playing with string. "You are a Thread because you are dyphoros, just like this strand of time. That is what it means to be of the Weaveborn. Time is not a river; it's a whole ocean of currents, happening all at once. You two; you are like shimmering stones thrown into that ocean, rippling out, connecting timelines that have been estranged."

My head spun, the words pressing into the fibres of my being as truths I had already known that needed to open. I thought about how time sometimes slowed to a hush when Cae and I shared quiet moments, and how it sped like a wild horse when we were in danger. I had felt these ripples but never named them. I thought about what it meant to be a timeline connector, a Thread. I was a part of the Weaveborn, and I didn't yet know what that would really mean. Was I supposed to do something different now?

"What are we to do with this knowledge?" I asked, almost a whisper.

"Stop trying to control time," the Weaver giggled, her eyes sparkling. "When you surrender to the flow, it becomes a dance. Don't grip the moment, let it move you. That is how you connect timelines and open new pathways in the current of life."

My heart buzzed, every cell vibrating with something that felt both terrifying and comforting.

And then, as quickly as it started, the crystal room evaporated around us, dissolving into a thousand shards of pale pink light. We found ourselves gently lowered onto the mossy ground back in the forests of Simsora. I brushed the moss off my knees, dizzy but alive. I felt the shift still humming through me, a new layer of understanding not quite settled but pulsing softly like a secret heartbeat.

A sudden sharp pain shot between my brows, making me double over. It wasn't just a headache; it felt like an unknown sound being played right inside my skull.

Cae's hands shot out to steady me. "You alright?"

I nodded weakly, though my eyes swam. "There's... music. And something else, like two melodies fighting each other in my head."

At the same moment, a soft, lilting tune drifted through the forest from the direction of the sea.

"You hear that?" Cae asked, eyes shining.

I nodded again. "East, by the water. Let's go."

We followed the faint, lilting music east through the forest. Each note slipped between the trees in wafts of tonal radiance, coaxing us deeper. My headache pulsed with every step, a rhythmic echo matching the tune. Cae stayed close beside me, his fingers brushing mine now and again, a silent reassurance I clung to like a raft on stormy seas.

As we descended toward the shoreline, the ground softened underfoot, moss giving way to damp sand and drifting seaweed. The scent of salt and brine thickened, curling around us like an old friend. Somewhere above, the moon sliced the night sky into silver ribbons, each ripple on the waves below catching her light like shy glances.

"There," I whispered, spotting a figure perched on a jagged rock that jutted into the tide.

The creature shimmered in and out of sight, like a mirage at first; skin rippling with the hues of twilight ocean water, hair floating around them as though still submerged. Its eyes glowed softly, reflecting both the moon and something deeper, some ancient knowing that tugged at the edges of my memory.

"That's a Thelassi," I breathed. Even though I grew up as Daer in this dimension, I had never encountered one; it was breathtaking.

The Thelassi turned toward us fully, its gaze gentle but piercing. When it spoke, its voice wasn't heard; it was felt, like a vibration inside the chest, a note that echoed on the inside.

"It is an honor," it sang, each word woven with harmonics that bent the air. "Our kind have watched you both from the Deep, from the places beyond."

Cae stepped forward, "We're honored too," he said, his voice quiet but steady, as though afraid a loud sound might shatter this delicate moment.

The Thelassi inclined their head, seafoam hair cascading like a waterfall. "You have come to a precipice in the weave of time," they continued, fingers dancing lightly over the rock as though reading its memory. "The Revetron is more dangerous than you can grasp. It does not merely reset; it devours. Erases the structures of souls that holds the multiverse together in union, in love's resonance."

I felt my pulse spike, an icy wave crashing through me. "But... I thought the Revetron was just a time device. A tool to pause or rewind," I stammered.

The Thelassi shook their head slowly, droplets of water flicking into the moonlight. "A tool, yes, but wielded by beings who misunderstand its true nature. You, Daria, Daer — D, are meant to be its counterweight. Your bond with Caelan, your merged souls, was foretold as an anchor that starts the reintegration of galactic unions. And to help return the balance to the other dyphoros beings, connecting souls to true freedom throughout the galaxies."

I stood there, rooted to the sparkling sands of this dimension, feeling the dimension tilt beneath me. All the timelines I had glimpsed, the broken cities, the oceans of light, the silent echoes of a thousand forgotten futures and pasts in the same woven fabric of time; they all thrummed now in my being, in the liquid fluids of DNA and stardust, like a hidden chorus rising.

"What are we to do now?" Cae asked. His voice was firmer this time, protective, as if he might wrestle the Revetron itself into regret if it tried to harm me.

The Thelassi's eyes softened even more in a kind of benevolent gesture. "There is a key. It was not built in this timeline, but by another version of Daria, a timeline where she stayed fully Human, never merging. This key is not simply metal or magic. It is an artifact that holds the frequency of creation and the memory of dissolution. You must find it, and only then can the Revetron be fully deactivated."

I swayed slightly, my legs threatening to give way. The Thelassi noticed, their gaze sharpening. With a graceful movement, they lifted a translucent orb from the waves and held it toward me.

"Take this," they intoned. "A Lumin glass gem. It will stabilise your inner harmonics as you move between realms and timelines. When your mind weighs from possibility, this will help."

I reached out, my fingers trembling, and took the shining rose coloured gem. It felt oddly alive, warm, pulsing softly in my palm like a newborn heartbeat.

"Thank you," I whispered, my throat tight.

The Thelassi dipped their head once more. "Do not delay. Every ripple widens, and already the outer currents tremble." Their voice softened further, echoing around us as though the ocean itself were repeating the words.

I turned to Cae, who nodded, understanding flashing in his eyes. "We'll find it," he said, his hand finding mine and gripping it tightly.

Just then, my phone buzzed violently in my pocket, an almost absurd sound amid all this oceanic grace.

Jeanie.

The sound jolted me back to my Human edges. I fumbled for the phone, nearly dropping it into the wet sand.

"Jeanie!" I gasped, answering.

She was panting, her voice sharp. "Daria! You alright? You sound weird, echoey."

I almost laughed and cried all at once. "I'm fine. Well, sort of. Listen, don't go to your cabin. It's not safe, Grison came through. I'm so sorry."

"What? Are you okay? Is the cabin… oh god," she choked out.

"It's a mess. We'll fix it later, I promise. But right now, I need you to check the lab. There's something hidden there. A key. Please, can you do that for me?"

There was a pause, a heavy one. Then she exhaled shakily. "Yeah… yeah, okay. I'll go after work. Call me in a bit?"

"Yes. FaceTime me when you get there, okay? I'll guide you."

"Okay. Be careful. Please."

I swallowed hard, trying to steady my voice. "You too."

She hung up, leaving a static hush in my ear. I stood there, still holding the Lumin seed, its gentle thrum somehow matching the new, terrified beat of my heart. Cae slid an arm around my shoulders, pulling me into his warmth.

"It will be okay, I promise," he murmured.

I pressed my face into his chest, the salt air sticking to my skin. "Are we really going to be able to stop an entire intergalactic agency?" I whispered. His warm hug made me feel like we had a shot, even if it was delusional to hope. That was the part of being part-Human that was enduring. Our constant ability to be hopeful despite unbelievable odds against impending doom and chaos.

CHAPTER FIFTEEN

Caelan: Key

"The key should look like some type of object, not of this world," the Thelassi explained as D tucked her phone back into her pocket, her hands trembling slightly. "The Revetron originated from another dimension, perhaps not on Earth, but we are unclear where it's from."

"Ro, the IGSTA agent we know, he made it sound like your kind invented it," I replied, tilting my head slightly, studying the Thelassi's luminous gills.

"I will pretend you didn't believe such nonsense of my kind," the Thelassi snapped back, its translucent fins fluttering in dismay. "We would never invent something so dangerous."

My cheeks flushed, heat rising up my neck. "My apologies. Of course. I should have known better. Ro is about as trustworthy as a soggy box of cheese rolls left out in a storm."

The Thelassi's stern expression softened, like a wave calming against the shore. It waved a delicate, webbed hand dismissively. "It is quite all right. Let us move to the more pressing topic at hand."

"Yes, the key!" Spitz blurted out, nearly bouncing off my shoulder in his excitement. I had to steady him with a palm, his little feet drumming a tiny rhythm against my sleeve.

"Yes," the Thelassi continued, its voice slipping into a gentle song-like cadence, turning to address D. "It is likely a found object your parallel self used as a foundation for the time travel device. A muse, if you will. A strange object that doesn't belong to this plane, yet inspired something revolutionary."

We were closest in proximity to Jeanie's Rekel-inflicted cabin to

FaceTime her back on the North Island and find the key. So we said our goodbyes to the Thelassi and promised a speedy return within the next few nights with the multiverse-time-altering found object in hand.

The road to Jeanie's unraveled like a quiet spool of green and salt. The earth smelt like rain-soaked wood and crushed wild mint as if it didn't know what was at stake. We kept low under our hoodies until the bracken gave up and the cottage shouldered into view. Jeanie's place looked like it had survived by haggling; roof tiles sulking but still present, garden fence tilting in a way that said don't you dare, and the letterbox wearing a scrape like a war medal. The yard had that combed-by-giants look still, branches stacked in wind's handwriting, grass matted into swirls that would, in a week, pretend it had always grown that way.

D shrugged off her damp hoodie, hair catching what light the place could spare. Spitz hopped onto the bench and immediately began judging the biscuit selection. I set kindling with the practiced reverence of someone who had only recently learnt that Human fires respond to encouragement. The fireplace harrumphed itself into cooperation.

"Right," D said, already moving, hands steady even though the edges of her were ragged. She pulled out her cellphone contraption and dialed. The call connected, and Jeanie appeared in Daria's science lab, already half-distracted. Her cat was sprawled across a stack of notebooks like it had tenure, while Jeanie batted it off with her elbow.

"Ignore him, he thinks he's head of research," she said, before adding, "and yes, Riley's fine; took her for a walk this morning, brushed her too. I'm basically her life coach now."

"Thank you! Side panel over there," D said, looking relieved to hear an update about her sweet bff in fluff. Somehow, she was intuiting where to direct her for the key from some other worldly wisdom. "Cabinet, bottom drawer."

Jeanie wobbled the phone in one hand and muttered, "So bossy, this one." She propped the phone on the kettle, forgot she'd done that, and we stared at her ceiling for a full thirty seconds while she swore at a recalcitrant handle. "There we go."

We watched the drawer roll out in jolting, phone-camera motion. Screws, pencils with teeth marks, a postcard from somewhere that required sunscreen, two rubber bands tied in a lover's knot, and then the not-light of it. Hook-curved and oil-glossed. Black that taught black to behave.

Jeanie held the phone close. "Well, that's ugly," she announced.

"Looks like a cursed pirate prize. Does it come with tetanus, or do I have to pay extra?"

D went very still. "That's it." Her voice had gone low and round, like speaking to a skittish animal or a god with poor impulse control. "Please lock it back up. We'll come get it."

"Gladly," Jeanie said, and didn't touch it with her bare hands. She used the end of a wooden spoon like a bomb disposal technician to nudge it back into the drawer, then turned the brass key with a crisp little click. "There. In time-out. If it starts singing, I'm moving to the Chathams."

"You're a gem," I told her.

"I'm a hostage to your plot," she shot back. "Now stop video-calling my ceiling and get yourselves up here. Ferry's running; barely. Wear your sea legs."

The call cut off on her sigh. The Motueka cottage exhaled with us. Then, like the sea reminding everyone who had the biggest vote, the wind put its shoulder to the weatherboards, and the glass gave a polite rattle.

"Tea?" Spitz suggested, already in the tin.

"Travel," D said, already rolling the map in her head.

We left the cottage as we found it; warmed, slightly less haunted, kindling doused, and made for the water. The strait that day was in a mood. Not quite feral, but not friendly. The ferry did its ungainly dance, steel trying to remember how to be a seabird. Gulls heckled us from the rails. A toddler with jelly on her fingers informed me with great authority that wings belonged outside, not under hoodies. I accepted this feedback, gravely trying not to draw too much attention.

Waves shouldered up under the bow and slapped down. Spitz pressed his tiny face to the gap in the door and inhaled enough salt to season a rugby team. D stood at the rail and watched the horizon as if she were trying to read its handwriting. "I feel this key, like it's... calling to me," she said, "It's... aware. Of me."

"Great," Spitz said. "I love it when artifacts have opinions."

"Better than boyfriends with opinions," a stranger muttered as she lurched by, squeezing to get off the ferry first.

We arrived in the evening of a day that had done too much. The North Island showed its glimmering hills and its particular way of pretending cities are not happening. We took to the skies to finish the route back to the apartment. D's hand found mine in the clouds like a metronome choosing kindness.

Jeanie met us at the door with a wooden spoon that had seen combat from her recent cooking endeavor. "I put it in a drawer, and then I put that drawer in a bigger drawer," she informed us, standing aside. "If it's still keen, I'm calling a priest, a lawyer, and a plumber in that order."

D's eyes looked glazed as she panned her apartment. "What is it?" I pried softly.

"Oh, nothing, it's just strange to be back in my place after everything we'd been through," she explained, "Like it was another life. And now I'm so much more than just Daria."

We made our way quickly to the locked drawer in her lab. The bottom drawer sat there with the assured posture of objects that understand they matter. Jeanie unlocked it, and we looked down at the hook-shaped, strange metal that had waited like a patient argument. D didn't wait for permission. She reached.

It wasn't shock. It was a note; cello-low, bridge-wide; struck somewhere beneath all these beakers and chemical agents. The room leaned toward her. The light became softer. The key (if we could dignify it with that mortal word) settled into D's palm like a shape finally remembering where it goes.

Her pupils swallowed most of her irises. Beneath her skin, hues of blue shifted between pearl and ember-rose; patterns I had seen only in water at dawn. They arranged themselves under the thin boundary of Human. I put my hand between her shoulder blades and felt not bone but span; something made for this moment.

"Oh," she said, not in surprise, but recognition. "I'm a shard."

Jeanie's spoon clinked the desk. "A sheila what now?"

D's gaze had gone far and faded, lost in a memory of lives. "A shard. Not just a Weaveborn or a Thread. Most of my parallels learnt the trick; they stopped returning here. They moved out of the loop, out of this distorted timeline here, the broken blueprint that's been fragmenting old and false ways on Earth for centuries. But one didn't. One kept getting hooked by duty, by love that was really a leash. The curse dressed as a kiss. That one is me, well, it's Daria. I think as D I'm more of a bridge." She blinked, and something behind her eyes flipped like a book to a page it had been saving.

She breathed once, hard. "I thought I was homesick for my dyphoros self, but it was so much more." The object thrummed in her palm. "Yes, this key can control the Revetron, it can start it. But somehow it's tied to something far bigger than that, and versions of me have been trying to stop the Revetron, the IGSTA for far longer than I realised."

Jeanie looked at me, mouth agape and eyes a little dazed. "Right. Well. That's beautiful and horrifying, and I'm totally lost."

D tucked the key in my pocket, and I caught my breath a little, with the level of trust that must have took. "You hold it until we get back to the Thelassi. I don't want to feel all of those things right now." Her piercing gaze never failed to take my breath away, even when she was being more serious than normal.

That's when the humming began. At first, it was just a bee behind glass. Then it remembered ambition and filled the study's corners with a low insistence.

"What's that noise?" Jeanie glanced around the space, "It's not the key, is it?"

"I don't think so," D had sat down on an errant stool for a moment, steadying herself after feeling the pulse of the key.

Then I saw it, out of the corner of my eye, an old radio on the sideboard, a thing that had given up seeking attention years ago, shivered in its dust and decided to audition. It was buzzing with some type of language, foreign to me.

Spitz squinted at the radio the way a jeweler looks at a very rude diamond. "What if it's friendly?"

"What if it's the power company from another dimension?" Jeanie countered, catching up quickly that one. She was always up for my flavor of weird. "We are not paying two bills for the same lightbulb."

The kitchen light flickered; one, two, three. It felt like a pattern, like it knew what it was up to. Was it just teasing weary travelers, or was it something more? The light flickered again, and the clock on the radio that was buzzing, which had been dutiful at 8:11, sniffed and skipped to 8:13 without the courtesy of passing through 8:12. Then it went back to land on 8:12. Finicky timepiece, that.

"Did you see that?!" I pointed to the clock, "Did you see time jump around on it?"

"Skip pocket," D announced, paging through a tiny leaflet she had pulled out of her pocket. "Page four, right under Time Trickery. Time's gotten lazy; copy-pasting bits, and then forward-skipping when it gets bored. We need anchors."

"What is that manual you have?" I stared agape at the tiny Time book she was referencing, "When did you get it?"

"I know it's going to sound crazy," she giggled a bit, "But what doesn't these days? Daria from that other dimension, the one that had the key, she gave it to me when I touched it."

"And what's an anchor?" I pressed, "Why do we need it?"

"Anchors?" Jeanie demanded, already marching to the stove. "I've got soup, a frog named Darwin who went AWOL, and a mortgage. Pick three."

"Those are actually brilliant," Spitz told her, delighted. Then, seriously: "Three things that keep you you. Say them, hold them. Or this skip pocket might eat you and alphabetise the bones."

"You are not far off," D confirmed Spitz's eerily accurate joke assumption, "We need to have things in our memory log, in our agreements of what is real and true, or the skip pockets could distort even our memories."

D was already moving, touching the tiny notch she'd filed in her bracelet months ago. "Scratch on my bracelet," she said, voice steadying as it spoke the familiar. "Smell of moss on my skin. Cae's laugh when it sounds like it got arrested for loitering."

"Aye, okay," I muttered. "Mine: the fleck in your eyes, regardless of which D you are being more of; the hum of my wings even when folded; your face when you know you're right and pretend it was an accident."

"Which is always," Spitz added, preening. "Anchor: me. Forget me, and I haunt you; tastefully."

Static swelled like weather moving furniture. Under it, clicks arranged themselves: three short, one long, two soft. Not random. Pattern. Weaver business.

"The Weavers are helping from afar," I said, spine remembering something before language did. "Recall code."

"What do we do, return the multiverse to sender?" Jeanie asked. "Because I don't have the receipt."

"Hold the anchors," Spitz told us, softer now. "Breathe like you mean it."

We did, which is harder to do than anyone realised. The pressure in the room unbuttoned, the flicker heartened. The clock steadied: 8:14, then 8:15. The soup stopped smelling like regret and went back to warmed tomatoes with delusions of grandeur. I could feel the skip pocket's looping teeth withdraw, sulking.

We had maybe three breaths before something else decided to be brave. The next hum wasn't lazy. It came in clean and high, like a wire pulled tight between two cliffs. The radio didn't repeat; it opened. D didn't touch the box. She stepped closer, hands down by her sides in that way she does when she meets something wild and refuses to flinch. "Easy," she said to it, to herself, to time. "We're listening."

Jeanie stood with the spoon like a sceptre. "If it asks for my password, I'm going to the pub."

She had a point. The hair along my arms had already voted to stand. Something was otherworldly about this noise, unfamiliar, completely not of this world. We all felt it. There's a kind of quiet that isn't absence; it's attention wearing its holiday best. The entire lab room was wearing that kind of quiet.

The voice came thin, bent in transit, then found itself. A voice that was clearly translated from another language, just as I used the Eurometer, this sound was clearly from another dimension as well. "Hello? Is this on? Can you hear me?"

D's hand found mine again. We were all breathless and waiting for someone to speak.

"We can hear you," D said finally, her voice so soft it could have been meant for a sleeping infant or a moment before leaping into the void. "We're here."

Static smoothed, almost shy. The voice drew breath we couldn't see. "I'm… "

Part Two

Recall

CHAPTER SIXTEEN

Adera: Dilemma

2135 AFE Spiral Time (After the Fall of Ether)
Planet: *Drual* **Dimension:** *Gael*
Galaxy: *Andromeda, Dioma Arm*

I was born in the wrong dimension.

That isn't self-pity, it's logistics. Dimensions stream alongside each other in the same wave, each vibrating in its own pitch. Think of it as a cosmic orchestra. Far off in a galaxy a long way from me, there is a wee planet named Earth. The Human dimension moves slowly and is dense as hammered iron, the Fae dimension faster and more reminiscent of Gael's, in its distinct hues of silver-bright lights and crystalline ways. And me? I woke in another timespace and galaxy altogether; quick, fine-threaded, luminous, and patterned at resonances the Earthlings wouldn't understand. The melodies of Drual and Earth hardly overlap. And yet, I've always felt the pull.

I was supposed to wake in the Fae. At least, that's what every rumor insists, and what my dreams refuse to let me forget. But at the last instant, Nuvious, meddler, iridescent nuisance, tilted my casting sideways. One flick of his claw, one delighted snicker, and I landed here instead: in Drual's resonance field, the wrong note in a song that otherwise played in tune. Sprites are allergic to straight lines. They skip through timelines like the innocence of Human children tossing stones in ponds, delighted by the rings of trouble. I should have known better than to expect my arrival to be left untouched. And yet, I never thought anyone would meddle this deeply with me.

The proof of misplacement lives in my fibres. My kin, the Kyrae, are swarms; fractal mandalas singing memory forward. They dissolve and recombine with ease, carrying past and possible futures as a chorus. When a swarm passes, you hear bells and the subtle click of patterns solving themselves.

I am not a swarm.

I am singular. Condensed. A thread that refused to dissolve. The hole in the mandala. To some, that makes me fascinating; to others, cursed. To me, it makes me lonely. And lately, it makes me broken.

Every dyphoros child undergoes integration when the age comes, or at least, we did before the Fall of Ether. Coming of age as a dyphoros on Gael was a deeply honored rite. It was precise, almost always seamless. Complications were so rare that they were more myth than fact. The selves from parallel realms are supposed to merge; two notes braiding into one chord. It's precise, almost always seamless. My elders prepared everything as tradition demanded: sacred geometries glowing in fractals, soundscapes tuned to the exact microtones of my soul, and herbal vapors to soften the walls of the mind. It was flawless, on the outside.

But inside, I unraveled. My other self was supposed to step in fluidly, their memories aligning with mine, our lifelines weaving into one. Instead, they sat in me like an awkward neighbor: close, but not connected. Their memories came fragmented, constellations without the lines to bind them. Sometimes I felt words I didn't know catch on my tongue. Sometimes I woke from half-remembered scenes; heat, flame, wings; and couldn't tell if they were theirs or the Fae's. Instead of fluid movement between versions of me, I stumbled. I was supposed to be a river. I was a tide pool, trapped in conflicting currents.

To admit it felt like betraying my lineage. Dyphoros are revered on Drual; guardians of the multiverse's weave - the Weaveborns were keepers of story and memory. They'd been persecuted for so long, contributing to the Fall of Ether itself. The IGSTA had grown relentless in its task of separation. But here, in Drual, we were protected. And Avaris, in Pyron, was safe too, for now. These disparate planets had still managed to resist the complete disintegration agenda of the Galactic Separation programs. And since we'd been persecuted for eons and needed to restore what was now broken beyond immeasurable repair, I knew it was my duty to merge. If I confessed failure, I'd risk shattering the trust placed in me. To start the lineage once more. To repair Ether, to repair the unions of the cosmic origin stories. But the pull to the Fae dimension was too distracting, too all-encompassing, and I could not for the life of me figure out why. Not to mention that I didn't really want to merge. Duty aside, I wanted to remain who I was, lonely but still somehow whole.

So I kept silent. And the silence ate at me. When the ache grew unbearable, I sought Ora.

The Halet's corridor glowed with dewy light as I vibrated through. Elders of Form Yesmet passed, palms pressed together. "Mehan's blessing upon you in the all."

"Yesmet," I replied, bow steady. My voice sounded braver than I felt.

Ora opened the door before I could knock, glowing warm as home. "Aedra," they said. "Come, child. Tell me."

I sank into a cushioned chair, spine sighing relief.

"Gream?" Ora asked.

"Yes, please."

The steam smelt like when I was a tiny thought form, just coming into any amount of physicality, but it had been a long time since I'd indulged in this scent. I wrapped my fingers around the cup and let its warmth hide my trembling.

"The truth is..." My voice wavered. "It didn't work."

Ora's eyes narrowed slightly, not in judgment, but in careful listening. "Go on."

"I can sense them; my other self, but they are fragmented. There's interference. We're not merging. There's a wall I can't get through, there's dissonance I can't place."

Ora nodded, lips pursed. "Perhaps they are the ones resisting?"

The idea jolted me. I had blamed myself, Nuvious, the pull to the Fae dimension, the IGSTA, ritual error; never Avaris. "What do you suppose would be a reason?"

"Not every self longs to dissolve," Ora said gently. "Not every story wants to braid. Have you tried speaking to her?"

"I wouldn't know how, not with this much interference."

"The dasant," Ora suggested. "Old, yes, but faithful. Write to her. Sometimes words open doors, pure resonance cannot bridge between dimensions."

I hesitated. The dasant had gathered dust in my den for ages. An ancient device; part channel, part mirror; used before telepathic refinement made it obsolete. Could such a relic help me?

"Has this happened before?" I pressed.

"Not to my awareness," Ora admitted, honesty sharp as glass. "Integration is meant to be absolute."

A swirling pinch surged in my fibres, hot and sour. I gripped the cup harder.

"Try," Ora urged. "If she put up a wall, ask gently."

I nodded because anything else would be collapse. Returning to my corridors was instantaneous; it was only for story that we created form in the first place. My den was quiet when I placed the dasant on the low table. The surface woke at my touch, emitting a soft harmonic ping. I stared at it, words locked behind my vibration.

Finally, I wrote:

Are you there? Please answer. I can't keep breaking like this.

No reply. Only the glow of the device, humming softly, recording refusal.

I wrote again:

Do you know we're meant to be one? That the others watching? That I am unraveling without you?

The dasant flickered, but nothing came.

I buried my face in my hands. Maybe Ora was wrong. Maybe my other self wasn't resisting. Maybe she wasn't even there at all.

Or maybe she was somewhere else entirely.

The thought came like a fissure in stone: the Fae.

That's where I was meant to belong. That's the home my dreams replay. If I could reach them, perhaps the ache would make sense. Perhaps the unfinished song inside me would finally resolve.

I placed my palms on the dasant and whispered, "Show me the Fae that are pulling at me."

The air shivered. Drual paused mid-breath. Bridges locked their spans; swarms froze mid-spiral. Koryph knots stilled like stones. Even the Veyadra ribbons coiled tight, listening from lightlands afar. The dasant's surface flared, spilling silver light. My denaeta ignited at my wrist, threads crawling up my arms. The world sharpened, edges too precise. A tone pressed against me, unmistakable. A soft sort of humming buzz.

Could it be?

Forests of twilight, glowing blues, and blinding lights at a distance, spilling silver when the wind sings. Lakes composing symphonies. Cities grow from patient branches. All of it; suddenly close, not dream, not memory, but invitation. A corridor opened. My light betrayed me, reaching. My edges blurred. All I had to do was step, let go of my center, and surrender. The denaeta hummed like joy and grief at once.

But memory clawed in: IGSTA boots on corridors, heavy and merciless, closing doors the moment they opened. Harmony silenced by decree. Bridges unplugged in the name of order. Dimension bonds collapsing until Ether itself dissolved. If I proceeded, they would feel it. They would hunt. It's not just a regular merging, it's the first one after the fall. Yes, we were veiled, but who knew what they would do, only that they would find out. Fear surged. At least I knew what was really underneath my resistance. It wasn't just Avaris, if she had hesitation in the first place. But I needed to find out where she stood.

"Not today," I whispered, wrenching my light back into myself.

The corridor snapped shut with a thunderclap. My body staggered, wafts of fibres aching from the recoil. The dasant dimmed to an innocent glow. The room smelt of potential and disappointment. Outside, Drual herself exhaled. The swarms clicked through vibrations; she brightened. As loud as I was, the swam was louder still. I pressed the denaeta to my skin, forcing it to record in its piecemeal ancient ways: Alive. Stubborn. Curious. Not today.

I fled to the Fold, Drual's pocket of quiet. A pale basin of light, scarred by a ripple where a Veyadra once pressed too close. No chaos, no chorus; just silence. The denaeta was warm at my wrist, quickening the burn, a star that refuses to dim. The bracelet's shape around my glistening form felt weirdly comforting, like it was an anchor to something more real, more lasting. It replayed the Fae vision: leaves brushing my cheek, rivers making a choir, cathedral-trees. Home I never had, and yet mine. I breathed until the ache softened just enough to survive.

"Why?" I asked the silence. "Why did you deny me my rightful home among the Fae?"

No answer, except a shy shimmer along my being, a kindness from some unseen Lythari. I accepted it. Sometimes you take kindness without knowing its sender. By the time I returned to the plaza, Drual had resumed its performance of normal. Bridges unfurled. Swarms spun. The Veyadra conducted like nothing had been interrupted. But I knew better. I had tried to reach the Fae. I had almost succeeded. Maybe it would help me with Avaris and the merge, too. I wasn't sure how many refusals I had left in me. As I wove my way along the steam basin, my denaeta cooled, but the ache still pulsed inside me, unfinished, insistent.

CHAPTER SEVENTEEN

Avaris: Vigil

I was born in the wrong dimension.

Somewhere between a comet's wink and Nuvious's coffee break, timecards were shuffled, and I slid into the wrong lava paradise. I was meant to open my eyes in the far-off earthly realm, where green foliage's glory is matched only by the buzzing heights of bioluminescent tech. Don't ask me why I've been drawn to them since before memory; there is not too much I would want to let go of in my present life anyway. Instead, I cracked into Ignara, pink and flaming, a scandal with wings. My cradle, a cozy basalt bed, my lullaby hissed typhoon winds.

Honestly, I adore being me, I'm not going to lie. But the pull to the Fae has tugged at me since hatchling days; colours in dreams that don't belong to our fire, songs that twist their notes sideways, trees that look like glass woven through dawn. When I argue with myself (which I do with admirable volume), I swear I can smell that realm's breath: cool, sweet, a little unruly. Not better than Ignara, nothing is better than Ignara. But haunting me the way a half-remembered riddle does. And then today, the blip, teased too. Taunting me with promises of what felt like the Fae dimension. As if it knew it would get under my scales. So yes, if anyone has been flirting with fate across realities, it's me.

I live on the Isle of Ashborn, where lava writes poetry in cursive and the cliffs banter louder than the elders. Ashborn suits me. Everything is alive, always shifting in its form, even if through fiery means that would disorient softer creatures. I have room to spread out my wings, to be all of me, fire and I are one. When I stretch, the ground stretches. When I brag, the vents applaud. Outsiders call it a catastrophe; we call it rhythm. Ignara and I are a matched set: playful, temperamental, and glorious in our ways.

So, naturally, the dyphoros integration, the merge, got staged on my ridge. Thirty-five cycles is prime age, the Field says, for tying yourself to your "echo" across dimensions and calling it transcendence. The elders polished their pride. Incense drew circles in the air. Aedra, my assigned echo, my Thread across the veil, was prepared as well. I stepped into the spiral like it owed me homage. Wings high. Scales and sparks alight. I planned to honor my duties despite enjoying my solo life.

But the land's rhythm had other thoughts.

Lightning, which usually keeps a clean line on Ignara, squinted sideways like it had seen an ex. The lava under the ridge hiccuped. Sparks rose from my scales and… paused. The wind, helpful, nosy wind, slid a whisper between beats: *two-and-two, miscast*. I'd heard that before. Yesterday, when the Isle and I encountered the blip. Now I knew what it meant, the merge, it wasn't going to work. I looked down just in time to see my sparks twitch like dancers forgetting their step.

Aedra was there, just on the other side: not hostile; more like a steady hand testing door hinges. I felt her at the base of my wings, at the notch of my throat, inside the bone where stubbornness lives. Not a voice. A memory. I drew a breath, large, gorgeous, and the weave… slipped. Interrupted mid-knot, like a ceremonial ribbon cut by a razor-sharp lava rock.

Laws unbound, the frozen sparks hissed. Ashborn simmered a breath beneath me. I exited the spiral smiling like I meant it and pretended I had choreographed the whole disaster for effect. (It would have been very like me.)

The elders took it as a sign to postpone the merge; the lands were never wrong. There was no shame, but certainly a lot of weird things had been going on lately between this and the blip. I returned to my nest to rest for the night and restore my embers to glory.

******

The dasant chimed in my nest at dawn, a harmonic ping sliding through stone walls in a drawer I had long forgotten. I ignored it. Bit into firefruit. Let juice run down my claws in a way that communicated "unbothered." The chime gave up. Silence remained, impressed this time with my lackluster nonchalance. I could almost hear it taking notes. Next dawn: another chime. Persistent. Predictable. Absolutely Aedra.

I sighed, which is not dignified, and therefore I did it alone. Finally, I gave in, dug into the edges of the dusty drawer, and pulled up the device.

Avaris? Are you there?

I considered ignoring her again. The irony of communicating through non-telepathy with your other self seemed ridiculous. The memory of the failed merge flashed in my mind. I couldn't avoid this forever.

"I'll be direct," I replied. "I do not want to integrate. I reject this union."

There. Clean as obsidian.

Impossible. I want to reject it, too. But how can we reject ourselves?

I laughed in Ignaran: smoke first, then flame. "It's not you, it's me. Accept this and move on."

Another pause. I could feel Aedra giggling at the absurdity of my joke.

You know it's inevitable.

"Good day," I wrote, and set the dasant down with ceremonial finality.

It should have ended there. Of course it did not. As I stacked ember-pendants in the trellisa at our family shop, I kept feeling a tidy little nudge at my elbow: move the red ones higher, no; higher. In the market, while haggling with a Brothorean over a heat-carved bowl, a sensation like breath leaned near my ear and suggested, politely, that I not mock their counting out loud. Not a thought I would normally have. She got me to hydrate when I would have otherwise stayed parched. Aedra wasn't haunting me. Haunting implies at least some form. This was more like a persistent ember that refuses to stop chewing on the edge of your wing until you do the sensible thing. Infuriating. Effective. Also: sometimes funny.

Right on schedule, Vorlec arrived to poke at my vulnerabilities. He landed on my shore with a cinder-spray entrance and a grin that had sharpened itself at an angle. He didn't come alone; five of his circle fanned behind him, clearly excited for the flames to be stoked.

"Dropped, were you?" he said, gesturing at the entire island like it existed to set up his punchline.

"Careful," I answered, watching the lava ocean. "The shore eats side kicks." He didn't get my punchline.

"You aligned," he said. "Everyone felt it. But the seal broke. Hesitation?"

My wings snapped open just enough to sting the air. "I don't hesitate."

"Hesitation burns worse than failure," he recited, pleased with himself for remembering the law in order.

"If you're here to recite, sing," I said. "If you're here to race, race."

He brightened, always up to a challenge. I'm sure he knew I would be in a mood. "Strideline."

The strideline waits where the lava lies too thin and dares you to trust it. Vorlec launched first, carving arcs so tight his sparks came back around to check on him. His crew followed in formation, all charm, no talent. I dove last. Heat slapped me up; my wings drank the red. Every stride rang in my ribs. Halfway across, he cut my lane; curved just so and buckled me out, classic Vorlec. Magma bubbled a blatant giggle at the show. I banked hard and landed on the far ridge with steam popping under my claws. He beat me by a breath and bowed like he'd just explained flying to me.

"Close," he said kindly, which is his cruelest tone. "Just like your merge."

I smiled with excessive teeth. "You were dazzling for three steps. Then I remembered who you are."

His circle laughed the way trained laughter does: too correct to be fun. I folded my wings slower than my pride advised, because restraint is fashionable.

I left Vorlec in my tailwind as I made my way to the Zeths Hall. I had no time for mockery.

The Zeths Hall was full of grunts and whispers; when the dyphoros norms hiccup, the elders call a meeting. We gathered beneath arches ribbed with cooled lightning. Smoke coiled in deliberate flourishes. The constancy-flame stood at the caldera rim, ember-lines drawn by centuries of staying lit. We sang the Lava Hymn because that is what you do when you want reality to remember its assignment.

"Avaris," the constancy-flame sparked a warmth of invitation.

I stepped forward. Heat leaned against my shins to see better.

"Your merge flickered because of the false," they said. "Mimic signals. Counterfeit currents. Interference."

I heard the echo again, but now it felt like a warning, faint as insolence: *two-and-two, miscast.*

"Was this the agency?" I questioned.

"Likely," flames don't mince words, "they will not stop what must be. This is far bigger than you know."

"Am I to do anything to clear this mimic signal?" I asked.

"The Glass Pyres, attuned for only fire beings; they use sacred flame to burn away mimic signal distortion," the constancy-flame explained, "But remember, you're not responsible for the distortions, only for what you do with your own energy and life."

"Where do I find the Pyres?" I inquired.

"You will be shown them when the time is right." Always mysterious, the constancy-flame.

Returning home, I was feeling confused, which is unlike me; I prefer confidence. Night crept up the ridge wearing storm-light. Ashborn sighed and arranged its lava in flattering curvy lines. I climbed the basalt tower that pretends to be a lighthouse. And again, contact at the edges of my thoughts. Not words or images. Just a gentle insistence doing what it does best: rearranging me. Wings wanted to open wider. Throat wanted to swallow smoke. Aedra was there, the exact way a chord is there when you are foolish enough to hum at the right resonance.

"Stop making sense," I told the air, because it was being smug. "Aedra is here. Not there. Here. She persisted when I pushed away. She annoyed me into drinking water. She pushes at my wings with decent timing. And when the knot slipped, the place that hurt was not some hypothetical forest of crystal; it was the space inside my ribs where a second rhythm had already started to sit."

This time, the rhythm consented, the air was softened, if that was possible on the Isle.

"So here is the arrangement," I declared, to Ashborn, to winds, to any nearby eavesdropping: "I will chase the source of the mimic signal, or its cure perhaps, and figure out what's going on with this blip. I will find out whether it's Fae or fraud or Nuvious's lunch. But I will not treat Aedra like a misdelivery. Next time the knot shows itself, I tie it. Not because the Hall hums. Not because the Field likes tidy lines. Because I *choose* her. That is the joke thrown back at the agency, at the false energy trying to thwart us. I understand now, this is the only way I will feel truly at home."

The Isle was surprisingly quiet in response. There was not so much as a disturbance or a rumble. I guess the lands finally know not to mess with this eternal flame. I made vigil that night until morning's glow, flames and ember sparks dancing around me for hours, never stopping to breathe anything but new life into the lands.

The following cycles behaved themselves only in the way patience does when it's planning a coup. I worked the market. Aedra nudged preferences like a domestic breeze; this rune higher, that lantern lower, yes, that price is fair. Vorlec hovered like a superstition, materializing whenever my expression hinted at comedy. He challenged me to strideline after strideline until our claws learnt each other's timing. We split wins with rude generosity and bowed like dueling orchestras. Ashborn remained on my side; the island is vain that way. When I slept, vents adjusted their lullaby to flatter my breathing. When I flew at dusk, the cliff faces brightened to catch my silhouette in nice angles. I accept devotion where I find it.

I folded my wings, which to me is the same as bowing. Aedra pressed at the edge of my breath, patient, amused, infuriating. "Tomorrow," I told her, which in Pyron means "as soon as the world brings me a knot that won't slip." She pressed back the way promises do when they intend to be kept.

I flew home along the ridge, Ashborn lighting my way. On my ledge, the lava below played a little overture because it cannot help itself. I lay down on black glass and let the island cool my fevered pride to a pleasant simmer. The winds nudged one last line at me, pleased with themselves: *an infinity bond warps time.*

To my tired ears, it sounded like prophecy.

CHAPTER EIGHTEEN

Aedra: Fragment

The light vine flickered strangely as I eddied, pulsing in irregular rhythms; not quite out of sync, but off enough to make my essence buzz. Drual usually breathed in harmony, each frequency calibrated to soothe the vessel and recalibrate the mindform. But tonight, something inside me, or maybe around me, was off. I had barely slept since the dasant exchange. Avaris's refusal echoed louder in the silence, unsoothed by the planet's steady breath. Her words hadn't just unsettled me; they had dislodged something. My core felt like a circular cave trying to echo back its own song and failing.

I paused before Ora's door, unsteady in my purpose, not sure what to say. The flora lining the entryway shimmered dimly, recognizing my signature. I wafted inside. Ora was already arranged on the cushion, gream in filaments. They looked up, not surprized. "Your energy is a storm tonight."

"I can't settle," I admitted, collapsing into the cradlehold across from them.

Ora motioned to the second cup beside them. "Drink. Then speak."

The warmth seeped through my filaments holding the gream. I didn't sip yet. "I tried the dasant. Avaris answered. She doesn't want to merge."

Ora's brow creased. "She said that explicitly?"

"She said... It's not me. And also it is me. But mostly it's her." I took a sip. "She said she wants to stay separate."

A long silence stretched between us. Finally, Ora said, "We've seen anomalies in the past. But nothing this intentional. This is a soul resisting unity. It's a dangerous game to play."

"I know," I whispered. "What's funny is I don't really want to merge, either. But I keep being there in her field in spite of myself, supporting her, helping her soothe the flame, shift things that are imbalanced. As if the almost-merge sort of worked but didn't."

"And yet… there's power in that kind of clarity. Maybe she's seeing something we can't yet. I was informed by the council of the mimic signal's influence; the IGSTA didn't coordinate this on their own, it was the false energy itself, the Megalight is getting stronger, reinforced by separation."

I stared into the gream's wafts of steam. "The ceremony wasn't faulty. But maybe we were wrong to assume it was the right time?"

"Don't blame time, that's an easy way to avoid your truth. Time is a friend to those who are willing. Do not let the mimic get to you; it's already distorting your desires. Reach further into your heart, find what is true."

The wall flora flickered again, rippling through my filaments. "Did you feel that?"

Ora stood abruptly, moving to the center chamber. "The dimensional field is vibrating a response to something."

We stepped onto the terrace. The sky above Drual was usually a calm prismatic wash. Today, it pulsed violently in narrow bands, like stretched strings under pressure. A sonic tremor shook the air.

"The agency?" I asked, already knowing.

Ora's jaw tightened. "They're not just watching anymore. They shouldn't have been able to breach our protections."

A dark ripple passed overhead. It wasn't a ship. It was too fluid, too organic. A displacement shadow. The kind that follows time-siphoning tech.

"The Revetron?" Ora breathed.

I turned sharply. "That's not possible. It was banned after the Ether collapse."

"Exactly," Ora said grimly. "So if someone's using it now… It's not from within Drual."

Before I could speak, my wristband flared to life. An urgent missive from the Halet Council. Unauthorised use of interdimensional tech. Location: outer ridge.

Ora looked at me, eyes wide. "Go. Find the source. See if it's really the Revetron, or something worse."

I nodded, my aura flaring slightly. I wasn't trained for conflict, but something inside me, the thread of Avaris, the echo of the Fae I'd felt in dreams; all of it tugged me forward. The flora parted as I flew. The outer ridge was crawling with energy. I approached on softly, avoiding detection. Something buzzed in the clearing that felt like a sour sort of intention.

At the center, hunched over a sideways slab, was a figure I didn't recognise. Tall, cloaked, and radiating IGSTA. I gasped, stumbling backward. In that moment, I saw her face. Pale, sharp, calm, and calculating, with dozens of sets of eyes evaluating the surroundings and the task at hand.

A few of her eyes flicked to mine. "Ah. The fragmented dyphoros."

I backed away, readying a defensive sigil. "Who are you?"

"You'll find out," she said coolly. "But first, you'll need to remember what you've already forgotten. Your friends on Earth certainly won't forget."

And with that, the cube flared. Behind us, the sky cracked. It wasn't the Revetron, but this tech was oozing with not-friendly. Time to leave.

The benefit of being mostly non-physical is that travel between places in my dimension is a breeze, and losing a denser creature like the agent was child's play. I made my way back to my quarters quickly. I knew time was of the essence, and I needed to get in touch with these Earth beings to understand why the agent had mentioned them and what they knew.

The dasant beeped quietly as if encouraging me to try again. This time, with the Human dimension. What did I have to lose? I tapped a message and directed my intentions.

"Hello? Is this on? Can you hear me?"

Moments passed, and nothing happened. But then, static began to reverb from the device, pulsing until the signal picked up a slight noise, a distant voice.

"We can hear you," the voice said, barely above a whisper. "We're here." The timbre of it had an odd brightness, like sunlight filtered through water.

"I'm known by Aedra. Have I reached Earth? I am from another galaxy; I sense your kind calls it And-ro-meda. Do not be alarmed; I mean you no harm."

I heard a soft shuffle, something tapping in the background. Silence. Then a collective intake of breath, several minds moving to the edge of one thought.

"Hello Aedra, I'm D. Yes, you have reached Earth!" the voice confirmed, "And I have more friends here with me."

"Are you a Human?" I tried not to sound too excited.

"It's a bit complicated," D replied, "We have Human, Fae, glowbug, various other adorable creatures too, actually."

I heard some type of squawk in the background. "Ignore that," a light voice muttered. "I'm Jeanie, the Human holding down the fort."

My heart did a little dance; this was what I had dreamt of all my life. To finally meet the beings of Earth. "Oh, this is delightful!" I laughed, an undignified bubble of joy that surprized me, because it rose from a deep well. I was speaking to Humans across time and space. The frequencies sparkled in my filaments.

"What made you contact us, Aedra?" D asked.

"A very confused intergalactic agency called IGSTA," I said. The name, a resonance mismatch as it left my vessel. "They breached Drual. Not with a device you'd recognise, more like a shadow of their presence. A displacement. They left a… message. About Earth. About 'friends and forgetting.' I thought you might know what it means."

"We know of the IGSTA! Why were they after you?" D sounded concerned.

I paused, a feeling I couldn't name that translated closest to the Human word for shame flushed through me, "I was not able to complete my sacred task," I began, "You see, where I am from, the IGSTA do not like what I am, what I am supposed to be, if it went to plan."

"What do you mean?" D sounded cautious and curious at once. "Please, it's safe to share if you feel comfortable. We mean you no harm."

"I dare not speak it through the radio," I was cautious, despite their promises, "my kin would not approve."

"Take your time," a lyrical voice said gently. "No pressure. We're professional waiters and snackers. I'm Jeanie, by the way."

"I understand," D's voice was harmonic and echoed at different chords of sounds, like a symphony, not unlike some of my kin, in their multiplicity. Who was this D, anyway?

"It is a fragment, indeed," I whispered, more to myself, in realizing that the agency somehow knew, how did they know?

"I'm sorry?" D replied, confused now, "What is fragmented?"

"The sacred task I referred to did not go as planned."

"Is there any way we can help?" the other, deeper voice asked kindly.

"We have more pressing needs," a softer voice taunted, playfully, "You know, like the teensy-weensy task of getting this key to the Thelassi to stop them reversing time with the Revetron."

"Spitz, you are being rude!" D scolded, lightheartedly.

"I'm keen to get on with it!" he retorted.

"You know of the Revetron?" I was aghast. How did they know of that device, on Earth?

"Yes, it's here, the IGSTA has it in the Fae dimension," D explained.

"Which dimension did I reach?"

"It's the good 'ol Human one," Jeanie confirmed.

"How do you know of the Fae dimension, then?" I was getting very curious now.

"Um, well, there was a tear initially," D admitted, "Between dimensions."

"A tear, you say?" How delightful this Human+ crew was proving to be. "You travel between dimensions often?"

"Little bit of a hobby, little bit of an occupational hazard," D said. "We had a tear at first, but now we can portal-hop quite a few mix-and-match ways. Well, when the portals don't sass back."

"The portals… sass back?"

"Some have attitudes," Spitz confided. "You just never know when you'll walk on a portal you thought was a bridge or through a tear you thought was a forest."

"Stop telling this friendly intergalactic emissary our portals have personalities," a deeper voice said wryly. "We sound unserious."

"We are unserious," Spitz countered cheerfully. "That's why we're still alive."

The levity undid something in me. The feeling was not exactly relief; more like a loosening of a knot I didn't know was tied.

"We probably said too much," D hesitated.

"I appreciate your trust, and for that, I will extend mine." I felt good about this crew. As I was speaking, I received a pounding telepathic message from Ora, and had to pause a moment to integrate the news.

Twin Spires: confirmed anchor sites. Counter-oscillation ritual available. Thelassi can assist. Recall protocol recommended.

I closed my eyes as the information settled in my mind. Suddenly, there seemed to be a hidden meaning to the agent's warning about forgetting. What had I forgotten? What would the Recall protocol help me remember?

When I spoke again, my voice felt different, steadier, like I'd solidified parts of my non-form ways just slightly into something I could latch onto long enough for the task at hand. "There is something you must know that will help."

"About which thing?" Spitz poked.

"The Twin Spires in the Fae dimension," I explained, "they can help anchor time to be stronger than the Revetron, so that it will not have the power to shift its way ever again."

"The key we have," the deeper, but still harmonic voice explained, "it's supposed to disable it, but time is not on our side."

"Time is our friend, and does not pick sides. We must anchor time itself," I reiterated. "I would like to help you find the Spires."

"That would be wonderful Aedra!" the deeper voice continued, "I'm Cae by the way. There's a Fae land called Faierodon where I am from. If you can reach it, we'll rendezvous. The Thelassi will take the key off our hands to intercept the IGSTA, and we can find the Spires together. Do you have a way to interdimensional travel?"

"I should be able to access the Tercel Gateway tonight and set it to your location and frequency of the Fae dimension if you can tell me the mathematical coordinates. But there's a second component I must explain before we part. A… Recall."

Cae's inhale was small but sharp. "Recall?"

"The word means many things on Drual, where I am from," I said. "Memory, retrieval, a summons, a re-singing. In this context: a gathering of what was distorted to reset it." I saw images of their planet, of suffering and hurt, eons of slavery and cruelty to each other, flash through my system. There was much to restore and heal on this planet. "If we perform a Recall ritual at the Spires, the field could stabilise, allowing dimensions to intermingle, repairing the tear."

"We also love a plan with steps. So: we deliver the key to the Thelassi." Cae confirmed the plan, "We consult a Lerali for the Spires' exact location. We prep the counter-oscillation ritual. Aedra, you get yourself to Faierodon. Then we do the Recall."

D's tone brightened, the smile audible again. "Sweet as. And if any portal's being a muppet, Spitz will bring the retorts."

"Effective nine times out of ten," Cae agreed. "The tenth time, we bribe it with the Human dimension's most annoying music. Works like a charm."

I found myself deeply amused once more, making noises I rarely had the chance to create with my kin. The IGSTA operative's taunt still rang. Remember what you've already forgotten. But now it felt less like a threat and more like a promise. Perhaps forgetting was not a failure but a strategy I had adopted to survive the waiting.

"Faierodon," I said. "I will meet you there."

"Choice," D said softly. "We'll be there. We'll bring snacks and questionable decisions."

"And the key," Cae added.

"And my good side," Spitz said.

"You don't have a bad side," D told him. "You are the bad side."

"Compliment accepted."

"I'll stay at the Human basecamp," Jeanie added brightly, "doing my best to keep us vaguely on track. Emphasis on vaguely."

Something like laughter tugged at my wavelight. "Thank you," I murmured. The words were too small. The feeling behind them, a burst of unfamiliar.

"Go to your Thelassi, I will meet you shortly." And with that, we disconnected, the intergalactic transmission complete. In a matter of moments, my life had turned upside down, and I felt enlivened, despite the failed merge lingering in my "to fix" list.

CHAPTER NINETEEN

Avaris: Singularity Wound

The blip had not left me.

Just like Aedra was always a whisper away, it, too, stalked my breath, folded itself into my wings, whispered in the pause between heartbeats. The elders spoke of it as if it were some anomaly of rhythm; a disturbance, a mimic current, a hazard to be watched until it passed. But I knew better. Lava may lie, but it never forgets. The Isle remembers when something foreign touches its skin. And the Isle was restless.

Ashborn's ridges split fresh each dawn, and the smoke carried no warmth, only warning. The sea hissed louder at night, as though it was pushing me to be cautious. Even the constancy-flame had flinched when I asked about the blip. Glass Pyres, it had told me. Cryptic, infuriating. Typical.

Still, I could not sit in my nest waiting for revelation like a cinder waiting for wind. The blip had messed with my rhythm; it pulled at me with a persistence, the way the Fae realm haunted my dreams. And Aedra's echo hummed the same dissonant chord, thread and pull, fracture and ache. Why were they intercepting one another? What was it about the blip that was related to the merge? Did it have a hand in stopping the merge? I had more questions than answers.

If I wanted to know why, I would have to walk into fire older than my kind.

The Pyres called me already; there was no waiting. At dawn, as I crossed the obsidian bridge to the western ridge, they beckoned with smoke that did not belong to Ignara. Glass fire leaves no ash, no char;

it singes light into itself until the world bends around it. And bend it did. My path turned strange. Valleys curved where they should not. A cliff face appeared twice in succession. The world folded to lead me, and I was relieved for the direction.

Then, something even stranger emerged. The lava below froze mid-wave. Sparks hung in the air, still as glass. Like a drum forgetting its beat, the moment repeated. My foot hit the stone twice. The same breath left my throat twice. My wings shifted in the same arc of air, identical, uncanny. I felt disoriented, unnerved. Did I make it up? What was happening? It felt like time and space were… stuttering, rewinding, and repeating briefly. Was this from the blip's echo? And where did it go?

By the second night, I was disoriented and tired of the quest, wishing I were back in my cozy lava bed. Time kept stuttering, and my memory kept the log. I wasn't sure if I was making much progress at all. After what felt like an eternity of stutter and repeat, I finally saw them, shadows emerging from the distance.

The Pyres. Jagged spires of molten crystal, alive with flame that was not flame. They did not burn orange or gold, but silver-white, starfire enlivened in iridescent form. My wings recoiled, and warmth of recognition raced through the rivets of my singeward spine.

This was no mimic; the Pyres' resonance felt like truth.

"Why bring me here?" I asked aloud, voice scratching against the hush. "To sear me clean of the blip? To show me it lives in me?"

The Pyres did not answer in words. Their fire bent toward me, folding my shadow into impossible shapes. Behind me, sparks froze again. Ahead, the glass-light curved and time distorted into itself for a moment, shifting forward, rewinding, reshaping. It happened so fast, I couldn't tell if anything had happened at all, besides my memories, which were quickly becoming my only anchors.

And then I felt her once more, tugging at the edges of my aura. Aedra. Her presence slid along my bones, quiet but undeniable. She was not here in form, but the pull, the same magnetic ache that lived in the blip, lived in her. I staggered, wings catching the air. The realization seared hotter than the Pyres. The blip and Aedra were behaving as anomalies, not accidents. They were of the same phenomenon, the same weave. The inability to merge was because of this: a singularity wound in timespace; all of it sang the same note. And it called not to Ignara, not to Drual, but to the Fae.

The Pyres swirled flames of rainbow hues in shimmering circles around me, dancing in union and then separation, as if to confirm my new awareness in celebration and woe at once. The flames hissed, curling into a portal of storm. Aedra was singularly thread-woven into Drual form. The blip was showing me the anomaly, a promise, and a prayer to help. Whatever had caused this blip to distort my lands, whatever had prevented the merge, it was because of this wound. And the Pyres made it clear to me that I was an integral part of the healing of the wound.

With the message received, the current settled, and I found myself standing in a quiet flatland, the Pyres nowhere in sight. I was relieved the time skipping had stopped, and grateful for this new understanding, though it was immensely perplexing. I had answers, but from them only more questions. I didn't know if the blip was still in Ignara or on the Isle. I didn't know how to help heal a wound that had impacted such a driving, polarizing, and all-encompassing energy as a singularity. How had I not known that Aedra was a singularity thread? She was supposed to be from the land of swarms, the complete opposite of singularity. A tug pulled at my heart, compassion for her, being so different and holding so much inside of her. And in that same moment, I felt her soften ever so slightly at the edges of my awareness. Maybe healing was possible for her, for us?

Returning to the Isle was a much less violent journey, as if Ignara was taking a breath, having handed me the torch and flame to carry for healing an anomaly in timespace. No big deal, I'm sure I'd figure it out before breakfast tomorrow. Now, I needed to find the blip, on purpose, and have a few words with it. I spread my wings, preparing to circle the lands in search. The Isle crackled beneath me, lava applauding my efforts. Approaching the west ridge, I noticed unusual behavior in the lands once more, a good sign I was getting closer.

Suddenly, the skies opened above, swirling a waft of circulating clouds in a cyclone of chaos and energy. This had to be the blip. With one breath, I dove into the storm-mouth, silver fire streaking my scales. The moment stuttered. Reality bent, and the cyclone swallowed me whole. The storm-mouth was not empty. Its edges crackled like ayre struck against glass, lightning folding back into itself in loops that made the sky stutter. The air smelt wrong, like rain that had never touched ground, sweet and sharp, a taste that made my teeth ache. I hovered in the current, wings trembling from vibrating winds. The clouds swirled too deliberately, like a throat swallowing light. And in its center: a hollow dark that wasn't absence but density, a weight that bent everything around it.

The blip.

The same signature I had felt on my ridge, when sparks froze midair and lightning doubled back. But this time it had grown in power. I held myself together as I approached the core. The first brush of its pull clawed every ember inside me into stillness. I am Ignaran, flame is my blood, storm is my breath. But the singularity did not bow to fire. It bent fire. It bent me.

Time wavered. The storm flashed once; then again. The second flash was not a continuation of the first, but the same moment replayed. I blinked twice and saw two of myself, wings spread at slightly different angles, each dissolving as the other took hold. The stutter rattled through my bones. The Isle below answered with a groan, stone splitting as though it too had been caught in the skip. I probably should have turned away. But I had never said no to a challenge. I leaned forward and touched the blip's core.

The world inverted.

Heat abandoned me first. Fire should have clung to me, loyal, but here even flame stilled. Sparks that bled from my scales did not fall; they hung in place, scattered like a constellation. My wings beat, yet each motion lagged behind itself, ripples of after-image chasing me. The air folded. Each breath was not one, but many: shallow, deep, none at all, a chorus of lungs disagreeing. And sound, sound fractured worst of all. The storm should have roared, but instead it pulsed, a single thunderclap drawn thin and repeating, warped into harmony with itself. The sky sang like a broken bell.

Inside it, I was prey, an unfamiliar feeling for a fire-breathing dragon. And still, I burnt with awe. Then I heard the whisp, a murmur riding the wind, reminding me of my place.

An infinity bond warps time

And through the looking glass of the warp, I saw her. Not Aedra's body, not even her face, but her resonance; threadlike, luminous, a filament drawn from the same wound that birthed this storm. It pulsed in me, as if my fire had remembered another half it had always been missing.

The singularity did not distinguish between us. The blip's pull was her pull. The same chord vibrating in two instruments. I reached. Not with claws, not with fire, but with something more raw, something bone-deep. The moment I did, the storm shuddered as if it had been waiting for me to admit it.

Images flashed through me. Not visions, not dreams; possibilities. A forest of crystal trees that sang when wind moved them. A city grown from silver vines, towers bending toward one another like dancers in mid-bow. Water that shone with starlight even in shadow, whole seas woven from reflections. The Fae.

I knew it before the thought finished. This storm, this singularity wound, was not an accident. It was a doorway. Not to void, to invitation. And Aedra, stitched of the same anomaly, was already leaning toward it. I wanted to soar over my Isle with joy and anticipation. What madness was this? Instead, I let the fire of recognition sear me silent. Even my dashing, confident ways had moments of abashed awe.

The storm tightened. Clouds coiled inward, dragging me closer to its throat. Bolts of lightning electricity circled back upon themselves, their light suspended in the air as if time itself had congealed around them. My body resisted, every wingbeat straining against the impossible gravity. Flame flared from my chest, searing my skin in protest. The singularity tugged harder, bending not just matter but meaning.

For a moment, I wondered if it would unravel me; turn my fire to stillborn embers, fold my name into nothing. Then I remembered: fire does not surrender. It consumes. It transforms. I pulled my wings tight, let the storm drag me through. The throat of the blip spat me into silence. Not darkness, not void, but silence vast enough to pay tribute to the idea of empty. It had weight. My own heartbeat sounded foreign, too loud. The emptiness shimmered, full of structures that only half-existed; bridges of light that collapsed when I looked at them, rivers of shadow that hissed when I moved.

And threaded through it all: the hum of Aedra. She was here. Not in body, but in resonance. And the hum bent toward one direction, pulling me like a magnet toward a horizon I could not see.

I knew where it led. I landed hard on unfamiliar stone when the storm spat me out again. Not Ignara; too cool, too silver-lit. The ground hummed under my claws but did not burn, which felt ghastly and unusual. The sky was aglow, the scent of the air crisp, where in the galaxies had I landed? I stumbled, wings twitching. I could breathe, I could blow flame. But in my chest, the truth burnt steadily: I assume the blip was the portal to the Fae dimension, had I arrived?

Not quite.

I may have landed, but something was still tugging at me, pulling me forward. I was no longer chasing answers, destiny, or prophecy. Somehow, I knew now I was being written into them. The air jittered; one heartbeat fast, the next missing entirely. Light fractured into thin sheets, slipping over one another like broken lava shards trying to remember their origin. I felt myself stretch; part in Ignara, part in someplace unmade.

"No," I hissed. "This isn't right."

The blip had moved me somewhere, but not entirely; there had to have been something that intercepted my intention to arrive in the Fae dimension. Layers of reality seemed to echo around me, folding my wings through themselves. I tried to pull free, but the current had learnt my frequency and would not let go. Ashborn called distantly, her volcanoes dimming as if holding breath. Time twisted, and for one blink of existence, I saw my own reflection stretching between two worlds: one scaled and burning, one made of light green, blues, and crystal structures.

The space in the blip, this portal, had been hijacked. The static and distortion spun in my head; this had to be the Megalight. The blip flared, dragging me through a thousand half-moments, until even my fire couldn't keep up. And then there was nothing; no ground, no sky, only interference.

CHAPTER TWENTY

Aedra: Recall of a Skip

After the transmission, the room held its breath. The air thickened with the echo of voices from another space, another timeline perhaps? I wasn't sure how time worked here. Even the flora along the ceiling glowed a little warmer, as if the walls themselves had listened and approved. The faint whir of the dasant subsided into something that sounded almost like rest.

I sat with my hands in my lap and let the quiet settle around me until my pulse matched its rhythm. Recall. The syllables felt old in my mouth, as if I'd been saying them in dreams for years. On Drual, recall is more than a rite; it's a way of turning toward the thing that turned away because it was not safe to be seen or heard for a while. It was not remembering, not chasing, not claiming, but listening so wide that what is lost finds itself inside your ability to hear. Only when you are a safe resting space, and not a moment sooner. A sacred site to be honored and honor that which was in remission until the time was correct, until you and time were ready, together. And only then, recall was a way of tapping into the Field and anchoring a forgotten chord, being, memory, or truth through your vessel. I wasn't sure how this ancient practice would help the situation with the Revetron, but there was one way to find out.

Ora was waiting on the terrace, eyes on a sky that flickered in places, light stuttering as if uncertain which moment it belonged to. The horizon wavered in a recognition of movement and sound, the current carried a faint scent of potential cascading in circuits of golden hues.

"You reached them," they said without turning.

"I did. They're… unconventional." My smile came uninvited. "But aligned."

"Excellent." Ora's shoulders eased, and the relief moved through them like a chorus of harmonic vibrations adjusting to a new rhythm. "The Council approves the Spires plan. They warn: the IGSTA will not like you moving closer to the Fae. The mimic feeds on forgetfulness; Recall starves it."

"I thought as much."

I told them about the operative's message, "remember what you've already forgotten", and watched Ora's ebons tighten, a small quake contained by will.

"Old script," they said finally. "They're trying to make you doubt your own timing, your deeper relationship with it. Don't let them hand you their timeline. Your alignment with these creatures must have been a recall also of a previously lost connection of souls. This is a victory, a reunion of something once lost during the fall. We will discover more soon, I'm certain."

"Yes, but I have still failed with the merge." I swallowed, the words sitting heavy. "Ora… what if Avaris says no again?"

"Then Recall will become Witness," they said, voice low, steady. "Not the union, but the seeing. Sometimes the seeing is enough to move what was immutable."

I closed my eyes. For years, perhaps lifetimes, I'd been told unity was the only end worth chasing, that to be one was to be whole. But my experience had been otherwise. I'd never felt more myself than when I was split; facing Avaris, feeling her meet me across the distance. Maybe our people's fear wasn't of division; maybe it was of the music division makes. An unfamiliar chorus. But not wrong. Just different.

"I'm going," I said. "To Faierodon to help. Then I'll find Avaris."

Ora stepped closer, transmitting a telepathic warmth of connection. The contact sent a small, grounding pulse through me, like a key turning in the lock of my form. "Prepare the Recall. The rest will sort itself out."

******

Later, in my quarters, I gathered courage. The dasant rested quietly, its faceplate reflecting the room in a forgiving blur. I gathered the tools for Recall to bring on the journey ahead. They were simple, unambitious things that carried weight because of their heritage. A thin bowl of springlight, caught at dawn. A strand of my early feathers braided with starthread. A sliver of bark from the Listening Trees, still breathing their slow sap. And, because I could hear D's teasing in my head, what she would equate to a 'biscuit' in Human terms, but from my dimension. Snacks seemed reasonable for the journey ahead, right? I laughed at myself, feeling foolish, but kept it anyway.

After I prepared for the Recall, I decided to try to contact Avaris one last time, before I dimension-hopped and distracted myself with IGSTA business once more. I tapped the dasant.

"Avaris," I said.

Speaking her name cooled the air, the way the room chills when a door opens to night. The shadows along the wall deepened, and a hush rippled through the space.

"I am not asking you to be me. I am asking you to be you, where I can see you."

Silence. Then, a rustle, not sound but knowing, a wing that didn't exist moving inside my filaments.

"I know," I said. "You refused. You were right to. I would have swallowed you and called it love. I'm still learning how to be all that I am. I know it's a lot."

A prickle of energy brushed along my scalp; neither warning nor blessing, just contact. The bowl trembled. The springlight flickered and dimmed, then brightened again, a heartbeat finding a new, unfamiliar pulse.

"Join me in the Fae dimension, join the mission if you can? If you stand with me at the Spires," I whispered, "we can Recall together. Perhaps our song is different, but it's ours. The Megalight cannot erase our song. It may be hungry, but it has no mouth. Our music matters, Avaris, even if it's not the norm."

The light flared once, then steadied. A thought, not mine, arrived, wearing my voice.

And if I stay separate?

I hesitated only a breath. Recall doesn't entertain pretense. It dissolves it until you're naked enough to be heard.

"If you stay separate, I'll keep the door open," I said. "Either way, we must help reverse the Revetron. You know you are pulled there, too, to the Fae."

"And what do you want, Aedra, if I never come?"

I paused, deepening my breath.

"I trust your choices," I replied, wholeheartedly.

Then I will stand near you, she said telepathically, *her voice confident and defiant, but playful. At the Spires. I will not be gathered, but I will be counted.*

My laugh cracked open, full and unguarded, the kind of sound that makes walls sigh. "Thank you," I said. And added softly, "When I see you, I won't try to be you."

Another chime from the dasant and it clicked off. It was immediately followed by a telepathic message in Ora's voice, calm and distant: The Thelassi await. The Lerali have mapped the Spires' next clear phase. Travel now if you want the open chord.

I rose, dizzy with gratitude and anticipation braided into one. The multiverse felt held together by a few kind thoughts, and I was content not to know whose.

I packed light: the braid, the bark, the bowl, and the biscuit. My filaments stirred as if remembering their own reason. The portal locus outside my quarters woke as I approached, humming the childhood note for safe crossing; steady, bright, unafraid.

Before stepping through, I pressed two fingers to my lips and tapped the dasant, orienting it to the Earth beings.

"D, and team" I murmured. "I'm coming to you. Please be there."

The reply came like overlapping chords:

The wee glowbug first, breathless, wind in their voice. "We're flying fast, IGSTA on our tails. There may be snacks involved."

Cae, clipped but warm: "We've got the key handed over. The Thelassi are fussy, aye; but they hum in tune when it counts."

And D, soft, anchoring: "We kept the door open, see you soon."

Something flickered at my back; not wings, not thought, not fear. Avaris, close as breath.

"Then let's go," I said. "I'm bringing my version of biscuits."

The glowbug whooped. "Sweet as! Leadership I can get behind."

D laughed, harmonics light as a bell.

I stepped into the portal. Drual reached for me, not to hold me back, just to know it would be there when I returned. Color unspooled, space folded, and I fell into a soft song.

******

The first breath felt cooler: ozone, rain, and green, fragrant, and alive. I was grateful for the acalte which allowed me to dampen the magnitude of my forcefield and convert my body to this dimension's form waves; so much slower than Drual. Being the equivalent of a black hole would draw a little too much attention at full force here. I dimmed to twenty percent to 'fit in.' To get my bearings. To have a shot at completing my task. Faierodon rose before me in braided towers, each one carved by sound and glimmering with its own melody. The city's welcoming chorus pressed against my being, low and inviting.

On the plaza ahead, three figures ran toward me; three notes I'd hoped I aimed properly to align with when I arrived.

D reached first, hand outstretched, eyes bright, voice warm. "Kia ora, Aedra."

Cae followed, precise and assessing, scanning my edges like a craftsman checking for cracks. I knew he could sense I was dimming out of respect for this dimension; Eura's could feel everything. "Welcome. You look like someone who did a big thing and pretended it was small."

Spitz skidded in last, arms wide, hair in full rebellion. "You brought the vibe! And, is that some kind of cosmic biscuit?"

I blinked. Laughed. Held it up. "For negotiating with portals and otherworldly gods."

Spitz pressed a wee glowbug foreleg to his heart, solemn. "Perfect. Cosmic carbs."

D's palm hovered near my forearm, a question without words. I nodded, and their touch was feather-light, anchoring, unexpectedly familiar. The realization struck like song through stone — D was a dyphoros. A union balanced in harmony, having merged between two realities. No wonder her energy carried that dual resonance, earth and ether intertwined. I was comforted by this, somehow. Despite not having merged, I was not alone. Singular, not a swarm and not a merged dyphoros. But at least I knew another more like me than the rest now. It was miraculous that a dyphoros union had occurred here, no wonder I was pulled to this place.

"Jokes aside, there's been something off here," D said, "Events erased, unions broken, even creatures missing. Something is very wrong. We need to talk to the Thelassi to figure it out."

Cae angled his chin toward the far horizon. "The Thelassi are three alleys south. They have an update for us, and we need to see what's happened since delivering the key. The head of the Lerali just updated the phase map; we've got a countdown before the open chord closes."

"Plenty of time," Spitz said, already bobbing in anticipation. "We'll fly."

We flew. The city opened for us, streets softening, doors bowing, music rising in wafts of steam. The air bent around our motion, Faierodon seemed to cheer us on. The Thelassi were waiting where Cae predicted, through the silver door etched with a thousand mirrored glyphs. Inside, the light shifted into slow spirals, each colour a language. The Thelassi met us eagerly.

"The key helped us; thank you. We were able to deactivate and retrieve the Revetron. We have hidden it from the agency, where they cannot find it."

"That's great news!" Spitz exclaimed.

"It's not all great news," the Thelassi continued, "We attempted to anchor the Revetron rift, but the IGSTA had already begun to reverse time. The wound is not linear anymore; it loops back into itself. We cannot heal it with symmetry alone."

D's jaw tightened. "So we need to patch time."

"Something like that," said the Thelassi, inclining its head. "The Spires can stabilise the loop. But they will require resonance, not force."

The Thelassi extended a shimmering filament of light toward me, pulsing faintly. "Your signature carries the singular frequency. The Recall will need your chord to open the anchor sites. At your full power."

I took the filament; it sank into my wrist and disappeared like it had always belonged there. "Yes, I have brought other items to anchor. We'd better reach the Spires before the chord closes."

The Thelassi continued, "Time is malleable, but of the essence now."

"C'mon, we're in the fast lane of the multiverse," D teased. "We've got this."

"Keen as, let's go!" Spitz gestured for us to leave.

We stepped back into the streets, the Thelassi's final notes trailing behind us like a gentle blessing. The Spires waited on the horizon; two towers of living stone that shimmered as if illuminated from beams of every dawn that ever happened.

As we drew nearer, the air thickened. Gravity loosened its grip. Colors began to bend around us, hues rearranging themselves into frequencies I could hear. My acalte burnt gently against my wrist as I attuned to full power.

Then, time hiccuped.

It started as a tremor underfoot, a loop in existence. The same moment repeated twice, then at warp speed, like an infinity loop. Spitz's laugh echoed, fractured. D blinked; once, twice, and the second blink left a trail of her eyes lingering behind. Cae's device sputtered and read the same second again and again. Everything around us blinked, distorted, repeated itself in a fracture of time ad nauseam. I wasn't sure how long it lasted, because time was not clear. Then, relief. Regular time, whatever that was here in this dimension, returned momentarily.

"Skip loop pattern," Cae muttered. "Agency's trying to hijack us so we can't reach the Spires. But what on earth sort of device are they using now?"

The Spires towered before us now, throwing off rings of light that cascaded in every which way, bending geometry around their bases. They weren't still structures; they were events. Every surface sang with oscillations of gold and blue.

I reached out, palm open. The nearest Spire's hum leapt into my being, resonating with the thread at my wrist. A sound like breath drawn through glass; pure and vast. That's when it happened, a different sort of recall: a skip that felt more like a gift. A fragment frozen in time, from somewhere else. The light around the Spires bent sharply, rippling into concentric halos. Every sound turned liquid. The city behind us slowed, trees mid-sway, raindrops pausing mid-fall. The world held its inhale. Time folded once more.

Across that fold came the echo; her.

Avaris.

She appeared not as form, but as a geometry of flame, her voice woven through the resonance of the Spires themselves. The skip had been hers; the moment she was confronted with my own singularity, and didn't give in. The moment she sent me something that shifted me forever: compassion. Compassion for my burden of being a singularity, of the vastness I carried for so long, completely alone. Was it happening now? Or had it already happened? I couldn't tell.

Her memory poured through the skip like sunlight through water, refracting everything it touched. It flowed through the Spires, rippling outward; healing fractures, stitching timelines. It was breathtaking; a cosmic pulse of empathy so radiant that even the earth's gravity bowed to it. My body trembled with the resonance. Every cell felt rewritten by understanding, not from her words, but from the way she saw me. Just like Ora had said, her Witness. The singularity wound in me; it was gone. And wherever it hid, I could feel the Revetron's reversal pulse once, then steadied, a wound like my own, ready to unwind. Suddenly, I felt different. Transformed. Softer. Where there had been resistance in me, in her, there was now ease.

From afar, I heard Avaris, her voice like starlight in liquid form.

You are not a black hole. You are an acute and volatile substance, yes, but it's made of love. I see that now, it's why I didn't surrender, it's why I didn't run from what I am, what we are made of, in the end. I am flame, volatile as well. Molten and infinite in movement. You are the substance that holds the stars together. The absence is what allows matter to matter. And we are that which births new laws of creation, separate but always together. Always as one.

The words moved through me, steadying the currents. For the first time, I felt expansion without collapse. I felt vast, but not empty. I was ready to perform the ritual.

I placed my anchors; filaments of gold unfurling from my palms, each one sinking into the ground with a shimmer of star residue. They spread outward, weaving through the dust and stone until the whole plain began to glow with faint geometry. The Spires responded in kind. Their surfaces shifted, once-solid stone turning translucent, veins of molten light running upward in intricate patterns. New colours, new patterns, new shapes emerged. New creation from the void - from me. The gold deepened, thickening into something almost tactile; enlivened radiance blending back into itself.

The glow moved in waves, rising from the base to the pinnacle, reflecting off the air as if the atmosphere had turned to mirrored glass. Every ripple redrew the world; sky curving, towers stretching, shadows bending toward the light. Then came the shiver. The time loops faltered, flickered, then began to fold in on themselves. Colors split and reunited, motion stuttered, then smoothed. What had been repeating finally slid into alignment. Above us, the light from the Spires braided together in a slow spiral, forming patterns that pulsed across the horizon, luminous fractals dissolving into clarity. The ground steadied. The distortions eased.

And for the first time since the Revetron began to reverse the Field, the world felt balanced, breathing in its own rhythm. I hoped that the memories would be restored, the creatures return to their rightful homes, here and wherever it had begun to erase them.

All around us, Faierodon exhaled. The sky rippled with aurora threads as the damage mended itself. The Thelassi's light signals shimmered from distant towers, signaling success.

Spitz, dazed, muttered, "Did Aedra just reboot the multiverse's proper timelines before brekkie?"

D, eyes wide but smiling, answered, "Looks like it. All in a day's work."

I laughed, voice breaking with relief and awe. "That was just us warming up. I think we're ready now. For the Recall. To restore what was lost before the Fall."

Cae nodded, adjusting their gear. "The anchor sites are open. Spires are in harmony."

The city around us hummed approval, the melody of healed time folding into a serene chord.

We took our positions in the circle at the Spires' base, each of us glowing faintly with our respective resonance. The air buzzed with the low-frequency hum of power re-learning how to be gentle.

I raised my hand, the braid at my wrist shining like dawn.

"Let's begin the Recall protocol," I said.

The Spires shimmered, their hum traveling past sound, past sight, into whatever waits when time stops needing to be counted. The macro logs outside time-space, far beyond the anthologies of varying dimensions, even farther beyond the great forgetting, closed quietly behind us. The opening from before the Fall of Ether had just begun.

CHAPTER TWENTY-ONE

Avaris: Molt of Mirrors

The air shifted, whirling in madness and empty chaos, unlike the familiar sizzle chaos of my Isle. It reverberated through the edges of my wings, sending sparks flying unwillingly every which way. The portal had not opened; it had cracked. I hung in the split, half-formed, light dragging at my bones. The sound of my own pulse doubled in my ears, a hiccuping drum that refused to pick a single style to the beat.

Below me, the Isle of Ashborn pulsed in and out of focus. I saw her mountains once, then twice, then backward. Lava froze mid-spurt, a red fountain turned sculpture. Even my roar came late, chasing me through the delay. I was caught between heartbeats, as if the multiverse itself was stuttering to determine what would be next.

"Don't you dare," I growled to this distorted space, though my voice sounded distant and echoed by a stranger.

The portal tightened, deciding how long to keep me in the in-between. I was caught between worlds, though I wasn't sure it would have let me go to the Fae either way at this point. Sparks peeled off my body and hung there, trapped in the air like a constellation that had lost its sky. For a moment, I thought I would dissolve into those points of light, but then I heard the Isle call for me.

It was not sound but tectonic memory. The volcanoes roared to life, their vents spilling white-hot demands that reached for me. My Isle, my cradle and crown, was calling me home. The pull yanked me down through the clouds of distortion. I hit the surface with a crash that shook mountains. When the dust settled, I was lying in a ring of molten cozy home. The sky above was fissured like a cracked mirror, edges of the failed portal still oozing blue filament and fragments. I tried to stand, but my claws slipped through my own reflection. My scales, my pride, my armor, were flickering like faulty stars.

A shape rose from the nearest vent: a Cindren, molten form, eyes like twin cores of magma. I recognised him; it was Theren, the oldest of the Isle-guardians. His voice was a rolling quake.

"What have you done, Flame-Born?"

"Good morning to you, too," I rasped. "I fell through an existential malfunction, no big deal."

He hovered above the flow, staring me down. Behind him, more Cindren emerged; dozens of ember-bodies whispering heat. One smaller than the rest darted forward, light quicksilver. Vosk. I remembered his laughter from younger centuries, back when Ignara still danced for festivals instead of omens.

"She's different," Vosk murmured. "Her fire sings in two keys."

Theren raised a molten hand, paused to listen. "Distorted harmonics."

"Or evolution," Vosk countered.

Their argument vibrated through the ground, and the Isle shifted uneasily. I spread my wings; a storm of cracked scales fell like coins around me.

"Enough." My voice echoed through the magma tubes below. "The portal had mimic distortions; it blocked me from my destination. This is just residue. It's clearing. Contain me, and you'll burn for nothing. Grace still works here, too, you know."

Theren's molten brow furrowed. "Then prove your flame still answers the Constancy."

He struck his staff against the ground. Fire leapt toward me in a spiral test. Reflex took over. I breathed; not ordinary breath but a column of silver fire threaded with mirror light. It met his challenge midair, and for a heartbeat, the two flames wrestled. Then mine swallowed him whole and turned it to glass.

The Cindren fell silent.

Vosk stepped forward slowly, his molten shoulders trembling in wonder. "The Constancy sings in her again," he whispered. "But not the same tune."

"No," I said, lowering my head. "A truer one. I was shown something in the in-between."

"What were you shown?" Vosk pressed.

"I was shown a seed of some kind, radiating blue flame," I explained, "only for a blink of a moment, in the Fae dimension. But I was blocked from going."

The Cindren gave each other concerned glances and said nothing. The Isle began to tremble, not in threat but recognition. Lava streams redirected themselves, carving a new path toward the western ridge. The message was clear. Come.

Theren gestured for his kin to follow as escort. "The Cradle of Glass calls you. If it consumes you, I will not interfere."

"Appreciated," I muttered. "Hospitality as warm as ever."

We walked. The land reshaped beneath our feet; valleys closing behind, ridges bowing ahead. Even the ash seemed to be tenser, tiny grey motes whispering my name in the old tongue. The air thickened with the formidable taste of change. By the time we reached the Cradle, the portal scar above the island had faded to a thin trace in the sky. The chamber gaped before us, half-cavern, half-wound in the world's crust. Its walls were molten mirrorstone, reflecting me a thousandfold. The reflections didn't agree with one another: in one, I was whole; in another, skeletal light; in a third, nothing at all. The Constancy Flame burnt at the center; tall, blue, patient.

Theren and the others stopped at the rim. Only Vosk dared step closer. "Do you know what happens here, Flame-Born?"

"Yes." My throat tightened. "Dragons molt here when the old shape won't fit."

He nodded, solemn. "Then we will bear Witness."

I stepped into the Cradle, the air inside weighty and relaxing, not threatening at all. The Flame flickered, lowering itself as if to meet my gaze. I felt its heat enter me, crawl up the hollow behind my sternum where the mimic echo had nested. The interference shrieked; my vision doubled. The first scale broke with a sound like thin glass under stress. Another followed. Then a dozen. The pain wasn't sharp; it was memory, every version of myself being peeled away. I saw them float upward, each scale holding a scene: my arrogance, my isolation, my refusal to merge with Aedra, my fear of being less. They circled like ghosts of light, whispering accusations.

"Not today," I said through clenched teeth. "You're beautiful, but you're done."

The Constancy Flame flared. The molten mirrors on the walls began to sing; a deep harmonic that wrapped around my scales. My body responded instinctively. I reared back, wings stretched wide, and let the molt wash over me. Heat rolled outward in concentric waves. The Cindren at the edges knelt, their forms flickering in reverence or terror; I couldn't tell which. My wings cracked open along their seams, spilling rivers of liquid light. I couldn't keep track of where my body ended and the Isle began; my veins were magma lines in her skin.

The sound changed. Beneath the roar I heard whispers; thousands of them; the lands themselves. They spoke in tone, not word: pride, grief, release. Ashborn had waited centuries for this. The molten scales that fell to the floor hardened instantly into mirrors. In each one, the mimic signal distorted and died, like trapped static finally starved of fuel. When the last piece left me, I felt lighter than ash. I collapsed to my knees, trembling. My wings were translucent, refracting the chamber's light into ribbons. My fire burnt silver-white, quieter but infinitely hotter. I inhaled; and the weight of the air lifted.

Theren was the first to approach. The molten giant stood at a distance, cautious as one who approaches a newborn sun.

"Is it done?"

I looked at my reflection in the nearest mirrorstone. My eyes no longer burnt gold but deep indigo, streaked with faint lightning veins. "Done enough to begin," I said.

Vosk came closer, cupping a shard of cooled mirror in his hands. "The interference; gone?"

I nodded. "The mimic fed on what I refused to see. It can't eat acceptance."

He stared at me, wide-eyed, then at the Isle itself. The volcanoes had quieted. Only a single plume of white smoke rose straight upward, pure and steady. "The land hums with you. It hasn't done that since the First Age, before the fall."

I managed a smile. "She's proud. She raised a stubborn daughter."

Theren grunted approval that almost sounded like laughter. "Then, Flame-Born, you are restored."

"The flame reminds us of the cycle of death and rebirth," I said with a new softness I didn't know I had in me, "every breath is an ending, every spark a beginning."

The Constancy Flame flared once more, taller than before. In its heart appeared the spectral figure of Elder Sen'kai, her form shaped from molten vapor. Her voice resonated through every stone.

"Avaris of Ignara. You have remade what we could not. But know this: when you leave, the balance shifts. The Isle's pulse is tied to yours. If you cross, we change."

I bowed my head. "Then let us change together."

"And if you fail?"

"I'll be the myth that tried."

The elder smiled; an expression like a volcano remembering warmth. "So be it." The vision dissipated, leaving the mists of the lava flow humming and bubbling with their approval.

The Cindren retreated as well, murmuring to one another. Only Vosk lingered. He turned a shard of mirror obsidian over in his palms until it cooled completely, then offered it to me.

"Take this. Reflection is not reversal, nor truth of who you are," he said. "You'll need the reminder."

I accepted it carefully; it glowed once, attuning to my new resonance. "You always were the poet among lava lumps."

He laughed, a sound like small eruptions. "And you were always the troublemaker who made prophecy nervous."

"Still am."

He backed away as the chamber began to rumble. The floor cracked in a perfect circle around the Constancy Flame. Lava rose, not wild, deliberate. It spiraled upward until it formed a ring of fire suspended in midair. Inside the ring, light condensed into a clear, pulsing void.

The portal reborn.

I stepped closer, wafting a breath of air that tasted of stardust and possibility. For the first time since the in-between incident, there was no interference, no mimic distortion; just pure, open resonance. Through it, faintly, I heard the harmony of another realm: Aedra's Recall, singing across the dimensions like a lighthouse through fog.

My chest tightened, not from fear but from recognition. Her note matched mine now. Separate, equal, complementary. It didn't pull me; it invited. Behind me, the Isle sighed, an exhale of steam through every vent. The volcanoes dimmed to a gentle red. She was ready to sleep again.

I looked up at the clean blue ring and spoke to my world. "You've kept me alive, old girl. You've burnt my temper into wisdom, more or less. When I come back, we'll see what evolution feels like."

The ground rumbled a fond growl in reply. I spread my wings. Light poured through them, painting the cavern walls in every hue of aurora. New sparks emerged from my back, but this time they had less singe; they danced and played with a new lightness. The reflection in the mirrorstone no longer argued; it simply followed. I felt the thrum of readiness in my blood, the clean line between before and after.

The portal pulsed once, responding to my breath. Not yet, I thought. Let Aedra finish her Recall. Let the dimensions remember themselves first. I lowered my wings and stepped back, letting the heat settle around me. The Isle's lullaby rolled through the molten channels like a heartbeat. I felt my energy there with her, at the Spires, supporting her.

"I will not be gathered," I told the silence, "but I will be counted."

The Constancy Flame flickered in agreement. I knew Aedra heard me. I sent her a message of comfort and truth, assuring her that she was not the repelling energy she believed herself to be, but the magnificence of creation potential itself. Outside, lightning danced on the horizon where sky met molten rock; the mark of a world listening for what comes next. I watched it for a long time, breathing with the land that made me, until the tremor of the portal's song aligned perfectly with mine.

CHAPTER TWENTY-TWO

Aedra: The Loom

As Recall protocol unwound its vibration and found its energetic within the vast Spires, Faierodon enlivened with song. Every chord the city held resounded against itself, tuning and detuning in the same breath. The sky was alive in the reverberation of light, unable to decide which timeline it belonged to. Creation was learning how to speak in a new language of sound. Across the plaza, D and Cae moved inside the trance-like state amid frequencies, guiding the stabilisers into resonance. Each pulse realigned a sliver of the cosmos.

I extended my field outward, feeling the vastness of the distortion. Timelines overlapped like competing melodies.
Stars flared in the wrong order. Even the memory of this dimension's physics, silly things like cause and effect stuttered, repeating themselves in a sympathetic echo.

The Megalight had tampered with the architecture of creation, embedding counterfeit harmonics into the Field, false symmetries that bent time around obedience instead of play. What we had grown to call the mimic signal was many vibrational tones, not a singular pulse. Every distorted beat had severed another connection between dimensions. Not just separating dyphoros unions, but unions of true love, unions of families, unions of passions, and creation acts of beings throughout the multiverse. The separate dimensions were not where the false had stopped with the influence of separation. It was simply where the Weaveborn could help restore union potential, within the overlaps of dimension unions and activated by the dyphoros reunions that were now underway.

Recall could change everything. The Recall wasn't just memory; it was reactivation and restoration. It could tap into the Fall of Ether itself, draw from the first fracture, and remember how love truly vibrated. Linear time was frayed through this galaxy; the Human systems flickered with asynchronous decades of advancement and decay, endless loops of stuck progress. It was particularly frozen in the Human dimension and a few other higher-density dimensions throughout the multiverse. In my galaxy, our spiraltime was much more flexible, but here, the full timeline needed a reset. Eura and infinite creatures throughout the galactic homeworlds hung in harmonic suspension. If the Recall succeeded, time would not just heal; it would reset as a new format, flexible but coherent.

I steadied my frequency. "Initiating full Recall field," I told the others. I let the tone of my frequency increase slightly so I could fully participate without overwhelming the beings of this realm with my resonance.

D flashed me a grin, supporting the proper placement of the ritual offerings.

"Here goes everything."

A harmonic wave rolled outward, layering itself over Faierodon's Spires, through its crystal rivers, into the surrounding plains. The ground sang back. Reality began to flicker, seams of pure resonance opening between air and intention. I felt them; all the timelines bleeding into each other. The worlds that had been, the worlds within worlds that might have been, the single moment where everything had diverged.

Within the Weave, I could taste the distortion: thin, sharp, metallic. It had the scent of faulty mathematical equations burnt into stagnation. It was the echo of the Fall. The Recall field deepened, pulling from the fractures that once divided empathy from logic. Through it, I sensed the same wound everywhere: planets that aged too fast, species erased mid-thought, stars flickering off-beat in the galactic chord. All of it carried the same harmonic scar, the residue of the Fall of Ether.

And beneath that scar, something sleeping. An origin beat, a pulse. A rhythm that belonged to none of us, yet to all.

I felt it; not through the body, but through frequency alignment, the way a chord feels itself completed. Something was humming beneath the city's recovered order. Something alive.

Just then, a glow flared across the horizon; a curl of heat that uncoiled into flame braided with moonbeam. Avaris stepped through it. Her light burnt steadily now, healed from the distortions she'd been mending. Around her, reality steadied; frequencies flattening into calm. I was overwhelmed with joy to see her here, beside me, in the Fae dimension. Her power and grace were beyond words. I had to concentrate on the Recall, but I held a momentary pause to greet her.

"You feel different," I began, "Softer. How did you get here?"

"I have had my share of cleansing the Megalight, it nearly blocked me in an in-between portal. The outer fields are stable," she said. "But there's a rhythm underneath; older than the distortions. I followed it."

"We've felt it too," I said. "It's running through the recall frequencies, directing them. It knows where to go."

She looked past me toward the horizon, where the woods caught the reflection of the hum. "Then we follow."

As I completed the protocol, the Spires released and returned to stillness, but Faierodon still shimmered like glass cooling; heat memories turning translucent, the world's edges smoothed by its own exhale. Every particle of air felt newly self-aware, cautious, as if rehearsing how to move in one direction again. The city's harmonic infrastructure, the great chords that held its gravity, re-tuned themselves in faint, hopeful intervals.

I drifted through the restored plaza, my frequency tuned to a fraction of its capacity to avoid disturbing the new stillness. Our calibration instruments pulsed in quiet satisfaction, blue-green readings steady across their surfaces. Time: linear, cooperative, slow; folded over us like cloth newly washed. Faierodon was already a delightful dimension with distortion mostly absent, until the IGSTA came, that is. But now, it felt gentle. I wondered how it had impacted their headquarters. Then the ground sighed. Not a quake, not a fault; just a resonant exhalation that rippled through the crystal strata underfoot. It was the sound of restlessness, the Field testing its voice after silence. I extended my awareness through the harmonic grid, and the vibration touched me; soft, familiar, ancient.

D lifted her head, eyes catching the invisible tremor. "Anyone else hearing that?"

Cae adjusted his wrist Eurometer; the device flashed in protest. "Sub-field resonance," he said, tone clipped but curious. "Nothing like the Revetron echoes. This is… heartbeat range."

It was time to follow the pulse. We flew towards the forest over the bay, Ekat territory not far behind in Ryheadyl. The Root Wells showed themselves to us quickly, as if they had been waiting for this chord.

They aren't wells the way Humans tell it; no stones, no buckets. They're living reservoirs: love-template resonances sunk deep into Faierodon's memory. When a world forgets itself, these wells give it back as Witness.

We stepped into the ring of Wells. The Spires' hum met the ground-song, and there it was, the Trace. A slow pulse rising from the center of the plain, steady as forgiveness. Avaris turned her face toward it the way flames turn toward oxygen.

"That's the call," she said softly. "The one Ignara kept for us safely here in the Fae dimension. It's why I was pulled here since I was little. I'd recognise that tone anywhere. They are living reservoirs of origin-energy; ancient 'roots' that connect dimensions. They're memory of the original template of love and connection before distortions."

I felt it touch my awareness; no pull or shove, only recognition. The Field asking us to listen wider. Ekat came out of the woods, ecstatic to see us, and this time with friends I didn't recognise. These cute green creatures with pointy ears looked like they had a twinkle in their eye of mischief, not unlike Sprites. I only knew of these creatures from reading up on the Faierodon creature Anthologies.

"Millie, Jis!" D exclaimed, giving the wee creatures big hugs. "I'm so happy to see you."

"And we you!" the one called Millie beamed.

"Do you know why the Spires sent us here?" I asked.

"The Wells assist in allowing civilizations to reset themselves against counterfeit blueprints," Jis chimed up, "like what the IGSTA had been creating from here. Thank you for coming. It's essential to activate them now that you've performed such a powerful reset."

"And how do we activate them?" Cae asked curiously.

"That is our specialty," Millie explained, "Root Wells are deeply ingrained in the fibers of the Earth, they are intricately woven into the mycelium and the creatures of the middle grounds beneath the surface. We must invite their support now by practicing a dance that calms the lower areas of her. She is a bit shy, you see, the Well. Not used to helping these ways with upper-world folk."

"I believe I can be of assistance," a wee voice bobbed from behind Jis.

"And who are you?" D asked softly.

"I'm Tes," the Hobgoblin was tentative in showing her face, "And, well, actually not me, per se. But I know who can help speak to the Wells."

The Hobgoblin and the Ekat gathered together to converse amongst themselves, clearly deciding the best way forward before sharing with the rest of us. Eventually, Jis cleared his throat and spoke.

"It is a volatile thing, what Tes offers." Jis explained, "This creature is not really the creature that she seems, Verru. More of a collective wave of interconnection among the Fungi kind crystallised in a being only to communicate with other races."

"There is no honor in hesitation," Tes retorted, "Let us call the Verru."

Tes gathered a pile of stones and bark, carefully placing things in a certain pattern, then started to dance in a circle around it, pulsing heavy foot patterns in thumping rhythm. The Ekat joined in the dance. Thump thump, clap. Thump, Thump, clap.

From the looks of it, nothing was shifting. Yet. But their dance was creating a trance-like vibration, much more grounded than the ways of the Spires and my home planet. It was rooted deep into the veins of the Earth. The Ekats paused the dance and stood still, an echo of their thump reverberating slowly through the trees, their bark blended into the leaves, through the soil, deeper still, rooting further into the depths below.

Eventually, from the swell of the leaves, something rustled slowly. A gradual shift and settling, a movement the eye of a Human would have missed. Was something growing from the ground? Slowly, a lifeform emerged and took shape, a stalk of shimmering and off white shape.

"Verru!" Tes shrieked in delight.

"Where is that which is," the echoing harmonic voice responded from the white glow.

"We are honored you have arrived," I spoke softly, "We seek only truth."

"Which is why I have made the arrival presently," Verru whispered. "The Root Well is an ancient technology unlike most of the Fae dimension. It doesn't shine or announce itself. Connected to the vastest intelligent network of love, vaster than anything here, much like your Swarms in Andromeda." I was impressed with Verru's awareness of my realm.

"There is something else here for you, in the grove, beyond the restoration of the Wells. Yes, they will activate a cleansing of the timelines now that they have been reset, the blueprint renewal. I have activated it now."

"Thank you, Verru," I responded sincerely.

"But there is far more for you, Aedra and your friend here, Avaris."

"It's the seed, isn't it?" Avaris whispered.

"It is, yes," Verru replied.

The ground rose into a gentle bowl where wind pooled. Nothing dramatic; just a node of resonance so calm it made speech unnecessary. The air there was thicker with possibility; colours stayed a breath longer before becoming themselves. In the center: not an object, but a beat; a low, patient glow that expanded and softened, expanded and softened, like the hues of liquid pinks at dawn moving into blues as they unravel.

"That," Tes said, nose wrinkling happily, "is what your Recall woke up."

Avaris stepped beside me, her pink scales glowing the colour of sunrise. "The Luminarch Seed," she murmured. "I saw a glimpse of it back home in the in-between. It was waiting for this."

"It was waiting for Recall," I said.

I extended a filament of my awareness. The Seed answered like an old friend; no heat, no shock, just awareness returning through contact.

And then, an entirely different Recall began. A vivid show spun before us like a holographic movie.

Sound became colour; colour unfolded into memory. Through the Seed, the memory of Ether opened itself as it had been: beginnings made by curiosity, not control. Worlds made from love's true resonance. Stars tuned to one another for kindness. Every being spoke to every other in the tone of care. The Seed's vibration widened until it filled the Field around us, carrying us inside the first ages. I saw Ether when it was still laughter in motion; creation happening by curiosity alone. Forms improvised themselves into being; music built matter. Everything spoke to everything else, conversation as existence.

Then came the tightening. Measurement without mercy. The old architects of IGSTA, good intentions braided with fear, began to file beauty into numbers and file numbers into prisons. Empathy was flagged as inefficiency; play, as waste. Equations replaced questions. I felt the Weaveborn scatter; the architects of kindness breaking apart, hiding within stories and myths, veiling protections for empathy where logic could not reach. Time solidified, desperate to preserve itself by counting. Linear sequence became a cage built from good intentions.

Then, the Seed showed me a creature called the Loom; a Weaveborn that kept the harmony of Threads intact, the balance, connection between dimensions in flow. During the Fall, the Loom had folded into the void. Nothing was lost forever, but stored in memory and in-betweens. The Weaveborn left life spark in stories and hid inside children and plants and the small ways creatures choose each other over greed and violence. But the Fall had been vast, and the forgetting veils effective in separating dimensions.

Until now.

Beside me, Avaris's flame flared white, her resonance shaking through the recall.

"That's when we lost the Loom," she said, voice half-light, half-ache. "It wasn't destroyed; it forgot its own laughter."

"And we are its recall," I answered.

The vision folded, collapsing colour back into tone, tone into quiet. The Seed brightened. Filaments of gold and turquoise rose and wound around us both. No fusion; no merging of bodies. Flame and singularity simply agreed. We chose the same intention at the same time, and the Field took that as law. One word moved through every element, and the word was a door: Together. In that unsounded breath, I felt the shape of what I am. I am not a swarm; I am not a pair. I am a singularity because I am the Loom, the place where many can hold without collapsing. Avaris did not disappear into me. She ignited the spark of the lost Loom; of me. Her fire and her Witness gave the Loom heat and colour; my gravity gave her fire a shape to rest in. Union of intention. That's all recall required.

Our friends gasped at the understanding from what the Seed had displayed to us all; images like a distilled movie above our heads: the fall, the activation of the Recall, and my role as the Loom. The Seed flashed images, and it was unclear if it was memory or future. There were images of Threads of dyphoros uniting, of worlds restoring their harmonics. As if Ether was rebuilding from the void itself. Until this moment, time had paused to integrate from the Recall. But now, something shifted; it felt like a start, a jolt that had all of us rebalance our stance where we stood. We stood inside the Luminarch's glow, listening as Faierodon's heartbeat adjusted to its new flexibility. Time breathed with us; linear yet mercifully soft, the rhythm of art learning to be physics anew.

"What on Earth?" D pondered.

"Look at the Eurometer," Cae pointed to his device, which had reset the timepiece to a new rhythm, but was happily ticking along again.

"Linear time was reset," Verru explained, "With the recall and the activation of the Loom, we are given the gift of sequence without forgetting what has been lost."

And I heard it; the new rhythm of time.

Linear flow had resumed, but its rigidity was gone. It stretched, contracted, laughed, like something finally comfortable at creation's dance. Moments could now bend around compassion; cause and effect learnt to dance. I understood then what the Eura had always known: Time is not a ruler; it is resonance. Every action, every word, every kindness leaves a tone that lingers in the Field. If the note is benevolent, it anchors reality. If cruel or hollow, it fades.

"This is what the Eura have always known," Cae explained, "time is resonance and very alive. What rings with kindness endures. What doesn't, fades too fast to be counted."

Avaris turned toward me, her light steady. "So this is what we were for."

"Not to merge," I said. "To witness until collective memory could reveal itself again."

D reached into the small crevice of her pocket and pulled out the Lumin glass gem the Thelassi had given her. It pulsed once against her palm, then quieted when it felt my field.

"This has made my transition and timeline hopping much easier," she said, handing it gently to me, "I know you're dimming yourself Aedra, you don't have to, we can handle all of you. Take this, it's from the Lumins, and it helps balance a being between realms."

I had never received a gift like this. I was truly moved and felt so seen and understood. Far seaward, the Thelassi answered with a long, low vowel of approval; upriver, the Learali's crystal groves shifted into a gentler key. Even the Lumins pulsed beneath distant water, their light moving like a heartbeat through the quiet.

I opened the log inside the dasant, readying it for transmission to Ora back home.

Recall complete. Ether remembered. Loom has returned - it's me.

A momentary pause, then a reply,

I know.

The Spires breathed with us. The Wells kept time. Somewhere past the near stars, linear time exhaled; alive, elastic, steady, and waiting to be composed. The air rippled warm with something close to joy. For the first time since the Fall, creation was delighting in its own kindness and inviting it gently forward.

Part Three

Time as Art

Proverb

We measure time by the echo of kindness.
- Euran Proverb -

CHAPTER TWENTY-THREE

D: New Pulse

This was the moment the multiverse had just woken up and forgotten what it was doing before drinking a flat white. The clouds were rumpled, galaxies yawning, and someone definitely left the kettle of creation on the burner because it was buzzing. The Recall had ended. Frequencies were "stabilizing". Or at least Cae said so with his usual serene calm, wings flickering like a perfectly tuned harp. I wasn't convinced. My ears still rang from the resonance storm, and the plaza around Faierodon looked like a cosmic carnival halfway through cleanup. Sparks of dimensional light were swirling lazily, and the city was shimmering with the afterglow.

"Sweet as," I muttered, hands on hips. "Multiverse reset, reality un-borked, and yet somehow there's still glitter in my shoes."

A Hobgoblin trotted past carrying a broom the size of his body, muttering about "post-Recall overtime pay."

Once the worst of the luminescent chaos died down, Cae gathered a mixed crowd: Hobgoblins, Eura, Ekat, Thelassi, among others. Weirdly, even a few curious Humans gathered about who'd been caught in the dimension overlap during the reset. Jeanie would've loved to be with us, but she was still in the Human dimension, managing her Etsy shop and her pile of animals. And tending to Riley, thank goodness, I missed her so.

"Alright," Cae said, his tone the same one yoga instructors use before telling you it's about to get spiritual. Not that he knew what yoga was, unless he had gotten to that chapter in the Human Anthologies. "We're going to learn to hear time again."

A Hobgoblin raised a hand. "Do we need earplugs?"

Cae politely ignored him. "The Recall showed us that precision isn't what stabilises reality. Kindness does. Eura's have known this for eons; it's in our myths and legends. Every heartbeat that resonates with compassion anchors the Field. Every act of care is an act of physics."

He paused, his luminous wings fanning softly. "Time," he said, "isn't something we count. It's something we compose."

Someone clapped. Oh, that was me. Mostly because the whole thing was so earnest, it felt genuinely endearing. Everyone was enthralled with what he was sharing, and the message landed with open hearts.

"Beautiful speech," I said when the crowd dispersed. "But if time's art, I'm still painting with crayons."

Cae smiled that small, knowing smile of his. "You always did have a talent for colouring outside the lines and using mixed metaphors."

There couldn't have been a bigger understatement. I giggled and hugged him.

More Hobgoblins jogged past, hauling coils of cable and clanking tools, muttering half-jokes about "chronological spelunking" like it was their new sport. Tes waved a broom, taking a break from cleaning the debris of the sound waves. "If anyone asks, time is fine," she told me cheerfully. "Just needs a cuppa and a nap."

"Same," I said.

Aedra stood with her palms lifted, chin tilted as if listening to rain. Avaris hovered beside her, all quiet focus and fiery patience. The Spires thrummed underfoot: low, resonant, a heartbeat re-learning its rhythm.

"Do you hear that?" Cae asked, wings folded, voice like someone smiling mid-syllable.

"I hear a lot of things," I said. "Most of them are Hobgoblins swearing at the moment."

"No," he said, and touched the basalt plinth with two fingers. "Underneath."

I listened properly. Beneath the bustle and the clank, under the gossip and the jazzy buzz of a bioluminen
cent city finding itself again, there was a new tone: warmer, rounder, deeper in my chest than in my ears. It felt... kind.

"The Luminarch Seed is awake," Aedra murmured. "It was bound by the Recall. Now the husk has cracked. It didn't likely only activate me."

Avaris nodded. "And when a seed wakes..."

"It grows a whole garden?" I finished, yet another clunky metaphor, I realised. Then my stomach did a small drop, and not from poetry. "If the Seed's pulsing, what's it pulsing through?"

Cae's gaze had already gone far away, past the Spires, past the mountain line where Faierodon's ridges tore the sky into lace. He didn't answer me, which is how I knew he'd felt it too: the sideways tug in the gut that said something big was happening.

The pulse wasn't just here. It was going through them, too, the agency.

"IGSTA," I said, and wiped suddenly-slick palms on my leggings. "Headquarters."

As if the word were a switch, the air sharpened. A line of scarlet pinched the horizon, then spread; not lightning, not exactly, more like a thread dragged from the sky to the ground. The Hobgoblins went very quiet.

Aedra's eyes flared. "It's passing through their locus nodes," she said. "The old false-light chambers. They built them to quantify compassion and ended up in a destruction loop in memory distortion."

"Charming," I said. "We really must write them a review."

A red-gold ribbon radiated through us. It smelt like tin roofs in summer, and the first time someone meant it when they said your name. Every part of me lit and went soft at once, like I was a house full of lamps and someone pulled a single cord. Then the cord caught on something. Someone.

The lighting around the plinth in front of us flared. Not white, that would've been too easy. Not purple, obviously too mystical. Red, definite as a traffic light, and then it became a column, and then the column breathed, and I was on my feet, because it wasn't a column at all. It was a creature being stitched out of scarlet.

"Don't panic," the voice said.

"Nuvious?" I pondered, trying to connect the familiar voice to the blob of light.

He grinned, lopsided and guilty. The grin flickered; the edges of him fuzzed, then re-knitted. His hair was the colour of rerouted electricity. His outline vibrated with pizzazz. "In the flesh-ish," he said. "Would you believe I've been reshaped into the elementals?"

A Hobgoblin yelled, "Oi, D, your sprite mate's gone full disco ball!"

I squinted, and indeed, there was Nuvious, hovering mid-air like a living sparkler having an existential crisis.

"Witness," he said dramatically, throwing out both glowing arms.

"My new form: Spritetastic. Transient Luminous Event, personified."

He radiated a great red flare that lit up half the plaza. Every Hobgoblin dove for cover.

"Mate," I said, squinting through the afterimage, "you're basically a jolly hazard warning."

Nuvious preened, twirling like a ballerina made of solar flares. "At least I retired from IGSTA time-card swapping. Now I connect storms to the edge of space. I am the weather now."

This guy had a bit of an ego issue, but I was keen to get on with it. Cae, standing beside me with that patient teacher look, rubbed his temples. "And I was just starting to enjoy silence."

Nuvious looked down at his hands, which were there and then not and then very much there again. When he flexed, the air drew small red purses of light around his knuckles, as if the storm couldn't quite let go of its shape.

"I was still entangled in their systems," he said, not meeting Cae's eyes. "I told you everything I could before the Recall. Thought I'd done my one brave thing and could go back to being a clever coward. But the Luminarch didn't ask. It came through HQ, through the false-light stacks, right through me. There wasn't anywhere else to be."

He glanced up then, and there it was: the guilt, but also the wonder, the way people look after their first decent cry in months. "It burnt the metrics out," he said softly. "Left the... music."

Avaris stepped forward, an expression of the kind you wear when a wild animal refuses to bite you. "Can you hold form?"

Nuvious tilted his head as if listening to instructions from somewhere behind his left ear. "Mostly. I'm on probation from physics." He flickered, steadied, and gave me a sheepish look. "Still me, though. Still sorry. Still learning."

Cae's shoulders loosened a fraction. "Then you're just in time," he said. "We need eyes that can see what was erased."

"Ah," Nuvious said, relief and dread knotted into one. "About that."

He lifted his hand and pointed toward the far terraces. We followed his gesture with our eyes and saw it — a thin smear in the air where colour ought to be. The paving stones through it looked a little too clean, a little too new, as if they'd never known footsteps. The edges twitched, resisting definition.

"What am I looking at?" I asked, and already hated the answer.

"A kindness," Nuvious said. "Undone. They didn't just erase

events. They rewrote awareness. Whole afternoons where someone decided to be decent, removed like spam." His voice wavered, then steadied. "I helped build the schema that tagged those moments as noise. The Revetron had been engineered to do a lot more than reverse time before it was intercepted by the Thelassi. You can see the distortion coming back when things are too perfect."

Cae reached out, not touching Nuvious so much as affirming the space his confession made. "Then help us retune it."

Jis exhaled softly and spoke up. "For this, we'll need the Mnorae," he said. "The Hidden Folk."

Tes perked up. "Finally, a decent adventure after all this time debris clean up."

"They surfaced the last time the Luminarch stirred," Millie jumped in to explain, turning slowly as if the world were a shell and she was listening for sea. "They live in the gaps between frequencies. They can stitch perception itself."

"Which is fantastic," I said, "except for the part where they're unfindable."

Nuvious's outline smoothed. He looked brighter for a moment, less in danger of sloughing back into ions. "I can follow the absences," he said. "The places that should feel like memory but don't, they ring wrong to me now. Hollow." He gave an awkward shrug, then winced as his shoulder briefly forgot it existed. "Side effect of being half made of resonance. Handy for a search party. Less handy for couples dancing."

A shape flitted above us and landed on the nearest rail with professional casualness. Quinley didn't bother with hello. He gave Nuvious one crisp look, then me, then Cae, then back to the horizon where the last threads of red were dissolving. "Right," he said. "If we're doing perception surgery, do it quickly. There's still static in the wires. Someone thinks they own the songbook."

"We hear you," Cae said. "But how did you get here Quinley?"

Quinley hopped twice, as if stamping a signature on the metal. "Dimensions are overlapping like crazy right now," he said. "Just came to clue you in. The agency has been rewired, but that doesn't mean you aren't in for a show. The mimic still does what it does best." Then he was gone, a black arc into the light.

I arched a brow at nobody. "The usual."

Aedra's gaze caught on something below the terraces—a patch of shadow that glowed with an impossible light. "Verru," she breathed.

"They're back."

We made for the slope. The fungi domed like small lanterns, clustered in crescents. Their skins were the colour of old cream and rainwater; their undersides glowed faintly as moonlight. When I crouched, they rose to meet me.

"Hey, mates," I said, grateful to see them again. "We're looking for the Mnorae. Any chance you could help us find them?"

One of the caps brightened, then went dim in a slow pulse that made me blink. Another answered. A line of them lit in sequence, forming a glowing trail through the trees, like a cosmic connect-the-dots drawn by mischievous sprites who'd discovered glow sticks.

Tes clapped softly. "Finally, signage."

Avaris gestured a massive winged claw toward her brow. "Gratitude," he told the Verru. They hummed again, which I chose to interpret as we love you too rather than please stop standing on our cousins.

We set off: Cae gliding with that unteachable grace, Aedra and Avaris standing out more than most, Hobgoblins trotting with their jaunty doomed optimism, and Nuvious floating at my shoulder like a lantern learning to be a being. Not to mention Spitz, buzzing along with his usual zinger one-liners and obsession with snack breaks. The Verru's light-thread walked us into the shade and then deeper, under branches draped with the aftertaste of the reset. Every now and then, Nuvious would tilt his head and point, and we'd skirt another thin place in the air where something had been scrubbed to sterile. Those were the worst, the spots that felt like a hospital smell: too clean to be alive. As if the IGSTA had been trying to reset their perfection mimic harmonic here, too. I was getting more concerned to see the overlapping energies so abundant and intermingled. I had thought the Recall would fully reset the mimic, but instead it seemed to have challenged it to a dance off.

As we moved, the pulse kept time with us; not a metronome, more haka: breath and footfall and a quiet joy of synchronised movement among us. The Field wasn't just healing; it was rehearsing. At least the dance was worth the journey, even if it was still filled with some new distortions.

"You feel it, don't you?" Cae said quietly, falling into step with me. "Kindness, not precision. It's what makes the rhythm hold."

I wanted, very suddenly, to cry and to laugh and to eat something fried all at once. "I wanted it to be all better," I admitted. "But I also feel the new mimic, the perfection illusion."

Aedra glanced back with a smile that made me feel nine years old and forgiven for reasons I couldn't name. "Precision is beautiful," she said. "It's just not the glue."

"What is?" I asked, though I could taste the answer like salt. I was pondering how mimic's attempt at precision was, perhaps, also worthy of love.

"Gentleness," she said. "Courage's quiet sibling."

Nuvious shimmered, approval making him briefly more solid. "And it confuses the metrics from the agency," he added with wicked glee. "Try quantifying grace. The machine chokes."

We crested a small rise where the trees opened into a sacred grove. The light didn't change, but meaning did. Colours clicked one notch closer to true. Sound took a step back to let silence speak first. The Verru dimmed in unison, as if bowing.

"Here?" I whispered.

"Here," Avaris said.

Nuvious raised his hand and drew a slow circle in the air in the middle of the sacred center of the grove of ancient trees. The circle stayed. Not a mark, a thinness. He widened it carefully until it was the size of a window. The wind shifted, and the dew of the dampened earth softened. And then the Mnorae stepped through the hole, and every story I'd ever been told about them, too solemn, too holy, was inadequate. They were half-perception and half-pattern. Their outlines wavered like mirages, a tapestry of patterns that felt eerily familiar, as if someone had taken the swirls from your grandmother's heirloom quilt and merged them with the cosmic dust of distant galaxies. They had eyes that crinkled when they smiled. One of them had a smudge on her cheek as if she'd been adjusting reality while cleaning chimneys. Another wore three threads around his wrist like friendship bracelets. In some ways, they reminded me of the Weavers, but they were so very many, and they were so small.

"Finally," the smudged one said, in a voice like soft wool. "You took your time."

"We have been developing a new relationship with time," I said. "On the way."

"Delighted to hear it," she said. "That's why we're here."

Behind us, far away but approaching, I felt a faint secondary buzz creep across the Field. A filigree of tidy, tinny logic trying to write itself over a song. I didn't turn toward it. The Mnorae lifted their hands, and reality arranged itself around the gesture like it was relieved to be told where to sit. "Come," the smudged one said. "Bring your genuine heart and your jokes. We'll need both."

"It's great to hear I'm needed," Spitz buzzed. "Also, I brought snacks."

We followed them through the seam and into the place that wasn't a place, where memory hung from the vastness, and what had been deleted waited to be named. The space inside the seam felt like the pause before a song starts. Every breath held, anticipating witness. Ribbons of light wove through each other like living calligraphy, each intersection enlivening new thoughtform. The Mnorae danced with the effortless synchronicity of atoms that had been arranging themselves into stars long before language bothered to name them.

Aedra and Avaris stepped forward at once. They knew the rhythm, the way you know the steps of an old dance, even if you've forgotten the name. Avaris reached into the shimmer and came out with a handful of light that behaved like silk. She began resewing a torn edge in the air, her claws steady. The Mnorae joined her, their laughter rippling through the threads until even the damage seemed to giggle.

"Look at them," Nuvious murmured. His own outline brightened in sympathy. "That's what repair looks like. No punishment. Just mending."

Aedra's eyes were closed, listening to the pattern. "They're re-threading perception itself," she explained, "IGSTA's false light didn't destroy memories; it unlaced the awareness of them. They are integrating the awareness so memory can be accessed."

Nuvious drifted closer to Avaris. "Can you feel where it's thinnest?" he asked.

Avaris nodded. "Here." She touched a space that shimmered and went dull. A memory bloomed: a boy in a workshop offering half his lunch to a stranger, the stranger smiling and then nothing. The image blinked out again.

Nuvious sighed. "That's one of mine. That was tagged as excess empathy in the IGSTA archive." He reached in, hand trembling with light, and drew the image back until it steadied. "Not noise. Not anymore."

The Mnorae melody had its own soothing tempo: thrum-pause-thrum. My wings began to copy it before I noticed. Kindness had a tempo; I could dance to this. A shape of warmth brushed my shoulder. I turned and found Cae smiling at me in his gentle way. The joy around us thickened into light, binding itself across gaps we hadn't even seen. Moments flickered back into being; people helping, forgiving, feeding, comforting. So many small mercies that had been scrubbed out by the false's obsession with efficiency were re-illuminated. The space grew brighter, steadier. Then the pulse faltered. A note went wrong; a cold hiss slithered through the pattern like static.

Nuvious stiffened. "That's them," he said. "IGSTA is trying to interfere with the restoration. They're sampling the frequency."

The smudged Mnorae frowned. "They never tire of measuring what can't be owned." She turned to Cae. "Take what you've learnt and carry it where it can grow. We'll hold the pattern here."

Avaris stayed beside her; Aedra too. Threads of memory glowed around them like vines on a trellis. I didn't want to leave, but the air was shifting; the feeling you get when a dream is about to end, whether you like it or not. Nuvious touched my arm, warm and bright and a little too real for someone half made of resonance. "Go," he said. "I'll help them finish the stitching. Call it community service."

"You sure?"

He smiled, all spark and sincerity. "If I disappear, it's only because I'm everywhere at once. That's progress for a former head of mischief."

I grinned. "Proud of you, bro."

He gave me a mock salute that shed a few sparks.

The Mnorae reached toward us; the seam folded, light bent, and suddenly I was blinking on the terraces of Faierodon again. The pulse underfoot felt stronger now, more like a heartbeat and less like a headache.

Cae inhaled sharply. "It's moving outward," he said. "Through the Fae dimension, into the Human layer."

"Then we'd better follow it," I said. "Jeanie's probably wondering why the Wi-Fi keeps achieving enlightenment."

He laughed, and the laugh became the jump. This time, the portal cracked jokes as we winked through dimensions.

CHAPTER TWENTY-FOUR

Caelan: Composing Reality

I felt the burst of popping out of the portal like a bell struck my wing, and just like that, we were in Jeanie's backyard in the evening. The new timeline made even teleporting feel casual. Dimension hopping used to feel like a headache; now it was a blur between cups of tea. Dare I say fun even? It still felt like classic Kaitaia; chickens chatting, earth damp and coffee-rich. Over the bay, soft pinks wafted calmly, reflecting off the clouds.

The back door banged open. Jeanie marched out in gumboots and a dressing gown, a kitchen utensil held like a sceptre. "Every time the sky does that hiss-pop, it's you two," she said, nodding at me and D.

"Hi, love," D gave her a huge bear hug. "How's Riley!? Long story short, kindness is the new physics." She seemed like she was finally used to seeing me as variants of my Human-Fae selves.

"You've been into the mushrooms again, haven't you?" Jeanie said, deadpan. "Riley's great, let me find her."

"Technically just the Verru," said Spitz, his glow flickering with laughter, "they were helping us."

I unfolded my wings just enough to glow, a soft field instead of a spectacle. "Jeanie, we needed your help. Time has been reset—linear, that is. Humans need to learn to hear the new pulse from the Recall reset before IGSTA re locks it to a mimic frequency."

She looked at me, then at D, and sighed like a parent consenting to a field trip. "Right. No idea what babble you just said. Kettle first, time-pocalypse next. You know, linear time's handy for nervous systems?"

Over tea, we told her about the Mnorae, the repaired memories, the

Field's new rhythm. Jeanie listened, shoulders loosening as if the explanation had ironed the world flat.

"So basically," she said at last, "be decent and sing along?"

"More or less," I said.

"Sweet as. I can do that." She started humming along to the radio while stirring the yummy-smelling pot on the stove.

To help us get started with Human awareness, within hours, she had booked the community hall for Kindness Frequency 101—flyers promising resonance attunement and snacks. Half the town turned up expecting yoga.

I stood up front, luminous and careful, Eurometer and a smear of makeup softening the sharper angles of my Fae-ness. Jeanie handed out tuning forks. I showed them how to breathe with the pulse: not to chase the clock, but to remember the last time they made someone smile and count from there. D translated me into Kiwi plain-speak. The walls hummed, the lights flickered, and even the old heater rattled along like it wanted to be percussion. By the end, everyone glowed faintly gold.

As we left and ventured outside, Quinley perched on the hall sign, bright black eyes keen. "Not bad for mammals and the like," he croaked.

"Thanks," I said. "We rehearsed."

"Keep it playful," he said, launching into the dark. "The Megalight lot hates laughter. Scrambles the algo."

He wasn't wrong. I felt the faint buzz of interference under the warmth, like a mic picking up a distant storm. Somewhere, in whatever glossy storage unit held the deactivated Revetron, a new apparatus was rebuilding, measuring, calculating.

I reached into the pulse and found a mathematical taste that made me frown. "They're still trying to measure empathy," I told D. "Harvest the resonance."

"Let them try," Jeanie said, arms folded. "Kindness doesn't run on batteries."

"Still," I said, "we should be ready."

The sky attuned its colours again, pinks, then gold, and the sea answered with a hush like applause. It felt good to have the lands, oceans, and skies of the Human dimension speaking louder now. They had been subdued before the Recall. The beauty took my breath away for a moment and settled into my wingspan, imperfect and utterly alive.

"Time's art now," D said softly.

"And art breathes life into all who allow it," I added.

The pulse rolled through us, bringing surges of play and laughter to this quirky group of mixed-dimensional beings. This crew felt like family to me—more than I had ever felt before back home. Somewhere above us, sterile sensors recorded nothing but noise.

The town didn't return to what it had called normal. The new normal felt like light-woven wings after the rain; too tight to fly, and learning from yesterday's glow. Kids skipping stones left rings that glowed a heartbeat longer. Old couples, mid-argument, paused and remembered why they liked each other. I waited for the novelty to burn out. It didn't. It slowly rose, like dough under a tea towel—warm, patient, alive.

Back at the lab, Jeanie started making a new jewelry line with Recall activation so she and D could work together. "What's with the buzzing?" D asked, plucking up a pendant that was sounding low resonance as she handled it.

"Check out the new line. It's story-amplifying." Jeanie lifted a bracelet, held it to the sun, and it refracted a pattern into the table—a brief, vivid re-enactment of someone's first kiss, the memory projected in translucent colour and sound above the teacups. The image flickered, then absorbed back into the crystal.

I whistled. "It recorded the feeling?"

"More than recorded," Jeanie corrected. "It resounded. Take enough of them, and you start harmonizing stories. Look." She pointed to a woman across the table, smiling.

D and I decided to camp out by the ocean for a few nights, to recover and reset after so much chaos and activity. The calm, the reset, the lack of IGSTA chasing us at every moment—it was a welcome relief.

A few days later, Jeanie rang to tell us her frog, Darwin, had hopped back from the cosmic abyss and was back to scaring the cats by hiding in their sandbox like nothing had happened. "Got snagged with the Crystal Converter during the first tear," she said. "Must have bopped home with the reset."

Spitz insisted on interviewing Darwin ("for science!") and returned with a summary: "He regretted nothing but disliked the way bugs tasted in the Fae dimension."

We built small rituals. Morning tea on Jeanie's porch when the pulse was strong. Check-ins with the Crow Network; Quinley reported that compassion spikes made Megalight's sensors skip like scratched records. Letters from Faierodon arrived on red light, Nuvious's handwriting a neat lightning-braid. We helped the Mnorae wherever we could, checking in on Aedra and Avaris's progress with the pattern memory recollection.

I was beginning to understand the benefits of linear time and nervous system regulation. When you get to live the life you desire and aren't constantly barraged by trauma loops and distortions, linear time can be a real bliss scenario. But peaceful moments did not seem to last forever. Eventually, the static grew. At first, it was faint. An off-beat tremor in the pulse. Jeanie cocked her head over tea and called it "someone tapping a pen during the good bits."

I named it plainly: the echo from mimic. Synchronicity began to distort again, imitating love but not true meaning. Coordinated deception plots began to show up in people's narratives. The Megalight had not stopped at monitoring empathy; the energies were predicting it, packaging it, trying to convert kindness into a stabiliser for mimic timelines.

One night, I walked the beach alone. A glint hung low on the horizon; a satellite, or an eye pretending. I raised my thermos in greeting. "You can watch," I said, not bothering to hide my wingglow. "Just don't think you can choreograph."

The sea answered with foam laughter. D appeared beside me with an extra mug, and Jeanie arrived a beat later, dressing gown flapping like a flag in a forgiving wind.

"Told you not to monologue at the ocean," D said, handing me the second mug. "It encourages it."

"Old habits," I admitted.

"Think they'd give up?" D asked, nodding toward the pulsing horizon.

"Control freaks never do," Jeanie answered herself. "But they can't hijack joy."

We listened. The pulse rolled through the dunes, slower now, deeper—the world's bassline. For a breath, I heard the Mnorae's laughter braided through it. The Field no longer lay smooth; it shimmered, improvised, alive. Every being, every memory, every small tenderness added percussion. The multiverse wasn't a machine anymore; it was a jam session.

"To imperfect harmony despite the noise," Jeanie toasted.

Somewhere far above, Megalight's instruments logged a spike of "unquantifiable noise," marked it red, and scheduled a meeting. Somewhere below, we started the next verse.

The next day was a gathering for the town, and Jeanie had big plans to spread stories of love. Townfolk arriving would see the entry sign: Story Magnification Fest. Jeanie had set up shop on a picnic table stacked with jewelry, crystals, and what looked like some of D's old fiber-optic science projects. "First annual event," she announced. "Registration optional; snacks compulsory."

The front lawn thrummed. We carried hope outside.

"Community story circle!" Jeanie declared. "If you can tell it, you could shift it. If you couldn't tell, listening counts."

People spoke. A lost dog was found. A first love at the supermarket. Each story manifested as a mesh of light and shadow above the teller's head, geometry that spun itself beautifully and dissolved into the air, leaving a coloured mist to soak into the grass. D told of her dreams coming true—of belonging in more than one place at once, despite never actually getting to shrink and ride on the back of a hummingbird. The air bloomed blues and golds. When I spoke, I told them about Faierodon, where stories were alive, relationships flighty, and the technology in harmony with nature. I spoke about Rekels and Ekat, Thelassi, and possibility. Eventually, I told them about how I had fallen in love with D, and how even dimensions couldn't keep true love apart. A sliver of light spun off my hand and settled on Jeanie's mug like a decal.

"That's a keeper," she said.

Unfortunately, our stories didn't keep the agency away. Moments after we finished, Ro showed up outside. Not in uniform, of course, but with that polished IGSTA posture that made every gesture look contrived. His wing shimmer had the faint metallic edge of someone who had given up on playing nice.

"Well, well," he said, voice bright with that familiar drawl that could slice or charm depending on the wind. "Didn't think I'd find you running a storytelling cult in a community hall."

Jeanie folded her arms. "It's called a festival, mate. We've got scones."

Ro smirked. "Cute. Headquarters called it narrative interference. You lot were bending harmonics again. Naughty."

D's shoulders stiffened. "You set us up last time, Ro. Don't pretend you were auditing for fun."

He gave a wolfish tilt of the head. "Fun was a side effect. I was here to make sure you didn't tear another rift. You know how paperwork got."

I felt the pulse thrumming under my ribs, matching his false calm. "You were still working for Gris, then."

"Someone had to keep the timelines tidy." He flashed that infuriating grin. "Besides, he misses you, Cae. Said you left glitter in the vents."

"Tell him it was love bombs," I said, stepping closer. "And it was contagious."

The light around us thickened. The pulse rose. Jeanie's teacup rattled.

Ro's smile faltered. "You lot are pushing resonance too far. You'll trip the sensors."

"Good," said Jeanie. "Maybe they'd learn something."

"The Megalight's pulling all your invisible strings, Ro," Spitz jotted in, "did you realise you've given away your free will?"

All of us were a bit stunned by Spitz's act of bravery. Ro paused a moment, and I wondered if that zinger had actually gotten through to him. Could he finally realise he was being played? He pulled a device from his jacket; sleek and humming with authority, he aimed it close to Spitz's eyes. "Don't make me use this. It's tuned to erase empathy frequencies and above."

D moved first. "There was a girl who could hear every colour," she began, voice steady, defiant. The pulse caught her words, prismed them into light, refracted them, and her story disarmed the device from Ro's hands.

Ro winced as the spectrum hit him, eyes narrowing, but his smirk held. "Still playing with fairytales to win arguments?"

"Still mistaking control for purpose?" I shot back.

The crowd joined in with tales, from kids to elders, their resonance calibrating new ways. Ro tried to recalibrate the device, but the frequencies blurred. The device pulsed red, then disintegrated into harmless crystal fragments in his hand. Ro cursed bitterly under his breath. "You're all bloody mad."

D grinned. "And aligned to a new harmony. Not going to be a frequency you can erase."

For a moment, Ro looked perplexed; just a tired agent stuck between duty and the beat of something older. Then his wings flickered, metallic again. "You're violating legacy narrative safety protocols; they kept the Human dimension properly looped into repetitive narratives, which suited the Megalight's energy requirements. You haven't seen the last of me."

He vanished into static that smelt faintly of ozone and regret. The sky seemed to sigh with his absence as the pulse settled. We stood there as the light folded over the bay, each heartbeat syncing to the world's rhythm; stories humming, giving me a new meaning to the Human word *resilience.*

"Well, that explains a lot," D pondered. "I can't believe he told us that—our fresh and enlivening stories were creating a breach in energy reserves for the Megalight. It's working!"

"It has been a long and complicated path, but we are making real change!" I explained to D, putting a hand gently on her back, grateful for her steady companionship through this journey. "I had always thought resilience meant you had to suffer and overcome in the Human anthologies I read growing up. Now I understand, it is far more. It was about creating strength, fortifying new ways together."

"You're right," D said, smiling up at me, eyes gleaming with hope. "Resilience isn't something we do alone; it's built with us all, in tiny ways of being. We *are* the stories, in the Weave itself."

Spitz let out a sigh; his sparkle dimmed to a dull flicker. "Resilience, yeah, sweet as," he buzzed, wings giving a tired hum. "But every time we think we've nailed it—boom! They whipped out some new contraption, new copycat, new sneaky agent. It's like playing tag with a Sophos who cheated."

"A Sophos—why, Spitz, you genius!" I smiled, a lightbulb going off in my head. "Didn't Ro say he was one back home when we first met him? They might just be the answer for what's next!"

Spitz's brow lifted. "They who?"

"The Council of Unwritten Things," D murmured. "They would have felt the shift."

"And who," Jeanie cut in, "or what, are the Sophos and this Council you speak of?"

"The Sophos, they are the wizards of the Fae dimension; they can stir up the weather and pull off tricks well beyond me," I said. "The best lot of them are the Council; they came about after the Fall of Ether, trying to stitch the forgotten stories back together by hand. A bit like tired librarians in the Human dimension, but running on starlight and stubbornness."

"And Ro was one?" Jeanie asked. "How'd he sour?"

"I don't know," D gazed off into the distance, pondering. "As Daer,

I knew him—though as a child, he was always getting into mischief outside of his understanding to fit in, to be loved. Perhaps he was just insecure."

"You knew him, eh?" I squeezed her hand. "There's still so much we have to catch up on when things settle."

"In the meantime," D breathed a soft acknowledgment, "we'd better bop back to the Fae dimension, check on this Council and the progress of the Mnorae, not to mention Aedra and Avaris."

The wind caught her words and carried them toward the sea, where the next chapter waited, listening, sharpening its pen. Perhaps the unwritten would have a new mythos to move from now. And we aimed to find out.

CHAPTER TWENTY-FIVE

D: Unwritten Things

Jeanie didn't make a fuss about us heading out; she was getting used to it. The dogs were doing anxious circuits around the compost bin. I felt terrible for leaving Riley behind so many times. Cae signaled to me gently the way his aura could; we didn't have to say anything. Spitz hung low over his shoulder, glow dimmed to a steady amber. I'd told Jeanie to keep the radio on, the one above the tea shelf, and she'd nodded like she always did. That was the whole farewell.

We stepped off the porch, and the garden stretched that little bit too far. The air thickened, heavy with that pre-crossing pressure that makes your teeth ache if you fight it. The fence at the back wavered, and then it wasn't a fence anymore but the sort of boundary you only notice once you've crossed it. The laughter and lightness of the portal hop since the Recall still had me in awe. The Fae side met us like a breath held too long. The light had different priorities here; soft from one angle, sharp from another. The ground felt alive but undecided about staying that way. Sound arrived half a second late.

Spitz did a quick loop, grumbling. "Still in one piece."

"Good start," I winked.

The Field showed bruises where the mimic had passed through; patches too neat, too polished, like someone had ironed the wildness out of them. We'd oriented our thoughts to land near the Mnorae, who were deep in those wrong spots, hands moving like they were untangling fishing line.

Aedra straightened when she saw us. Her face was calm, but there were soft shadows under her eyes. Beside her, Avaris stretched to full dragon height, scales shifting colour with her mood; bronzed pinks through the neck, molten gold along the wings. Smoke curled lazily from her nostrils in a visual sigh.

"About time," she said, voice low and amused. "We were starting to think you'd joined the Human nine-to-five."

"Tempting," I said. "Less fire hazard."

"Less interesting," she shot back.

Cae smiled, small and quick. That was as close as he got to banter before getting to it. "What's the latest?"

Aedra gestured to the torn stretch of the Field. "Localised instability. The mimic's residue blends with the organic lines. It's started rewriting context."

"Again," I muttered.

For a few hours, we worked alongside the Mnorae, hands and rhythm together. It wasn't fancy work; more like patching a net while the fish were still jumping through it. Cae took the north line; I anchored south. Spitz buzzed across the seam, feeding light into the gaps. When it settled, the hum went softer, less metallic, for now.

"Better," Aedra said, wiping her palms on nothing.

Avaris flicked her tail. "It is a patient testing process."

"We want to help more," Cae began, "but we have another mission at the moment." He paused to explain the Ro encounter and our idea around the Sophos helping us out.

"We've done what we can here for now," Aedra nodded, approving our plan, "Aedra and I will join you."

"We'll let you know what we learn from the Council," I said, bowing politely to the Mnorae.

The Mnorae nodded and faded back into their colours. We made our way across the Field toward the Council hall, a shape that grew from memory and habit rather than knowing. The air thickened into walls, and the ground coloured our path, underfoot. A gift from the Verru, no doubt.

The Sophos were waiting in a room full of mysterious objects and endless books breathing on their shelves. A handful of robed figures kept the usual Council faces on: calm, unreadable, slightly allergic to hurry. One particular Fae stepped forward, sharp eyes the colour of wet bark.

"I'm Esmion," he said. "Welcome. We've heard enough to know you matter."

"I should expect no less from a wizard," I said.

A flick of a smile. "I'm not a wizard. I'm weary of what happens when we act like we are."

Avaris stretched her wings, not to show off, just to remind the room who she was. Smoke curled from her nostrils in neat punctuation. "If this turns into a lecture, I'm walking out through the wall."

"Then I'll keep it plain," Esmion said. "You've felt the interference. IGSTA calls it stabilisation. The Megalight calls it progress. They're not just monitoring crossings; they're pre-empting unions."

Aedra's voice stayed gentle. "Explain."

Esmion looked between the two dyphoros beings; flame and stillness as the infinite. Avaris and Aedra, whom I now knew as friends. "The Loom is you, together. Your united field; the dragon's flame and the Drualan singularity; turning time toward mercy. When you two are aligned, dyphoros awaken across systems. Stories braid toward love. The Megalight can't metabolise that level of love or truth, so IGSTA is trying to disrupt it under the guise of safety."

"Do you know why Ro left you, why he became an agent?" I asked softly.

Esmion's eyes went somewhere else, remembering. "Ro believed the unions were unnatural. IGSTA showed him graphs. He doesn't like variety and prefers things to stay less messy. The Megalight knows how to weaponise tidy, that's how it recruits."

We let the room breathe. Cae found the practical thread. "We've known that the agency wants to block unions, but what can we do to help? The Mnorae have been working tirelessly, but the mimic's signal is still building."

Esmion gestured to the table in the centre; crystal blanks in a shallow bowl, each one humming like a throat clearing before a song. "The Loom sparks the pulse of love. These are carriers that can learn the Loom's pulse. If you tune them with lived stories, honest ones, they'll resonate with the Loom when it stirs. Think of them as invitations. They don't force anything. They make room."

Spitz hovered over the bowl, glowing bright with confusion. "These little stones can do all that?"

"Garden stakes," Esmion said. "For stories. We need to send the pulse through these and throughout the multiverse."

Avaris flicked him a look. "If a garden stake can help stop this tyrant Megalight, I won't weep."

"Gardens have protective thorns, like roses," Esmion explained, "These will adapt in the way kindness is not always nice or pleasant."

He didn't ask us to sit in a circle or hold hands. He just nodded at the bowl like it had been his grandmother's, and he trusted us not to chip it. I pressed my thumb to the nearest crystal and felt it settle to the pace of my heart. It was up to Avaris and Aedra to begin; they were the spark and the infinite birthing. Aedra's story was not a story so much as an energy of the all; her crystal learnt stillness that wasn't passive. Then Avaris leaned in, and every Sophos watched without blinking. She told the crystal about the way heat can hold when it isn't trying to punish. Her carrier flared red and softened embers, then settled into a steady breath.

"Good," Esmion said, voice lower. "That's the Loom's dialect."

"Careful," Avaris said. "You almost sounded impressed."

"I am," he said, without flinching. The room shifted, and the Council of Unwritten Things continued assessing the damage to narratives. Aedra turned, listening to spacetime like it was distant surf. One member shared concern, "They'll notice. IGSTA tracks any uptick in union-adjacent fields."

"They already have," Esmion said. "Two inspectors in the outer rings, one of them Ro's protege. The brief says 'containment.' But that is not what we must focus on. You were what we needed; you are the medicine that has ignited new intergalactic law. Despite their continued fragmentation attempts, they will not prevail. However, you are needed back home. I have heard from your elder, Ora. There is more to do in your galaxy before you return here. It is time for you both to return to your home dimensions."

"So we go," Avaris said, accepting.

Aedra nodded. "Soon. Before the next scan window."

Spitz's glow went dim. "That's... soon."

Esmion didn't reach for comfort. "The carriers will work in your absence. The Loom isn't bound to a room. When you breathe as one, across distance if you must; the invitations wake other unions."

Cae rubbed at a knot in his neck. "And the Humans? We plant these in places that don't look like temples."

"Especially there." Esmion's smile edged toward living. "Kitchens. Ferries. Barbeques, sporting events. Waiting rooms with terrible magazines. Anywhere the story already knows how to magnify love and share itself."

Esmion gathered the bowl and poured the tuned carriers into a worn satchel. He handed it to me with a bow. "Consent and curiosity," he said. "Those are the only rules. If someone says no, the crystal cools and waits. If someone laughs, it brightens. We'll be able to infuse origin resonance into the rain and waters, the elementals as well."

We moved for the door, but Esmion lifted a hand. "One more thing you should hear now, not later." He glanced at the Loom counterparts, pausing. "Ro didn't sell you out because he hated the Loom. The Megalight offered a version of love that never has to risk itself. It just isn't true love. Eura are often worse than Humans, not understanding love." His mouth shifted. "If we can change the course of the counterfit at its core, it won't be with better rules. It'll be with true love."

Aedra's eyes shone like wet stone. "Understood."

Avaris squinted at him. "You practice that speech a few times?"

"On the walk here," he said. I chuckled under my breath. After all, levity was the medicine itself.

"We watch over the unwritten, and heal the falsely written, that's why we have this council," Esmion explained, "Nothing is certain, and what's writing the unwritten is a precious thing to guard and tend."

We thanked the council and headed out, bringing sachels of charged Loom crystals in our hands. Outside, the Field had stopped buzzing like a fluorescent light about to die. Colours sat back in their chairs. The wrong angles softened. Aedra tilted her head. "It's quieter."

"Don't get sentimental," Avaris said, but there was no bite in it. "It's still a mess."

"Mess we can work with," I said.

We stood there awhile. Spitz drew lazy loops in the air, gold on gold. Cae's fingers found mine, brief and steady. The multiverse didn't fix itself; it just agreed not to need fixing.

Aedra was the one to end the quiet pause. "We'll head home before the next cycle. IGSTA's patrols won't miss us twice."

"You don't have to," I started.

"We do," Avaris said, not unkind. "You plant. We'll focus on the galactic agenda."

Aedra gazed into my eyes, a knowing we shared with the simultaneous burden and honor of being a part of something so vast.

"Plant quick, with love. Plant deep," she said. "Don't tidy it till it dies."

"Never tidy," I said. "Ask Jeanie."

"Just remember, D," Avaris turned to me, "Home isn't a dimension. It's wherever love echoes back."

She laughed a clean, crackling sound, and then they were gone, two bright signatures carving upward through the seam, folding into the dark where IGSTA scanners like to pretend wonder can be extracted and made into sensors.

Spitz pressed close. "They'll be all right?"

"They're them," I said. "They will reshape the galaxies into new stardust resonance."

We crossed back the way we always did these days: not with grand exits, just with the decision to be somewhere else. Jeanie's kitchen had kept our place. Riley was sleeping cozily among his chicken friends. I put a satchel down on the bench, which held hundreds of crystals with a mission.

"Don't start without us," I told them jokingly. It glowed brighter.

Cae leaned against the bench, relief showing up as tiredness. Spitz tucked himself into the fruit bowl to rest. The house settled around us. Somewhere between static, the radio found a laugh that wasn't in the room yet; Avaris, far but not away. I looked at the window. It wasn't quite dawn, and we knew there was much to do ahead.

The story felt like it belonged to everyone again, and the Loom — they breathed through that belonging even from afar, quiet as a held hand, strong as a promise made of organic truth and the residue of eternity.

CHAPTER TWENTY-SIX
Cae: New Fragments

The next morning, Jeanie's bench looked like the aftermath of one of D's field tests; cluttered, curious, chaotic, but energizing nonetheless. Crystals the size of marbles sat on a dish towel beside the kettle, each one humming at its own pitch, very loudly to my Eura senses; in fact, it was quite a symphony. D had sorted them into little families that made sense to her; steady, fussy, shy. Spitz hovered over the fruit bowl, pretending to supervise.

"We'll start local," D said, tying her hair back with a rubber band that had been a broccoli tie in a former life. "Ordinary places first."

Jeanie slid a small tin lunchbox across to me, the kind you give a kid when you don't trust their school bag. "Use that. No point scratching my table."

I packed the crystals, trying not to overthink it. Every time my fingers touched one for longer than a second, I caught a faint feeling off it, an instinct deciding where to go. Jeanie handed us gumboots and a cut-down screwdriver for wedging things where they belonged. "If anyone asks, you're checking the storm drains."

Spitz zipped to the doorway, glow up a notch. "Storm drains, aye. Very official."

We started at the local elementary school. The caretaker had left the side gate open, as usual. Children were already inside, practicing recorder in murky unison. We went around the back, where the art room vented out solvent and freedom from mindless ambition. D knelt by the bottom of the mural wall, where chalk ghosts layered over last term's projects. She pressed a crystal into a hairline crack between bricks. It didn't sink; it just settled, taking on the look of the mortar like it had been there since the school opened. Nothing flashed. No music swelled. We waited another breath anyway.

"Feels right," D said, standing up and brushing dust off her knees.

At the library, I set one under the counter lip where people rested their elbows while arguing about overdue fees. The woodgrain took the reflection of the crystal until the reflection became the object, and then it was gone. The librarian didn't look up from stamping returns. A kid at the nearest table had drawn a looped shape that almost closed but didn't; a figure-eight with a loose stitch. He coloured outside his own lines and didn't apologise. I couldn't help thinking of the infinity sign from the prophecy as he drew it.

Halfway through placing the third crystal, I got a flicker. Not a vision. A memory that I didn't recognise: standing in a different library, lime carpet, a colder kind of dust; a hand taking a book from mine and laughing at the wrong part of the title. I was confused why I was seeing this memory. Were there ghosts at this school trying to communicate?

"You okay?" D asked.

"Yeah." I rubbed the edge of the counter where the varnish had chipped. "Just thought of something I can't put a name to."

"Put it in the tin for later," she said.

We worked along the main street, quickly and ordinarily. A crystal under the corner of the café table that everyone drummed their fingers on while their order took too long. One in the bus stop bench, set into a cigarette burn where some teenager's boredom had won. One against the metal post that carried the lost-cat flyers, wedged behind a staple. The crystals didn't shine or beep. If they had, we'd have stopped. They just… took on the place and the place took them back.

Spitz kept a running commentary that helped keep us upbeat and on tempo. "Bench is good; steady foot traffic, high story content, mild chewing-gum hazard. Bus shelter glass is too tidy. Try the post. Oi, watch the spider. He lives there."

At the park, two kids were chalking a long hopscotch that turned into something else when they ran out of numbers. I set a crystal against the base of the low brick wall where parents rested with takeaway coffees. As my thumb left it, another fragment hit me; not dramatic, just sharp. Rain on a corrugated roof that wasn't one I had seen before. A laugh I recognised in my bones and couldn't place in my life. A name on the tip of my tongue that vanished when I looked at D. It left a small ache in my stomach that felt like I'd run too far and then stopped too fast. Strange.

By mid-morning, the street had picked up its usual choreography: couriers, prams, teenagers in hoodies trying not to be noticed while very much wanting to be noticed. A white van crawled by with a speaker bolted to the roof, droning out an ad for a "Clarity Programme" that promised "closure for every story" in a tone that implied only idiots wouldn't sign up.

"That's it," D said. "That's the mimic."

It was almost clever. The script didn't lie; it offered smoother outcomes. No awkward pauses, no regrettable words, no time lost to grief or second-guessing. All the scuff sanded out. People stopped to take the pamphlets because the font was perfect and the man handing them out smiled with both sides of his mouth at once. I took one and felt the absence of weight where the weight should have been. Jeanie, who'd appeared at my elbow without announcing herself, plucked it from my fingers and folded it into the shape of a paper dart. She set it on the nearest table and pressed a crystal into the fold so gently the paper didn't crease.

"Leave it," she said. "Let's see what it learns."

The crystals were enough; they would start the vibrational shifts and send them around the planet. We knew that, but it was still difficult to watch the ways the mimic was responding and distorting even after all the work we had done with the reset.

We ate pies in the ute because there wasn't time to go home. Spitz perched on the dashboard, stealing bites in a way he pretended was accidental. We'd brought the radio in the car this time, put it under the seat just in case we heard from them.

D tapped the casing. "You think she'll call?"

"She said she would." I turned the knob half a tick right, more habit than hope.

The radio sat there like it had since they left, doing nothing. Then Avaris: unmistakable even in the quiet of the transmission waves. Not the blazing version we'd met on our worst days, but the practical voice she used when there was too much to do and none of it allowed for drama.

"Tell me you're making good mischief," she said. "What's the latest?"

D leaned in. "We're placing. Quietly. How's your end?"

"Loud," she said. I could hear something, a low rumble that might have been distance or the way her chest worked when she was tired. "IGSTA's scanners are on every hour. They call it routine. It feels like being measured with a knife. Some of the Weaveborn are coming back wrong-footed. They flicker between their own pattern and the Megalight's trained smile. We're keeping the Loom steady, but it's heavy work when the auditors think love is a glitch. There's a lot of ground to cover in the whole of the cosmos, and parallel, we're setting up more origin networks to communicate."

"That's intense. How can we help?" I asked.

"Whatever you're placing, place faster." Avaris pressed, "IGSTA is writing stories backwards. They're starting with the moral and trying to rewrite anyone whose life doesn't match the mimic."

The van drove past again, the voice on the loudspeaker promising a future where no one ever said the "wrong" thing. I clicked the radio a touch left to cut the feedback. The crystal in my pocket pressed against my leg like a patient dog keeping track of me.

"What do we watch for?" I asked.

Avaris didn't soften it. "Anything too neat. People who agree with themselves in the same tone every time. Gratitude with rules attached. If you hear someone say a sentence that closes a door, wedge it open. Give the moment an out."

"Copy," D said. "We'll keep at it."

"We're here. Hold your end. Tell your little glowbug I appreciate the comms."

Spitz straightened. "Just here for the cosmic biscuits when you lot return."

"We'll get ahead of it, together," Avaris said, and the transmission quieted.

We finished the pies and kept moving. The dairy had a queue. The town didn't care what we were doing, and that helped. We placed another crystal at the base of the lamppost where kids locked their bikes and tried to look like they weren't waiting for anyone. One under the concrete lip of the skate park, where scraped knees and sweet talk lived. One at the hospital entrance, in the groove of the automatic door where you touch without meaning to.

The third memory hit when I was wedging a crystal into the crack of the bus shelter floor near the drain. It didn't look like much; just wet concrete and a dropped receipt. But as my fingers pressed down, I saw a different street at a different time of day. The same shelter, maybe, but with posters I didn't recognise and a different bus route number.

My jacket was different. My hands looked the same. Someone leaned into my shoulder like I was permission to relax, and I felt relief so clean it hurt. I blinked, and the shelter was ours again, empty.

D had that look like she'd noticed my breath change. "Still with me?"

"Mostly," I said. "It's like watching a video buffer out of order. I'm in it, then I'm not."

"What sort of creatures are there?" she asked.

"I can't tell," I said. "The jokes feel Human."

"Interesting."

We kept it up until the tin was light. At the noticeboard by the community hall, we tucked one behind the drawing of a lost budgie with the name Clampers. At the barber, I slid one under the rubber mat where little boys spun on the stool and tried not to cry. At the rugby club fence, D pressed one into the spot all the dads leaned on to talk about anything except the thing they'd come to talk about. By late afternoon, the town had the look of a job half-done in the good way. We'd left no marks worth noticing and planted more love resonance than IGSTA would know how to measure.

On the way back, we passed the white van parked outside the chemist. The man with the leaflets had removed his jacket and rolled his sleeves higher to show forearms that proved he went to a gym. His smile had the fixed edge of someone who didn't know what to do with their hands when they weren't holding a microphone. A woman asked if the programme helped with grief. He said, "Of course," in a tone that made grief sound like a missed bill. D touched my wrist.

"Let it go," she said gently.

At Jeanie's place, the house held our mess like it always did. The crystals we hadn't placed yet sat on the dish towel in a new pattern I didn't remember arranging.

Jeanie put bread in the toaster and counseled it to behave. "Any trouble?" she asked.

"Just pamphlets," D said.

Jeanie snorted. "That's the best they got?"

I took one of the leftover crystals and set it in the hairline crack at the corner of Jeanie's table. The crystal eased into the grain and went still. I'd brought the radio back in with us, just in case. It was near me all the time now. A few moments later, the radio cleared, and Avaris's voice came back, softer this time.

"One more thing," she said. "Keep your narrative loose. Let the stories breathe. If IGSTA tries to close a scene, open a window."

"Got it," D said.

"Good," Avaris said. "Tell Jeanie the jam was a smash hit." I hadn't realised she had sent Avaris back to Andromeda with jam.

Jeanie smiled at the bench, which, for her, qualified as an emotional display. "Tell her to bring the empty jar back."

"You can tell her yourself," I said into the mic, but the line had already gone. The carrier hum stayed, low as a cat's purr, then thinned to nothing.

We ate toast standing up because chairs felt ambitious. D wrote a list on the back of an envelope, where we'd been, how many crystals we had left, and which places felt empty. I wrote a different list on the corner: intervals, times of day, whatever my body had been doing when the fragments arrived. The numbers lined up in a way that made me itch.

"You doing equations on my bills?" Jeanie asked.

"Only friendly ones," I said.

"Good. I don't pay for unfriendly maths."

Later, when D took the rubbish out and Jeanie fell asleep in the chair she swore she never fell asleep in, I stood at the bench with a crystal in my hand. It didn't hum louder. It didn't hum at all. But there was a pressure in my chest that matched the weight of it; two pulses almost in time. For a moment, they locked, then one slid half a beat off the other and kept sliding until it found a new place to sit. It wasn't out of time; it was... paired. I felt someone else catch the same shift from somewhere not here. The sense of relief returned, clean as before. It passed. The kitchen beheld its usual problems: crumbs, a squeaky hinge, and a tea towel that needed retirement. I wrote the half-beat on the envelope and circled it, not really knowing what to make of it still.

We hadn't fixed anything, but we'd made a start at spreading more of the resonance of love in the Human dimension. The Megalight would try to sell a version of love that required a loyalty card. But when I stood perfectly still, I could feel the Human world running a hand along its own edges and not finding as many sharp ones.

D came back in with cold hands and put them on my neck to warm them. "Tomorrow?"

"Yeah," I said. "We keep going."

"Good," she said.

Spitz yawned half asleep in the fruit bowl like he'd done most of the work. The last crystal on the bench faintly brightened, then settled as if it had heard and approved. I counted the beats in my head and let the half-step between them stay as it was. It felt honest. We were planting, even if we couldn't see the roots.

195

CHAPTER TWENTY-SEVEN

D: Golden Equation

Sitting on a cozy chair in the bay window, I paused, reflecting on all that had happened over the last few months. It turns out that being born in the wrong dimension was actually the right springboard into a life I never imagined could be so meaningful. And I wasn't as alone as I'd thought, either. I'd found my team of creatures just like me, obsessed with learning what we already were made of from within. Plus, there was the added bonus of finding all kinds of forms of true love. All because I followed my heart, even when most of the world thought I'd lost the plot.

The remaining crystals sat on a tea towel in that casual arrangement Jeanie once called "deliberate chaos." We'd placed most of them yesterday. Today wasn't about a big push; it was about seeing if the world had noticed. It had started to, slowly. The dairy door had picked up a habit of catching itself before slamming. The playground bolt stayed fixed without anyone asking for credit. The school newsletter mentioned children drawing shapes "that appear to breathe," followed by a cheerful plea for more pencils.

The mimic tried to compete, but no one was really buying it anymore. Its resonance felt hollow, and people could tell.

Later that evening, Aedra came through on the radio, voice gentle and bright, like someone singing through wind chimes.

"You're closer than you think, D. Your side is remembering how to bend. We traced the same harmonic through three systems last night; it shows up with laughter. The Loom calls it the Melody of Ether. It's behaviour-shifting stuff, and all of it's playing a part. Time's truly moving like art again."

Cae scribbled time = behaviour in his notebook and underlined it twice, probably hoping it would sink in. "So the infinity sign isn't measuring distance or power," he said. "It's tracing a chord of repeat love."

"Yes," Aedra said. "Infinity as behaviour. The set that won't close because it keeps space for coming back. Sort of like grace always has, but with more fun and less shame and guilt."

Before we could answer, Riley padded in looking guilty. Darwin, the dimension-hopping frog, had somehow made it onto her shoulder blades without her permission. She froze, decided this was beneath her, and sat down carefully so as not to squash him. One of the crystals by the sink flashed strange rainbow hues, blinding us for a moment. When the light cleared, Riley and Darwin were gone — then reappeared as one, literally. A dyphoros union of frog and small dog was not something I had expected to see today.

Cae raised his eyebrows, his expression unmoved. "Dogfro level unlocked."

Spitz hovered above them, flickering like a tiny disco ball. "Ohhh, that's going to complicate walkies."

Jeanie let out a wheezy laugh. "Do you think they'll bark in croak or croak in bark?"

I tried to stay composed. "We don't decide who gets to be a dyphoros," I said, though my insides were doing cartwheels.

We decided to take it as proof that the day knew what it was doing. I needed air and a post-reset upside-down reality reminder, so Cae and I wandered down to the shoreline. The sea had that crisp, sensible smell that could sort out even a cosmic hangover. We walked until the conversation ran out of words and the path ran out of grass, and turned back toward the benches.

That's when I saw them; all three of the Weavers, sitting like they'd been there all morning, side by side on the bench, needles clicking, threads spilling over the slats. The usual galactic-knitting-party vibe had been toned down a notch, but only barely. Someone had thrown a picnic blanket over their laps as camouflage, as though that would stop people noticing three interdimensional grandmothers crocheting the fabric of existence beside the bins.

Cae and I exchanged a look. "Subtle, as always," I muttered.

The one with spectacles smiled up at me. "We don't do subtle, dear. It frays the thread."

"Figured as much," I said, sitting down.

"You've been feeling the difference," said the second Weaver, her needles glinting like starlight. "The world breathing in sync again."

"Feels lighter around here," Cae confirmed. "Like the Humans have remembered what they are for."

"Exactly," she nodded. "The Infinity Bond wasn't romantic, you know. It's structural. A set that permits return without erasure. The Golden Equation isn't a ladder; it's a hinge."

Spitz landed on the edge of her yarn basket, glowing bright yellow. "That's deep, but if you're the cosmic repair team, can we get a version with less humidity next week? My wings are sticking together."

The Weaver with the spectacles laughed softly. "Oh, the small ones always think they can edit weather."

"Hey," Spitz said, puffing himself up, "I once rerouted a thundercloud! I figure if the Sophos can, it must be easy for you all."

Cae, meanwhile, was writing again, chewing the end of his pencil. "So infinity isn't size," he said slowly. "It's how we meet again — like a cosmic law, not a number."

"Yes," the third Weaver said. "Infinity has breathing room for interpretation built in, but it really is just about dancing with and organizing sound waves."

Spitz gasped and held out his tiny glowbug palm for emphasis. "Wait, hang on, are you saying the multiverse is just... a big jam session?"

All three Weavers looked up at the wee bug, their needles pausing mid-air.

"Yes," they said in perfect unison.

Spitz blinked. "Huh. Explains a lot. Especially the sounds the pets make in Jeanie's kitchen."

Cae chuckled quietly, and one of the Weavers winked at him. "That one's got the right ear," she said.

"Oh, he knows," I added. "He's been listening to the same three chords of destiny since Tuesday."

Spitz cackled, nearly toppling into the yarn. "It's a classic!"

The Weavers giggled, resonant laughter that spilt into waves of starlight like time remembering itself. Threads shimmered between them, dancing in the air like soft aurora.

The Weaver with the spectacles leaned closer to me. "You've done well, D. You've brought peace to the lands for now, and love is vibrating true once more."

I shrugged, trying not to tear up. "Thank you, I had a lot of friends to help."

They stood, their threads folding back into themselves, and the air shimmered faintly with the smell of rain and jasmine.

"Wait," Cae said. "One more thing, the Golden Equation. We still don't really know what it's for."

"Oh, you do," the third said. "You're just pretending it's maths because that feels safer."

Then they poofed away in a shimmer of dust and smug wisdom, leaving us with the faint sound of distant knitting needles fading into the surf.

We sat there a while, just breathing. The sky felt clearer, somehow. Softer.

By the time we wandered back, the world had shifted again. The Human dimension was moving into more love in lots of little, nearly invisible, but mildly noisy ways. Two neighbours argued over a fence, then laughed at their own pettiness and decided to share the feijoas. Chalk drawings in the park had turned into full-blown maps of imaginary kingdoms. The dairy had a spare loaf on the counter with a note saying for whoever forgot theirs. Someone had tucked a crystal under the chessboard, and two players who usually raced each other with tension were now playing like the board itself was breathing. We hadn't planned any of it. The crystals weren't forcing anything. They were just catching what the day offered when no one was trying to score points.

At dusk, the radio crackled to life again.

"D, the Loom is waking across the spiral arms," Aedra said. "Little flares where songs had gone quiet. Not here yet, in Ignara, but it's happening. Keep going."

Back at Jeanie's, Riley-Darwin, now officially "Rida", was adjusting. Jeanie was crouched beside them with a treat in one hand and a lily pad water bucket next to her.

"They like the word snackles," she announced proudly. "Could be a new species trait. Also, they seem to enjoy flies still. "

Spitz hovered above her head like a tiny lamp. "You're doing great science there, Jeanie."

"Thanks," she said. "I'm thinking of publishing in Probably Not a Journal."

Jeanie squeezed my arm gently as I passed. "They seem happy, right?"

"I think so," I said.

She nodded, satisfied. "Good. I was worried I'd broken the space-time-pet barrier again."

Cae joined us, holding his infinity records notebook. "You know, D, I think we've learnt the ultimate lesson. That's what the Golden Equation was for: time warping to infinity. It was showing us that not every glow is guidance. We have to use discernment, pick the lights that leave room for the infinite to express. That's why we're all here. To protect the true light of creative expression."

"That's the most beautiful thing you've ever said," I murmured, though it felt too small for what he'd just revealed.

He smiled, drew a loop that wasn't a loop, a curve that refused to close, half a beat waiting for the next thing to arrive intact. He slid the paper towards me.

"Peace that has a nice tune," he said. "Not peace that sits."

"That's the kind of infinity I can keep up with," I told him.

Spitz dimmed his glow a little, unusually serious. "You lot make me wish I had a bigger brain. Or at least opposable thumbs."

Jeanie patted the air near him. "You're perfect, mate, even if your brain is too tiny to keep up."

"Oi!" he buzzed, pretending to be offended, then sneezed out a spark.

We weren't heroes. We'd just planted a handful of crystalline fresh starts in places where the earth already knew what to do. Maybe even after millennia, a lot of Humans still had some growing up to do to realise they were already free; that they didn't need to keep playing the old loops of limitation. But, for today, I had done my part.

My childhood obsession as Daria, trying to find the Fae dimension, hadn't really been about escaping to somewhere better. It was about being all of me, out loud and on purpose: Fae, Human, infinite. I'd wanted a doorway into that world, but it turned out the real trick was leaving one open behind me. Because I'd been there all along.

CHAPTER TWENTY-EIGHT
Epilogue

Birthrights as Weaveborn were reset to their natural unions once more. What began with the Recall in Faierodon became a wave far greater than anyone could imagine; an infinity bond. Time had warped in new ways, slipping through constellations and the thin seams of spacetime, seeding worlds with fragments of memory of what we all truly are: creation itself. Across the Milky Way, time stopped its skipping and stuttering and found a steadier rhythm; galaxies breathed in new harmony and adjusted their tune.

And on a rain-soaked hill in Wales, the Field lingered a moment longer on a particular name. Mine. Elspbeth.

My story's never been a subtle one; I blame the artist lineage. Those who saw me at all, well, it always went the same. Obsessive adoration. Marriage proposals. Tearful confessions. Pleas for forgiveness from people I'd only just met. I've had more "will you have my baby?" introductions than I care to count. If I'd been paid a fiver each time, I might've managed the rent without so many dreadful jobs or those cursed dating apps.

Friends, coworkers, strangers at the bus stop; the pattern never changed. Obsession, jealousy, collapse. Always ending with me alone except for Wally, my terrier, who at least never proposed but still had plenty of snippy things to say over breakfast. No matter where I went, a kind of chaos followed. It wasn't beauty; I'm ordinary enough. Hair like straw, eyes green as rain-soaked grass. Things just unravel around me; I don't even have to speak. Truth leaks out of me, uninvited. Even a simple "hiya" can undo someone's mind if they're not ready for it.

I'm not cruel; God, I try not to be. I measure tone and timing like doses of medicine. I've done all the work; shadow, ancestry, therapy, the lot. Still, the same pattern. The magnetism, the recoil.

Eventually, I stopped dressing it up. It's a curse. My great Aunt, Claudia, muttered about the Origin Point, the myth of the void before the Fall of Ether, but I never cared for such stories. To me, it wasn't destiny. It was decay. Every conversation went sideways. Every bond twisted. Every confession wasn't intimacy; it was someone emptying their wounds into my lap. The loneliness wasn't in being alone; it was in not knowing what was real.

So I tell people now, some version of: "If you stay near me, you'll have to face all your demons. There's no turning back. Do you still want to stay?"

Most don't. A few do. It rarely lasts long, but it's honest. I've made peace with it, mostly: an ordinary Welsh woman with an extraordinary affliction. I walk the dog, work my shifts, say as little as possible, and keep the volcano of truth banked quiet inside me.

Rain had been falling for three days; though in Wales, "falling" isn't quite right. It hovers, lingers, wraps itself round you like an old cardigan. I trudged up the hill, Wally bounding at puddles. The world was slate-grey except for the gorse, burning yellow even in drizzle. Then I heard the hum. At first, I thought it was a plane, then a migraine, until the ground answered. A deep vibration rolled up through the sodden soil and into me, not through bone but through that strange resonance I carry in place of calm. Wally froze, ears forward, staring at the hollow by the old stone wall. A waft of mist escaped the earth.

"Oh no," I muttered. "Not again."

The vapour thickened, shaping itself into a small figure; green-skinned, drenched, waistcoat patched with what looked like playing cards. A Hobgoblin, of all things, was polishing his hands on a rag that looked suspiciously like a map.

"Evenin'," he said. "You're loud."

"Sorry, what?"

"Your resonance," he said, cupping his ear. "Big as a cathedral. You've cracked half the ley lines in Carmarthenshire." He offered a hand. "Grin Ferrule. Maintenance division. Unauthorised but well-meaning."

I blinked at him. "Say what?"

"Time's been reset," he said, like it was the weather. "Linear's back to doing the polka. When the Recall ran, it woke the old Weaveborn, the ones left unfinished. You're one of 'em."

I gave a sharp laugh. "I'm just walking my dog."

"Not anymore, you're not." He tilted his head, listening to a note I couldn't hear. "Something in you's tied to the Loom itself; black-hole business, creative futures, all that cosmic nonsense. The multiverse remembered you, doll. Thought you could turn it off, did you?"

"I don't want it," I said. "Whatever it is."

"Too late, love. It's already buzzing through you."

The hill trembled. The rain flashed turquoise for a heartbeat. Grin squinted upward. "Right, that's my cue. Keep the dog close. And if things start lookin' too perfect, don't believe a word. The Megalight's partial to polish."

He tipped an invisible hat. "Welcome to the reset timeline, Elspbeth. The Loom's been waitin'."

And with a pop of air, he was gone.

The rain returned to its usual whisper. Wally sniffed the ground, barked once, triumphant. I stood still, heart hammering, the earth's vibration still humming through my ribs. One thought rose clear and certain: *It's started.*

Far above Wales, clouds blushed gold and pink, faint but visible to anyone who cared to look up. In Faierodon's sky, Aedra paused mid-thought as the same pattern shimmered across the horizon. Another Thread had joined the song, but not just any Weaveborn: truth wrapped in Human skin, born of singularity, lonely and luminous.

The Loom was awake across every world, but one note remained untested: mine. The Human resonance that could heal or shatter it all anew. I sighed and turned toward home. I'd been spotted, and I knew I couldn't hide anymore.

(To be continued in Book 2 of the Eura Trilogy)

Connect

Join the Journey

Other books by the author:

Reshape Vol 1 & 2
Kora Kelly & the Life Keeper

Social: @EuraTrilogy • by @CreativelyFreeStudios
More at EntwinedDimensions.com & CreativelyFreeStudios.com

Creatively Free Studios™ is also on Substack, Spotify, YouTube

About the Author

Ariel Grace is a tech creative director, photographer, and bestselling author-artist whose projects merge imagination and impact. Founder of **Creatively Free Studios**, she hosts the *Creatively Free Podcast* and creates art and stories that spark social and environmental awareness. *Entwined Dimensions* marks her debut in speculative fiction. She's a mom of two delightful daughters and a dog, Nova.